THE SILVER MIST

A Wild Hunt Novel, Book 6

YASMINE GALENORN

A Nightqueen Enterprises LLC Publication

Published by Yasmine Galenorn

PO Box 2037, Kirkland WA 98083-2037

THE SILVER MIST

A Wild Hunt Novel

Copyright © 2019 by Yasmine Galenorn

First Electronic Printing: 2019 Nightqueen Enterprises LLC

First Print Edition: 2019 Nightqueen Enterprises

Cover Art & Design: Ravven

Art Copyright: Yasmine Galenorn

Editor: Elizabeth Flynn

A Nightqueen Enterprises LLC Publication

Published in the United States of America

ACKNOWLEDGMENTS

Welcome back into my world of the Wild Hunt. This series has taken full hold with me and the world is expanding in wonderful and mysterious ways. I'm envisioning more of Ember and Herne's world with each passing day and I'm so grateful that my readers have taken it into their hearts. I'm loving writing this like nothing else that I've written in a long, long time. I'm also planning to introduce a spinoff series, alongside the original, this year.

Thanks to my usual crew: Samwise, my husband, Andria and Jennifer—without their help, I'd be swamped. To the women who have helped me find my way in indie, you're all great and so many thank-yous.

Also, my love to my furbles, who keep me happy. My most reverent devotion to Mielikki, Tapio, Ukko, Rauni, and Brighid, my spiritual guardians and guides. My love and reverence to Herne, and to Cernunnos, who still rule the wild places of this world. And a nod to the Wild Hunt, which runs deep in my magick, as well as in my fiction.

If you wish to reach me, you can find me through my website at Galenorn.com and be sure to sign up for my newsletter to keep updated on all my latest releases!

Brightest Blessings,

~The Painted Panther~

~Yasmine Galenorn~

WELCOME TO THE SILVER MIST

Life isn't easy when you bear the mark of the Silver Stag.

The Wild Hunt is on the trail of the Tuathan Brother-hood—a hate group terrorizing humans and shifters alike. Their investigation takes them over to the Olympic Peninsula, where they plunge into the heart of the haunted old-growth forest in a desperate attempt to stop the group before they strike again.

Meanwhile, one of Herne's friends turns to the Wild Hunt. He's unwittingly unleashed a terrifying spirit who threatens Port Ludlow with the fury of her storms. Now, they must not only locate Rafé, who has vanished while undercover in the forest, but they must also appease the Cailleach before she destroys the entire community and everyone within it.

Reading Order for the Wild Hunt Series:

- Book 1: The Silver Stag
- Book 2: Oak & Thorns

CHAPTER ONE

*H*erne stared out the window, his hands behind his back. The night sky held that soft silver sheen that came with a snowstorm, and the soft fall of snow drifted down through the night to blanket the ground and muffle the sound of traffic.

I curled up on the sofa with Angel, while Rafé sat cross-legged on the floor, staring at his tablet. On the covered patio, steaks were sizzling on the grill, and Angel had made hot cocoa for all of us. I leaned back against one arm of the sofa, pulling my knees to my chest as I held my mug and stared at the flames crackling in the fireplace. It was Friday night, and we were all trying to relax after a particularly grueling week.

"It's been a rough six weeks," I said, to no one in particular.

Herne nodded. "You can say that again. And I'm afraid things aren't going to die down any time soon." He glanced outside at the grill. "I'll check on the steaks." He ducked out the sliding glass door, armed with tongs and some barbecue sauce.

"He's worried, isn't he?" Angel asked softly as he shut the sliding glass door behind him.

I nodded. "Yeah, but aren't we all?"

We were on the trail of the Tuathan Brotherhood, a hate group that had claimed responsibility for a number of crimes around the area. At least forty people were dead, and dozens had been injured, including me.

A couple weeks after the credit union bombing, in which I had been injured, there had been an active shooter incident claiming eleven victims, the last one being the shooter himself. He killed himself before the cops could get to him. This time it had been one of the Light Fae—a student on the Washington Hills college campus who had apparently been recruited into the hate group the same way the others had—through drugging and brainwashing.

"Can we let it go for tonight?" Angel asked. "I just want one day's reprieve from thinking about it." She leaned forward and grabbed another marshmallow, popping it into her mug.

"I agree. We need a break. No more talk about the Tuathan Brotherhood tonight." I flashed her a smile and sipped my cocoa. "Instead, let's talk about Yule. Are you going to visit DJ?" Angel's little brother was living with a foster family, and she had seen him at Thanksgiving, but I wasn't sure whether she had decided to spend the winter holidays down there.

She shook her head. "No. Cooper is taking the entire family on a ski trip for the holidays, and I want DJ to go. Not only do I not ski, I simply can't take the time off, given we're headed over to the peninsula this week. We may not be back in time for Yule."

"Right. Well, he'll have fun. And yes, we'll probably still be over on the peninsula." We were out to infiltrate the hate group—or rather, Rafé was—and the entire agency was going over. We hoped Rafé would be able to feed us the information we needed in order to bust up the group right there. But I knew that Herne would have let Angel go if she asked. No, I knew there were two reasons behind her reluctance. The first was Rafé himself—she was worried about him.

And the second was while DJ had enjoyed having her there for Thanksgiving, Angel had confided to me that she felt like an outsider. Her brother was fitting in well with his new foster family, and she had felt like he had spent time with her just because he felt like he should. I tried to convince her that she was wrong, but the truth was—I had the feeling she was right. Angel was a strong empath and had a good read on people.

"Then we should plan out an agency-wide Yule party for the Solstice. If we get stuck over there, we'll celebrate when we get back." I drained my mug and set it on the table. "Rafé, do you go home for the Solstice?"

He glanced up, shaking his head. "No. My family doesn't welcome my presence."

"Then you'll spend it with us," Angel said, hastily adding, "If you want to, of course. I don't know if you already have plans."

He grinned at her. "No plans, and yes, I'd love to spend the holidays with you."

I let out a contented sigh. Angel and Rafé were getting

along. Herne and I were doing well. Leaving the work issues out of it, life was actually pretty good.

At that moment, Herne returned with a platter full of sizzling steaks. Angel reluctantly unwound herself and headed into the kitchen. As we gathered around the table, she returned with a basket filled with baked potatoes, and a salad. Rafé held my chair for me, then guided Angel to her seat. Herne placed the platter in the center of the table and I stared hungrily at the food.

"Dig in," Herne said, offering me a steak. He served Angel, then Rafé, and then took the last for himself.

"How's Danielle doing?" I asked. "Is she coming home for Yule?"

Danielle was Herne's daughter, whom he had only recently met. She was currently living with the Amazons on the island of Themiscyra, learning the ways of her mother's people.

"No, I don't think so, though she wants to come back during the spring for a week and we're working on arrangements now for that. She's made friends and her studies are going well. Myrna hardly ever writes to her, but I make sure to stay in touch. We're getting along better." He ladled more barbecue sauce on his steak and spread it across his potato, adding grated cheese on top.

Rafé glanced at him. "How long have you known about her?"

"Only about two months. We got off to a rocky start, but we're sorting it out. Her mother's absolutely no help, and now that Danielle is over in Themiscyra, Myrna appears to have washed her hands of the girl." Herne's expression darkened. "But better it happen now, than before I came into the picture."

I cut open my potato and added butter and cheese. The smell of the food hit me hard and my stomach rumbled. Ever since the Cruharach, when both of my bloodlines fully emerged, I had developed a love affair with meat that eclipsed even my former passion for hamburgers and hotdogs. It was my Autumn Stalker nature—the hunter within had fully emerged and she was hungry for beef on bone. On the other side, I had also noticed my singing voice had gotten better, thanks to my mother's Leannan Sidhe blood.

We set to eating but halfway into the meal, Herne's phone rang. He glanced at it and frowned. "Excuse me, I should probably take this," he said, moving away from the table.

I waved my fork at him, my mouth full.

Angel laughed. "Go on. We aren't going anywhere."

As he moved off toward the living room, I swallowed my food. "So, let's go get a tree tomorrow," I said to Angel.

"All right, but I want a fake one. A big, huge, beautiful, fake tree. My allergies aren't too bad but I don't think they'd be all that happy with a real tree in the house. And Mr. Rumblebutt would take every chance to climb it."

I sighed. I hadn't ever bothered with a Yule tree since I had been on my own—twelve years now—but this year, I wanted a big beautiful spruce tree. "All right. But if we do that, then the wreath on the outside of the door has to be real, and we decorate a couple of the trees in the yard, too."

"I'm good with that." She glanced up. "We'll need to go shopping and pick up ornaments."

Herne returned at that point, looking perplexed. "That was odd," he said, returning to his seat.

"Anything wrong?" I asked.

He gave me a shrug. "I'm not sure, but... Yes, actually. The call was from a friend I haven't heard from in a long while. Angus Lesley. He and his wife Fiona are originally from Scotland. I met them there, a couple hundred years ago. They're magic-born." He paused to take a bite of his food.

"What seems to be the problem? Brexit?" Angel asked with a grin.

Herne snorted, then rested his fork on his plate. "No. Angus wanted to know if we—the Wild Hunt—could help him. He's concerned about his wife."

"Is she ill?" Rafé asked, spearing another potato.

"Angus seems to think she's possessed."

That put a stop to the conversation. I finished my steak and toyed with my potato.

"Possessed? Like in...a spirit?"

He nodded. "I suppose. I'm not really sure. He just said that she's been acting strangely lately. He also mentioned that there are storms coming through the area that seem...odd. He used that word a lot—*odd*. Anyway, he asked if we could come over to give him our opinion."

"Where do they live?" Rafé asked.

"That's the thing. They live in Port Ludlow, which isn't far from Port Gamble, where Dr. Nalcops is located."

Ezra Nalcops was the doctor we suspected was in cahoots with the Tuathan Brotherhood. We hadn't done anything yet because we didn't want to tip him—or the brotherhood—off.

"Is Angus prone to paranoia?" Rafé asked.

"No, not unless he's changed over the years." Herne shook his head, a worried furrow lining his forehead.

"Angus isn't given to exaggeration. He's always been a steady man who has easily dealt with a variety of difficult issues. The fact that he's concerned enough about his wife to call me—that alone tells me this is serious."

A shadow seemed to fall across our dinner. I shivered, glancing outside. We were having an unusual snowfall for the Seattle area, and the entire world seemed white and cold.

"We were going over next week anyway," I said, glancing at Angel. She ducked her head, her lips set in a thin line. She was still upset that she had offered up the idea for Rafé to investigate the headquarters of the Tuathan Brotherhood, but it had been his choice in the end.

"Right. I'm thinking we'll stop in to see if we can help him out. I won't count this as a regular case, but we'll just see what we can find out, to help out an old friend," Herne said.

"How did you meet Angus?" I asked, finishing my potato. A blast of wind hit the trees outside and sent the snow swirling in a spiral and I shivered as a goose walked over my grave.

"Angus and I go way back. He was out on a hunting trip and I was in my form as the stag. He targeted me, not comprehending who I was. When I realized that, I changed back into my human shape and he almost fell over himself apologizing. He was hungry, which was why he was out hunting, so I offered him part of my dinner and we started talking and hit it off." He shook his head. "A lot of years have passed since those days."

"Is his wife Scottish, too?" Angel asked.

Herne nodded. "Fiona came over with Angus. As time

went on, they decided to try out the New World and just see what it was like. I had moved over by then, and I helped them find a place and get settled. They had three children, all whom have grown up and moved away. The oldest moved back to Scotland, one is living in Maine, and the third died on a fishing boat fifty-odd years ago."

I carried my plate into the kitchen, and Angel followed me. There was New York–style cheesecake with raspberry sauce for dessert, and I carried it while she picked up the dessert plates and we returned to the table.

"Well, if nothing else, it will be nice for you to see them again." I stood back, letting Angel take over cutting the cheesecake. I took the plates and poured the sauce on the slices, handing them to the men.

"Yes, it will," Herne said, sounding preoccupied. While Rafé carried their dinner plates to the kitchen, Herne glanced out the window. "This is not ideal weather to drive over to the peninsula, but we have no choice. I'll let Angus know we're coming."

"We're still leaving Monday morning, aren't we?" Angel asked.

"Right," Herne said.

"You seem really worried," I said, diving into my cheesecake, relaxing as the creamy filling dissolved in a burst of flavor on my tongue.

Herne shrugged. "I don't know. I just have an odd feeling about Angus and Fiona. As I said, Angus isn't given to exaggeration, so if he's worried enough to call me, yeah, I'm concerned that something is wrong."

We finished dessert and relocated back to the living room. Herne seemed restless, pacing around the room.

"Would you like to go out for a walk?" I wasn't looking

forward to the chill, but if it would help, I'd bundle myself into my snow gear and head out with him.

But he merely shook his head. "No, I fancy a run. I'm really not good company right now. I'm sorry, but Angus's call took me by surprise. Do you mind if we cut the evening short?"

Feeling concerned, but realizing that he needed space, I nodded. "Angel, can you and Rafé run me home?"

Angel nodded. "Not a problem. Why don't we all just call it an early evening? Rafé has to work tomorrow anyway, so you and I can tackle the laundry and catch up on *Rudding Place Northwest.*"

As Rafé and Angel gathered their things, Herne scraped off plates and put them in the dishwasher. I joined him in the kitchen.

"Are you sure you don't want me to stay? I'd be happy to," I said, touching his arm.

He tilted his head, his wheat-colored hair draping down his shoulders. The light in his eyes mirrored the depths of silent blue lakes, high in the mountains. He poured detergent into the dishwasher reservoir, then closed the door and started the cycle. Straightening, he wiped his hands on a dishtowel.

"Thank you, love, but no. I'm feeling the call of the wild tonight. There are times I need to race out in the woods and leave everything behind. Please don't think I'm pushing you away." He took my hands, drawing me to him. I leaned my head against his chest and he nuzzled my hair. "Do you understand?" His voice was trembling.

"Yes, I do. There are times we all need space. I'm not insulted or offended." I tilted my chin up, staring into his eyes. "Kiss me, though. Remind me that you love me."

"Always," he whispered, his lips meeting mine. They were warm, supple, and as he kissed me, he pulled me to him. I felt fully loved and cared for. Yet as much as he possessed me, Herne had never tried to remake me, never tried to change me. He let me be who I was, which only made me love him more.

Reeling from the intensity of his kiss, I pulled my head away, catching my breath. "I will miss you tonight," I said, reaching up to sweep a strand of hair away from his eyes. I traced the line of his face down to his jaw. The scruff of his beard was soft beneath my fingers, and he laughed gently.

"That makes me happy. That you want me. Perhaps tomorrow?"

"I meet with Marilee in the evening, but maybe I can drop over in the afternoon." I could feel his arousal as he pressed against me, but I could also feel something else— his longing to race into the forest.

Ever since the Cruharach, I'd been able to feel more emotions connected with the wilds, and had felt that same hunger in myself. Only for me, it was the desire to seek and hunt.

I had been practicing with a bow and arrow—the regular kind as opposed to the pistol grip crossbow I already knew how to use. I was also learning swordplay. I could fight with a dagger, in fact, I could wield two of them at once, but the sword was a different animal altogether.

"Call me in the morning and we'll see what's going on. For now, though, another kiss will tide me over." His lips met mine again, and I lost myself in the spiral of desire that spun itself around us. Finally, reluctantly, I pulled away.

"All right, if I'm not going to stay, I'd better go before you get me too hot and bothered." I laughed, gathering my things. Rafé and Angel were waiting in the living room for me as I headed for the door. "Let's get a move on, you two."

They made their farewells to Herne and we headed out to Rafé's four-wheel drive. As I swung into the backseat, I glanced back at Herne's house. The mansion was silent under the snow, and as I fastened my seatbelt, there was a glimmer as a silver stag came darting out from the side, standing tall and proud and luminous.

Herne. The Silver Stag. The Lord of the Hunt.

"He's gorgeous," Angel said, catching her breath.

Rafé nodded, his gaze riveted by the massive stag. "I still can't believe I know a god."

"You think *you're* amazed. I'm *dating* a god. That stag is my boyfriend." But my words fell away as Herne leapt ahead to race into the park that buttressed his house. He was faster than any normal deer could ever be, and a nimbus of silver surrounded him, a glowing fog that drifted from his body.

I watched silently as he vanished into the thicket. I hadn't been kidding. The fact that I was dating a god, one to whose mother I was pledged, left me wondering just where my life was taking me. But it was too late to back away, regardless of whatever consequences came from the relationship. I was madly in love with Herne, and he seemed to feel the same way about me. He held my heart in his hands, and all I could do was pray that he'd be kind with it.

Finally, after a moment, Rafé eased out of the driveway and we headed back to the house Angel and I lived in. All the way, I stared out the window, thinking. There were so many things I didn't know about Herne's background, so many hundreds—possibly thousands—of years that I knew nothing about. And yet, I was part of his life now, and every day I seemed to learn more about him. That brought my thoughts to Angus and Fiona.

Wondering what could be so wrong that one of the magic-born felt the need to contact Herne, I stared at the drifting snow as we traveled the silent road back to my house.

CHAPTER TWO

The next morning, Angel came racing into my room, waking me up. She was holding her phone and she looked like she had just been punched in the gut.

"Ember, Ember, wake up!" She shook my shoulders until I opened my eyes and blurrily pushed myself up against the headboard.

"What is it? What's wrong? Did something happen with DJ? Are you all right?" I rubbed my eyes, yawning as she sat on the edge of my bed, holding her arms across her stomach.

"No, I'm not all right. DJ's father called me." She stared at me bleakly. "DeWayne ran away from Mama J. when he found out she was pregnant. He's never had any interest in finding out about the child he abandoned. Why the hell is he calling now?"

That woke me up. I shifted, crossing my legs as I pulled a light throw from the other side of the bed and wrapped it around my shoulders. I loved my house, but it was proving chilly on the upper floor. I had quickly realized as autumn turned into winter that we needed central heating and air, but I wanted to wait for better weather before having it installed.

"What did he say?"

She shrugged. "DeWayne was looking for Mama J. He said he wanted to 'come visit her.' My intuition told me that he's low on money and has probably pissed off any friends who might float him a place to stay, so he's looking up old soft touches. I told him she was dead."

"How did he react?" I wondered how much of Angel's intuition might be her reaction to a man who abandoned his girlfriend and unborn child, and how much it was actually on point. She was usually spot-on, but this was personal.

She frowned. "That's the thing. He paused for a moment, then asked me what happened to 'the baby.' He doesn't even know whether Mama J. had a boy or a girl. I told him not to worry, that we were fine. He asked me flat out then what the 'kid's' name was, and if he had a son or daughter." She shook her head, staring at the bed.

"What did you tell him?"

"I asked him why he cared. That's when he said he 'wouldn't mind meeting his kid' and that he was planning on coming back to Seattle for a visit. I didn't know what to say, so I hung up on him." She shivered. "I think he just wants to find out if Mama J. left any money. He was a mooch when he lived with us, and he abandoned all of us, and men like that don't change."

I suddenly realized what she was afraid of. "You think he might want to take DJ with him? That he might come out here and take DJ away? He's not on the birth certificate, though—how could any claim hold up in court?"

"DNA. And he's a wolf shifter, remember. They can be canny and sly. He's a lone wolf—he told Mama J. that he got kicked out of his pack years ago. She felt sorry for him. That's how they met. He came to her soup kitchen one night."

Angel's mother—Mama J.—had owned a diner. She opened it to the homeless after hours, giving away the food that they hadn't sold during the day, and she always made a huge vat of soup and had bread to supplement it so that nobody went away hungry. Mama J. had also been an incredible card reader, and Angel had inherited her psychic abilities. I suspected if they looked far enough back in their family tree that they'd find a spot of magic-born blood, but I had never ventured the idea aloud.

"You know as well as I do that no court is going to give a man custody over a son he abandoned before birth, who doesn't have a stable life. Especially now that Cooper has him." I wrapped my arm around her shoulders. "We won't let him take DJ away from you. I promise, we'll figure out something."

She nodded. "It's hard enough having DJ living with Cooper. But I can handle that—it's best for DJ and I still get to see him. I couldn't bear it if some stranger dragged DJ away with him. I don't trust DeWayne. There was always something slimy about him and I can still feel it through the phone."

I slid out from under the throw, wincing as my feet hit the icy floor. A glance out the window told me it was snowing again. We had about three inches, which was a good amount for the Seattle area, and though they had actually gotten around to plowing the roads, it was slippery out there.

"I hope this stops before Monday or the commute is going to be hell." Shivering, I wrapped myself in my robe. "Come on, don't worry. We'll deal with DeWayne if and when he shows up. Chances are he won't bother. Today we're going to buy a tree and ornaments and everything else we need to turn this place into a winter wonderland." I paused. "You still up for it?"

Angel brightened a little. "Yeah, it will help take my mind off of DeWayne."

"How did he get in touch with you, anyway? He's been gone, what, ten years?"

"I still have the same phone number as I did back then. He had it because he lived with Mama J. Even before she got pregnant with DJ, I didn't like DeWayne. He was an asshole, and he kept making semi-suggestive moves toward me, but I knew if I called him on it, he'd gaslight me. Mama J. would have kicked him out—she was always on my side—but I knew she loved him, so I kept my mouth shut." Angel shook her head. "Part of me thinks I should have said something anyway, but then I wouldn't have my little brother, and I love DJ."

"I know you do," I said. "And you aren't going to lose him, regardless of what happens with DeWayne. We've tackled far worse problems before." I grabbed a pair of jeans from my dresser, along with a cobalt V-neck sweater and a black leather belt. Adding a pair of blue knee socks to the pile, and a clean bra and panties, I carried them back to the bed.

"I'll start breakfast while you change. Are you taking a shower first, or coming right down?" Angel stood up, thrusting her phone in her pocket. She was wearing a pair of green leggings, with a long golden tunic over the top. Angel could easily have been a model—she was five-ten, willowy, and had beautiful bone structure. And her rich brown skin was always clear and glowing.

"I took a shower last night. I'm clean enough," I said, grinning at her. "I'll be down as soon as I dress. Can you feed Mr. Rumblebutt?" I glanced around. "Where is the little booger? He didn't sleep with me, for a change."

"He slept in my room. He found my fleece robe and decided that it made the perfect nest." She winked at me. "Don't worry, I won't win his heart away from you."

"Go on with you," I said, waving her out with a laugh. Mr. Rumblebutt was my black Norwegian Forest cat, and he absolutely doted on both Angel and me. He was pretty much a tribble on legs, with tufted feet and ears, and he was my best buddy.

I quickly dressed, brushed my hair back in a ponytail and slapped on a quick face of makeup, opting for an icy look. Might as well match the season, I thought, applying a rainbow of silver, blue, and plum colors. After finishing my toilette, I slid on a pair of fleece-lined snow boots and headed downstairs, where Angel was making omelets and toast.

"Smells good," I said, sliding into a kitchen chair. "So I guess I'd better contact Ronnie about next week. I'm pretty sure she'll be watching Talia's dogs, and we need to arrange for her to care for Mr. Rumblebutt while we're over on the peninsula."

Ronnie Archwood was one of the Light Fae, but she had been excommunicated from the court long ago and was one of the few Fae who didn't look down on me because of my bloodlines. I was half Light Fae, half Dark. Most of the Fae called me a *tralaeth*—basically a dirty word for half-breed.

"Mr. R. likes her a lot," Angel said, sliding our omelets onto our plates. She added the toast and carried them to the table as I made myself a quad-shot mocha.

"He does, doesn't he?" I texted Ronnie while I was waiting for the espresso, asking if she could check on him and spend some time playing with him while we were gone. She texted back as I was carrying my mug to the table, confirming that she'd be able to watch over him as well as Talia's greyhounds. She could get my spare key from Talia, with whom we had exchanged house keys. Relieved, I checked that worry off my mental checklist.

"What do you think about our upcoming trip?" I asked as I settled in to eat.

Angel shook her head. "Not so much, to be honest. I'm not fond of going over to the peninsula. There are so many freaky spirits and creatures there, and I key in on their energy too easily."

"At least it will be a change of pace. I think we can all use a little time away. Maybe it will give Yutani a chance to sort out the crap he's going through." I paused, adding, "At least I hope so. He's been a tool lately."

Yutani, our IT guy, had recently found out he was the son of the Great Coyote, and he had been trying to contact the Trickster for a couple months now to find out why Coyote had never told him. He had also been acting out, and I was about ready to call him on it if Herne wouldn't. While Yutani could be overly sarcastic, it had reached a point where I wanted to smack him one.

"He doesn't know who he is now. He always had a

rough time, given his childhood, but now he finds out that the same god who claimed him when he was a child and basically threw him under the bus is his daddy. I know he's being a pain in the ass, but I don't blame him for being lost." Angel always looked for the best in people. It was a testament to her nature, but it could also be dangerous.

We cleared away our dishes and I stacked them in the dishwasher while Angel washed the table. Deciding to take my car, which was better in the snow than hers, we headed out to buy a tree.

"You realize we'll just get it set up and have to leave," Angel said. "How is Mr. Rumblebutt around trees, even a fake one?"

"I don't know. He's never had one to contend with before." I eased over to the left lane as we approached Wexworth's, a large department store that had anything and everything you could want, including groceries. A stab of worry ran through me. "Do you think we should attempt it?"

"I think we should buy everything today, decorate with swags and garlands and lights around the ceiling, where he can't reach them, then when we get home after the trip, we can put up the tree. That way there won't be any cat-astrophes to come home to," she said, laughing.

We pulled into the parking lot and I found a spot near the door—a miracle, given it was the Christmas season and shoppers were out in full force.

"Do you mind celebrating Solstice instead of Christmas?" I asked. "We could do both."

"I don't mind. Mama J. celebrated Christmas but it was always about family, never about religion. And given all the gods hanging around, we just went with the flow and adopted paganism. By the time I met you, Mama J. was basically a humanist more than anything else. I tend to follow her path." She shrugged, turning sideways to block a cold gust of wind that swept past. "As long as we have lights and a tree and pretty decorations, I'm good."

"How about DJ? I know he's celebrating with Cooper and his family, but…"

"Eh, he's good. He told me that he's learning about the Wolf Spirit, and I have the feeling he may be transitioning more into his Wulfine nature. Cooper's family are followers of Lupa, the wolf goddess. If he chooses to join them, I have no objections. They put a heavy emphasis on honor and keeping your word, and guarding the pack— which means family. Those are good qualities to embrace." She opened the door and held it. "After you, madam!"

"Thank you kindly," I said, ducking inside out of the falling snow. Seattle was coping rather well with this snowfall, though if it got any heavier we'd be in trouble.

Wexworth's was busy, but not overly so, and we managed to procure a cart without a wait. We headed for the home-goods aisles and proceeded to sort through the artificial trees. There were some incredibly good simulations, and we found a seven-footer that was pre-lit with multi-colored twinkle lights. The branches were full and sturdy.

"I like this one," Angel said.

"Then let's get it. What sort of theme do we want for the ornaments?" I wasn't too picky, but I knew Angel had a sense of design and I wanted her to be happy.

We looked through the decorations, and then I saw a

gorgeous blown-glass mermaid. "How about this? There's a unicorn too. How about a wonderland theme in blue, white, and silver?"

She nodded. "I think that would be lovely. Let's go for it."

We filled the cart with several of the ornaments—a couple unicorns, a mermaid, and faeries—then added an assortment of animals including an owl, a bear, several ravens, a couple bluebirds, a stag, and other assorted woodland creatures. Then we sorted through the blue and silver ornaments that were available, picking the shiniest, most glittery ones we could find. Angel dug through the garlands, coming up with a gorgeous flocked glittering garland to string around the edges of the ceiling, and we practically emptied the light section, opting for multi-color twinkle lights. After about an hour, we had filled two carts and, with the tree in tow, we headed to the checkout counter, adding various boxes of candy and cookies as we went.

"I think we've got enough to start," Angel said, grinning. "We can hang the garland and lights today, and set up the snow village."

"I want to make fudge, too. I have a feeling this coming week's going to be a bitch, so I want to spend the weekend relaxing and watching movies and having fun." As I paid the bill, with Angel giving me half in cash, I thought that we needed times like these—downtime when we could relax and forget about the death and bloodshed and mayhem going on around us.

By Sunday, we had decorated everything except for actually putting the tree together, we had made fudge and cookies, and stocked up on cat food. I had a good session with Marilee, though I canceled my appointment with her for the coming week. Even though the Cruharach was now safely behind me, I was still meeting with my mentor to work on strengthening my magic, and I was trying to learn actual spells now, like my mother had used.

I didn't have the knack for spellwork that I had hoped for, but I was learning how to direct the energy better than before. The innate abilities—like my Leannan Sidhe defense—were always there and ready, and my ability to talk to water elementals and summon the moisture out of the air had grown stronger. But actually manipulating the energy through spellwork? Not quite so easy for me.

However, my workouts were a different matter. Ever since the Cruharach, my workouts had become stronger and more intense, and I was finding that I could run faster, climb harder, and fight better than ever before. I was training with a martial arts teacher now, and he had me learning parkour, though I was still nervous about some of the acrobatics.

I called Herne on Sunday afternoon as I was sitting in my bedroom, trying to figure out what to pack. "Hey, we're still heading out early, aren't we? I'm packing and not sure what to take."

"Pack whatever you think you'll need for tromping out in the woods and snow. Don't forget to make arrangements for Fumblebutt." He laughed. He was fond of Mr. R. and had dubbed my cat with the nickname.

"Already done. And Mr. Rumblebutt kindly asks me to remind you that he is as graceful as the day is long, and he'll claw your nuts if you keep tormenting him with such cruel names," I said, inserting a formal accent into my voice.

"Yeah, well, tell the fluffball that I said hi." Herne laughed again. "Seriously, you and Angel need to bring winter clothing. Angus said it's cold over there and it's been snowing. They have five inches on the ground."

"It's been an unusually cold winter," I said, thinking about the roads. I hadn't been over to the Olympic Peninsula often, so this would be a new experience for me. "How many cars are we taking?"

"I don't want anybody driving over there who isn't experienced on the backroads. The highway can be dicey at times. We'll take my Expedition, and Viktor's going to rent a sturdy all-wheel drive big enough to pack equipment in. Yutani's vehicle is mighty, but too small. I'll pick you, Angel, and Raven up tomorrow morning. Raven's joining us, right?"

Herne had asked me to see if Raven would go with us, given the possibility of possession, and she had agreed to come with us. She would also come in handy if we met any of the Ante-Fae, given she was also one.

"Yeah, she'll be coming along."

"Good. Viktor will pick up Talia and Yutani. Rafé will meet us there—he's got an all-wheel drive so he'll be able to manage the roads. Charlie's staying here, of course. He has a couple tests and needs to focus on his schoolwork."

Charlie Darren was a nominal employee of the Wild Hunt, which meant to say that he was officially employed by the agency, but was focused on getting his accounting degree for the next year or so. After that, he'd be in charge of the Wild Hunt's ledgers. He did some data entry for us, but Herne wanted him to train into his position. Charlie was also a vampire, which meant traveling with us was potentially hazardous to his health if we got caught out in the daylight.

"Anything else we need to bring? Weapons, of course. I'll bring my pistol grip crossbow—I'm not conversant enough with the long bow yet—and my dagger."

"Just whatever you think you'll need for a few days to a week. We could end up there for a couple of weeks if things stall out. I hope not, but we need to be prepared." Herne paused, then added, "I talked to Danielle this morning. She'll definitely be coming to visit for Ostara. I'm looking forward to seeing her more than I realized."

"Then I'm glad she gets to come." I paused, then added, "Herne, I wanted to talk to you about Yutani." I wasn't sure what exactly to say, but Herne took care of that.

"I know, I know. I've been meaning to talk to him. He's been a PITA lately, and frankly, while I understand, it's not helping morale at work any. He can be as sullen as he wants on his own time, but when he's with the rest of us, he needs to leave the attitude behind. His aunt Celia called me the other night. She said that when she talked to him not long ago, he actually told her to keep her nose out of his business. And you know how much Yutani adores his aunt. So something has to be going on."

"Yeah, that is bad. Okay, well, given you already know what I was going to say, I'll leave it to you for now. But if he gets on my back, I'm not going to sit here and be his punching bag—metaphorically or any other way." I blew a kiss into the phone. "I love you. We'll be ready tomorrow. I assume early?"

"I'll drop by around eight. I won't see you tonight, I'm

afraid. I'm spending the evening with Morgana. She wants to brief me on some things she's picked up on that Saílle and Névé are doing. I think our fair queens are up to shenanigans, and they're probably not harmless."

I sighed. The more we dealt with the Fae Queens, the happier I was that neither wanted me to join their courts. I was about to say something when my phone dinged. I glanced at the screen.

"Hold on, Raven's texting me."

He snorted. "That could take awhile. Call me back when you're done."

I switched over to my texts. DON'T FORGET, YOU NEED TO PICK ME UP TOMORROW. NOT SURE WHAT GOOD I CAN DO BUT YOU KNOW I'LL TRY. SOUNDS LIKE A FUN TRIP.

CAN YOU BE AT MY HOUSE BY 7:30 AM? ARE YOU BRINGING RAJ?

I waited for a moment until Raven texted back.

YES, I CAN'T LEAVE HIM ALONE THAT LONG. I'LL BE THERE. SEE YOU THEN.

I called Herne back. "I just got a text from Raven. She'll be here tomorrow."

"Good."

I grinned. "By the way, she's bringing Raj."

There was a brief silence, then Herne snorted. "Why am I not surprised? All right. He's housebroken, right?"

It was my turn to snicker. "He's a gargoyle, not a dog. And yes, he's housebroken. Anyway, see you tomorrow, love. Wish we had time to get together tonight, but I need to do laundry, anyway. Love you."

"Love you, too."

As I pocketed my phone, I glanced out the window. There, perched on the roof outside my window in the snow, a lone crow was staring at me. A shiver ran down my back as I walked over to open the window. I leaned out, and the crow tilted his head.

"What do you want to tell me?" I whispered. I had come to realize that the crows were messengers for me. I touched the crow necklace at my throat that Morgana had given me to symbolize I belonged to her.

The crow let out a long shriek, then glanced up at the sky. I followed his gaze. There, the clouds were thickening, and I could smell ozone in the air—the scent of snow riding the wind.

"There's a storm coming, isn't there?" I asked, turning back to the crow.

He stared at me for a moment, then let out a single caw before taking wing. Circling outside my window three times, he then set out, heading west toward the incoming storm. I shivered as I reached out to touch the water elementals caught in the clouds. They were dark and twisted, and I quickly pulled back, shielding myself. Something was on the move, that much I could feel, and whatever it was, it scared the fuck out of me.

CHAPTER THREE

*R*aven was at the house by seven A.M. She
looked incredibly alert for that early in the
morning. Raven BoneTalker was one of the Ante-Fae, the
predecessor to the Fae races, and she was a bone witch.
She was somewhat of a firecracker—though Herne called
her a loose cannon—but Angel and I found our friendship
with her growing.

Raj was sitting patiently in the snow behind her,
staring at the house with a skeptical look. He wasn't afraid
—I knew him well enough to recognize his expressions by
now. Raj just happened to find strange places rather
daunting at first, and he was suspicious of them until he
figured out they weren't going to launch themselves
toward him. He had been over to our house with Raven
often enough, and though he had cottoned up to Angel
and me, he hadn't come to a decision about the house
itself. At least not yet.

Leaving him where he was with a stern, "Stay here,"
Raven followed me into the house, carrying a basket

covered by a tea towel. She was wearing a black velvet dress with a low-cut neckline lined in lace. The bodice fitted to her curves and the skirt flared out in an asymmetrical hem, with the front just above her knees and the back to mid-calf. Raven was a buxom, curvy woman, with hair about the length of mine, only her espresso locks were streaked with purple. I thought it was natural and not dyed, but it seemed rude to ask. Her eyes were the same deep brown as her hair, and she sparked off magic in her wake.

"Morning, ladies," she said, breezing past me as I opened the door. I was still in my sleep shirt and robe and I yawned as she brightly ordered, "Get dressed, Kearney. It's morning. Snap to it!" She brushed my cheek with a kiss, then hustled through the hallway to the kitchen. "What's Angel making for breakfast? I thought we could add these to the table." She set the basket down on the table and pulled the cloth off to reveal a bowl of muffins. "I made them. Blueberry lemon, with pecans."

I stared at the fragrant muffins and my stomach rumbled. "Yum," I said. I reached for one but Raven slapped my hand.

"Not till you're properly dressed. Good gods, don't be a slouch. Get a move on, woman." She glanced around. "Where's Angel?"

"She's finishing up her shower, I think. I'll go get dressed." As I started to turn from the table, I grabbed one of the muffins and, laughing as she waved me away, took off for my room.

I met Angel on the stairs.

"Raven's here, and she brought muffins." I held up my prize. "I scored one."

"Of course you did," Angel said, laughing. She was dressed in skinny jeans, a peach-colored turtleneck, and a pair of Uggs. "I'll get breakfast started."

I hurried to my room and decided to follow Angel's lead. Jeans and a sweater were good. We had packed for inclement weather and for tracking out in the woods, but I hadn't decided on what to wear for the trip itself.

I grabbed a fresh pair of low-rider black jeans, pairing them with an emerald green V-neck sweater. I dug out a pair of Doc Martens I had recently bought. They were platforms, ankle boots that laced up the front. The chunky heel was easy to move in and had good traction, and they were extremely comfortable. I slid them on, then did my makeup, brushed my hair back into a ponytail. Taking one last look around my bedroom, making certain I had everything I'd need, I saw Mr. Rumblebutt sleeping on the bed. He started to purr when I scooped him up.

"Hey you, be a good boy for Ronnie, please. I'll be back as soon as I can, and so will Angel. Meanwhile, you'll score—I know Ronnie gives you extra treats. Don't worry about us, okay?" I held him up, then kissed him on the head and let him down again. He zoomed away, thudding down the stairs. He must have heard a can opener.

I followed him down to find Angel making scrambled eggs and bacon while Raven was setting the table. Ronnie had arrived, and she was opening a can of cat food for Mr. Rumblebutt, who was all over her. He liked her, for which I was grateful, and she made it a policy to spend at least an hour a day with her pet clients, if not more.

"Have you been over to Talia's yet?" I asked, wiggling my fingers at her.

"No," Ronnie said. "She said she'd take care of them

this morning. I'll go over there at noon to walk them, then again at eight, after I've fed Mr. Rumblebutt here and played with him for a while."

"You don't know how glad I am that Mr. R. can use a litterbox." I frowned, thinking. "Raven, what does Raj do? I mean, I know you let him out, but if you had to leave… he's intelligent enough, can he make do inside somehow?"

Raven laughed. "He's quite intelligent, but gargoyles are wired differently than we are, so we don't necessarily understand their abilities. But no, he goes outside mostly. I could train him to use the toilet, though it would be harder for him unless I bought one low to the ground, but frankly, that seems more trouble than it's worth. I have a friend come over to take care of the ferrets while I'm gone. You remember Apollo? He's an animal lover and Vixen doesn't mind if I hire his services for this."

I blushed, my mind going to all sorts of places at the word "services." Apollo the Golden Boy was another one of the Ante-Fae. He was gorgeous, and one hell of a sexy dancer, and he belonged to Vixen, the Mistress of Mayhem. Vixen was possessive of him, but they—Vixen was gender-fluid in the most literal sense of the word— had no problems with Apollo making platonic friends.

"All right, let's eat," Angel said. "Ronnie, I made enough for you, too."

We gathered around the table and ate breakfast. By the time Angel had started the dishwasher, it was almost eight. A horn sounded from outside and I got a text from Herne, telling me it was time to get our butts out to the car.

"Lock up when you're done," I said to Ronnie, picking

up Mr. R. for one last snuggle. "We'll be back as soon as we can."

"You know he's in good hands with me," she reassured me.

Grabbing my suitcase—thank gods for rolling luggage —I headed outside, followed by Angel and Raven. Raven whistled to Raj, who came bounding over to her, and we descended on Herne's SUV en masse. As Herne stowed our luggage in the back, I slid into the front seat while Angel and Raven settled in the middle seat with Raj between them. Once we were all buckled in, Herne started the engine and we were off, headed to the ferry.

WE ARRIVED AT THE EDMONDS TERMINAL TEN MINUTES before boarding. *The Puyallup* was one of the jumbo ferries, over four hundred, sixty feet in length, capable of holding two hundred vehicles and almost twenty-five hundred passengers. It had an elevator to the upper decks, where there was a galley as well as vending machines and restrooms. The crossing would take about half an hour.

Luckily, Viktor was already there, and we managed to squeeze through. As Herne paid the fare and we drove aboard, parking halfway between the bow and the stern against the outer wall where we could see the waves crashing around the ferry, the great engines of the ship creaked and grumbled. I immediately felt a sense of connection with the water so close, and found myself breathing a little easier. My Leannan Sidhe blood was water-based, and ever since I had undergone the

Cruharach, that sense of belonging had increased every time I came close to any body of water.

Herne turned off the ignition and put on the emergency brake. As we unlocked our seatbelts, I frowned. Beneath the sense of connection, there was something else—something that was disturbing my senses. I slipped out of the car and, zipping my leather jacket, stepped up on the ledge that traversed the side of the ferry. I held onto the railing, staring out over the water.

The clouds that had been coming in from the west were closer, and though they hadn't yet reached us, I could feel them circling through the air, spinning and crashing into each other. They were raucous and rowdy, like frat boys gearing up for a party, and there was something shadowy about the energy that made me uneasy. I usually loved storms, but I was leery of this one—it felt too alive, too alert.

"Good morning," Herne said, swinging up on the ledge to stand beside me. He leaned on the railing. "Raven's opting to stay in the car with Raj, while Angel's going upstairs."

I nodded, still staring at the clouds. "There's something coming, Herne. Behind those clouds. I have an uneasy feeling about this trip."

"Could it just be your worry about Rafé?" He slid an arm around my waist, hugging me to him.

I thought for a moment. Could he be right? Was it merely my fears for Rafé behind my discomfort? But when I closed my eyes, trying to pinpoint the reason, my thoughts turned toward the peninsula, and in particular to the thought of Herne's friend Angus.

"I think…it has something to do with Angus. I know

he's your friend, Herne, but we have to be cautious. There's an energy caught up in the storms that are coming in, and they're coming from the direction of the peninsula. There's a twisted feel to it, as though they aren't natural."

"Weather magic, perhaps?" Herne said, frowning. "I hadn't noticed, I've been so busy trying to figure out how best to protect Rafé. I know you and Angel still think this is a mistake, and you may be right, but right now, this is the only choice we have. We *must* infiltrate the group and they're good at keeping out of sight. This could be our break to help us figure out who's behind the Tuathan Brotherhood, and how best to deal with them."

"I know," I said softly. "I didn't like the idea at first, but you're right. We don't have much of a choice when it comes down to it. I just hope that he's able to stay safe. Who knows where the hell they're going to take him?"

"That's why we fitted him with a subcutaneous tracking device. It should work in case he loses his phone. Yutani has him on trace, so barring any unforeseen complications, we should be able to track his movements no matter where he goes." Herne paused, then added, "By the way, I talked to Yutani."

I let out a sigh. "And?"

"And he told me that he doesn't mean to be an ass. He's been trying to contact Coyote for a while now, and he keeps running into dead ends. He's frustrated with both the situation and himself. I think he'll keep himself in check, though."

"I know he doesn't mean to be an asshole, but honestly, we've all had issues and we've all had to deal with them. Just because he feels at an impasse isn't an excuse for railing at the rest of us." I felt sorry for Yutani and was pissed at Coyote for not contacting him—for not telling him in the beginning—but I was running out of patience.

"Don't forget, he's been dealt a lot of blows over the course of his life, none of them for anything under his control. I think Coyote's silence reminds him of the rejection he felt when his village pushed him out." Herne shrugged. "Whatever the case, he promised to try to do better."

The ferry suddenly rose and dipped, the water spraying over the side. The winds were growing stronger and I shivered as they blasted the water around us, sending a drenching mist over the side.

"Do you want to go up top and sit with Angel, or back to the car where Raven is?" Herne asked as we pulled away from the railing.

I shook my head. "Neither. Let's walk up to the bow and watch the water from there. It should be okay if we don't cross over the safety lines."

The ferries were open ended on both sides, and so we walked along the outer railing to the bow of the boat. There were four cars there. The middle two were slightly forward, and there were ropes that crossed in front of all four, signaling where to stop when you pulled forward onto the ferry. I noticed that one of the cars was occupied while the other three were empty. The one that was occupied had a woman in it reading her tablet.

The next moment, the ferry lurched as a gust of wind shook the boat, cresting a wave high enough to splash over the hoods of the cars at the front. Herne caught hold of me with one hand and grabbed one of the safety rails on the side of the boat, pulling me off the deck and back onto the ledge. He held me tight as the boat rose up and then dipped abruptly on the rolling water.

As we watched, the car with the woman in it suddenly broke loose and began to roll forward toward the ropes at the front. The woman began to scream as the car skidded on the wet deck. Over the rumbling of the ferry engines, over the roar of the waves, I could hear the fear in her voice.

"No!" I broke free of Herne's grasp as the car went rolling toward the edge of the ferry.

The woman appeared to be frantically trying to start her car so that she could put it in reverse, but then next moment, the ferry rose again and then, abruptly dropping as the wave rolled out from beneath us, the nose tilted forward. The car teetered on the edge. Before anybody could move, it tilted and fell into the tumultuous waters.

I yanked off my boots and vaulted up on the edge of the railing as the ferry's engines slowed. There were screams and shouts as three of the ferry workers raced toward where the car had gone overboard, while two more tried to hold back the people pushing forward to see what the commotion was about.

"What are you doing?" Herne yelled, reaching for me.

"I can swim like a fish and I can call on the elementals," I shouted back at him before diving into the water. As I headed toward the rolling waves, I focused on my mother's blood and summoned my Leannan Sidhe side.

The shock of the cold water hit me like a brick, but I managed to come up for air. Then, narrowing my focus, I caught a lungful of air and dove beneath the waves, reaching out for any nearby water elementals. They were thick in the sound today, and I immediately felt one by my side. I projected the image of the car and the terrified woman trapped within, and then formed the image of me opening the door and getting her to safety, along with the need for help.

Communicating with elementals was tricky—they didn't think in terms of words and language—but rather, emotions and images. But it was one of my talents, and the elemental in front of me seemed to understand. As it encompassed my body, we went sliding through the dark water behind the ferry.

There, slowly sinking, was the woman's car. The inside light was on and I could see that she was pounding on the window, her expression one of absolute terror.

The elemental was huge, and I thought of a way that we could rescue her. I formed the image of the water element wrapping around the car and carrying it to the surface long enough for me to free the woman. After a brief moment, the elemental coiled one tendril around me and another around the car, and we began heading toward the surface.

My lungs felt like they were going to burst, and I must have projected the pain toward the elemental because then it forced my lips open and a bubble of air rushed through my body. I caught hold of it in my lungs and relaxed enough to focus again. Somehow it had managed to transfer a breath into me. Grateful, I embraced the elemental with my thanks.

The water around us was reeling, rolling in swirls and eddies that seemed to boil like dark clouds. I closed my eyes as the waves crashed against us. If the elemental hadn't been with me, I would have been pulled under by the churning waters of Puget Sound. Everything around me was bathed in silver and dark gray, and for a moment I couldn't figure out which way was up or down, and it felt like we'd never surface. But then the elemental broke through the water and the air rushed around me. I coughed, wheezing as I gulped breath after breath.

The elemental held the car steady as I reached the door and it used a tendril of water to shelter me as I pulled on the latch. The inside was nearly full of water but there was enough air for the door to release, and the woman came spilling out. She was either unconscious or already drowned, but I didn't have time to check.

I grabbed hold of her, and right then, heard shouts behind us. A lifeboat was chugging through the water, heading toward us. The *putt-putt* of the motor was the sweetest noise I had heard all day.

I gritted my teeth, holding the woman under one arm as I treaded water, keeping us afloat. The elemental gave me a gentle shove, pushing me forward, and in less than a minute, the tugboat was beside us and the men were pulling us aboard. As I tumbled in, I saw the car begin to sink again before it quietly vanished beneath the waves.

"Are you all right?" one of the men said.

I nodded, pushing back the hair that had plastered against my face.

"Check her. I'm fine." I shivered, but we were almost at the bow of the ferry and I knew I could get warm on board.

Another man in the boat began giving the woman CPR. The first few compressions, nothing happened, but then she coughed, spitting out water as the man rolled her to her side. She opened her eyes, still coughing, but she was alive.

As she sat up, groaning, the man next to me gave me a long look. "You had help, didn't you?"

I nodded. "I'm part Water Fae. I can commune with the elementals. I happened to find one willing to help."

"I'd tell you how stupid you were to do that, but the fact is, she'd be dead if you hadn't. So I think I'll leave that lecture for another time," he said, a smile on his lips. "You're a brave woman, you know?"

"Not always. But what else could I do?" I shrugged, realizing that's exactly how I felt. I had the ability, she was in trouble, and therefore the only choice I could make was to help. "My conscience wouldn't let me rest if I had just stood back, watching."

"I think we need to hire Water Fae for the ferry system. Hazard pay, but hey—it's worth it." The man smiled again as we neared the ferry, where we were hustled up a rope ladder.

Herne was standing there, an ashen look on his face. He rushed over to me, pulling me into his arms, covering me with kisses as he held me tight. Angel and the others were right behind him.

"I thought I lost you," he said hoarsely.

"No chance of that. I'm too stubborn to die," I whispered back, shaking as the cold hit me hard. "I'm freezing."

At that moment, one of the deckhands hurried over while a medic attended to the woman.

"Do you need help?" the deckhand—whose nameplate read "Julius Tirran"—asked.

I shook my head. "Just a blanket, a place to change, and

something hot to drink." I turned to Herne. "Can you get me dry clothes out of my suitcase?"

He nodded, but it was Angel who hurried back to the car. The engines started up again, only this time, heavy blocks were placed by the car tires of the front-most cars. The deckhand led us to the elevator and upstairs, where Herne guarded the restroom while Angel brought me in clothes. She had also brought in my blow dryer and she quickly dried off my hair, brushing it into a loose ponytail.

"I know you felt you needed to do that, but if you ever put yourself in danger like that again, woman…" She paused, her voice thick with tears. "I thought we lost you."

"I wouldn't have gone if I hadn't believed that I could save her. I'm impulsive but not stupid." I turned to her. "The woman would have been dead if I'd left it up to the ferry workers. They couldn't have gone down in those depths without scuba gear. I managed it because I'm part Leannan Sidhe, but it was still rough for me and without the elemental's help, there would have been no hope. So yeah, they would have tried but I guarantee you, they wouldn't have succeeded."

"I know," Angel said. "But let's hope this kind of freak accident never happens again."

"I'm with you on that one." I was still freezing, but at least I was dry.

When we came out of the bathroom, Herne and the deckhand were waiting.

"We're approaching the dock. There are bound to be reporters there. We can give you the option of remaining anonymous if you like." The deckhand glanced at Herne nervously, as though he was afraid to approach me. Herne was hovering around me protectively, and he gave the deckhand a dark look.

"I would prefer that," I said, not wanting my name splashed around in the news. "If the woman asks who helped her, can you please just tell her 'a good Samaritan'?"

"That I can do, though we need your name for our records." He was holding a tablet, and I reluctantly gave him my name and phone number. "Thank you, Ms...Kearney." He paused, still looking like he wanted to say something, but then the loudspeaker crackled and the captain was asking us to return to our cars.

"If there's nothing else?"

He shook his head. "No, we can contact you if there is."

Herne and I turned and, following Angel, returned to the car. Viktor, Yutani, and Talia had already buckled up in Viktor's vehicle, while Raven and Raj were waiting in the backseat of Herne's SUV.

I silently climbed in the front seat, exhausted and still chilled. I didn't feel like talking. Glancing at Raven and Angel over my shoulder, I turned back to stare out the window as we drove off the ferry and into Kingston. I had saved a woman's life, but it felt like an ominous beginning to our trip, and I believed in omens.

CHAPTER FOUR

Kingston was a small, picturesque community on Appletree Cove, which opened out into Puget Sound. With the ferry terminal, most of its business came from tourists and commuters on their way across the sound to Seattle, or up the peninsula to Port Townsend. The main street was decked out to appeal to nostalgia, with quaint shops and boutiques lining the streets, and the marina was home to boats of all shapes and sizes, including a number of houseboats.

We drove off the ferry, turning onto NE First Street, which curved around the parking lot of cars waiting to board. From there, the street curved to the left before merging with Highway 104, which was where we wanted to be. Within minutes, we were passing through a heavily wooded rural area, with occasional streets or driveways leading to nests of housing, and from there, we followed the highway as it curved north once again, through tall stands of trees. The storm had broken and it was snowing lightly, sticking to the roadways and grass.

"I hope we make it to Port Ludlow before it really starts to come down," Herne said. "I changed over to snow tires just in case, but the peninsula can get some fairly deep snowfalls."

"Port Ludlow is only about an hour's drive from Kingston, at moderate speeds," I said. "I looked it up on MapApp before we left this morning. But then again, the highway over here's not exactly the easiest."

"That's why I'm slowing down. Text Yutani and tell him to remind Viktor to slow down on these backroads. They're behind us." Herne nodded toward the rearview mirror.

I craned my neck, trying to catch a glimpse of them. Sure enough, there they were. I pulled out my phone and texted for them to be careful and slow down.

Less than fifteen minutes later, we approached Port Gamble, where Dr. Nalcops lived—one of our primary leads to ferreting out the Tuathan Brotherhood.

Port Gamble was like a cross between Kingston, with its quaint and charming design, and Port Townsend, an artistic community hearkening back to Victoriana, but it was mostly for show. Very few people actually lived here. Originally a mill town—a company town built for the mill workers—like Port Townsend, Port Gamble had aged poorly until the Olympic Property Group took over maintaining the entire town.

Though a few places were available for lease, Port Gamble had become more of a museum than anything, with a minuscule population. At least of the living. The town was rumored to be one of the most haunted cities in Washington State, with reports of over half the buildings in town containing some sort of ghostly activity. I was grateful we were approaching during the day, because the energy was odd enough as we were passing through during the daylight hours.

"Where is Nalcops's practice?" I asked.

"Yutani texted me his address. He's on the outskirts of town, on Milltown Lane, off of Wheeler Street. We're not stopping there just yet, though. We don't want to tip him off before Rafé heads up to meet the group."

"If they're so secretive, how does Rafé know where to go?" Raven asked.

"He received an email ten days ago that he's to meet with members of the group in Port Angeles. He'll be transported to the location at that point." Herne glanced at me, then in the rearview mirror and I knew he was looking at Angel. She said nothing, however.

"So they're picking him up? You have a trace-spell on him?"

"A magical implant. It's subcutaneous so they shouldn't find it if they search him. Of course, if they use a bug tracer, they'll find it, but we're hoping they won't think of that." Herne made a right, taking the exit leading toward the Hood Canal Floating Bridge. From there, we had another ten miles until we reached Port Ludlow, where we'd be staying with Angus.

Like the 520 and the I-90 bridges in Seattle, the Hood Canal Bridge was a floating bridge—the third longest in the world. Part of Highway 104, the bridge spanned Hood Canal, which fed off of Puget Sound, near the Squamish Harbor.

"We're lucky. The bridge is still open," I said as we approached it. That meant the weather hadn't gotten bad enough to shut it down yet, which happened during major windstorms or heavy snow.

It was a two-lane bridge, stretching across Hood Canal with an open view of the water. Street lamps illuminated the bridge at night, and the bridge could open to boat traffic when necessary. The traffic was light during this time in the morning, and we passed over it uneventfully, even with the falling snow. On the other side, we curved to the left as the road bent, passing a side road that led to the Shine Tidelands State Park.

We continued along the thickly wooded highway with sporadic pockets of housing peeking out from the trees until we turned right onto Highway 19. Another few minutes and we turned right on Oak Bay Drive, and a short time later, we pulled into Port Ludlow. Definitely a step up from Kingston in size, Port Ludlow had a thriving tourist industry and was located on Port Ludlow Bay. It was affluent, especially compared to a number of smaller towns on the peninsula, and had a resort that was known throughout the state.

"Where's Angus live?" Angel asked.

"He lives out on Olympus Boulevard," Herne said. "Near the end of the road shortly before Basalt Point. We'll be there in a few minutes."

I glanced at the clock. It was almost noon. "He's expecting us?"

Herne nodded. "Yeah."

Angel's phone pinged. "Rafé's about ten minutes behind us. He'll meet us there."

Suddenly, a pungent smell wafted forward from the backseat. I coughed and turned around. Raven was staring at Raj, shaking her head.

"I'm sorry. He got into the chili I made yesterday and ate about a quart. He's been farting ever since. I'm surprised we made it through the morning without him smelling up the car." She grinned and patted his head. "You goon."

Raj let out a soft sound, and tilted his head. "Urmph…"

"What was that?" Angel asked.

"Gargoyles don't talk. Not the way we do. They're intelligent but it doesn't translate to the way we think of intelligence. He's empathic to a degree, and he can understand what I say for the most part. He's like a cat in that they meow mainly to humans. The more you talk to cats, the more they tend to talk back to you to let you know what they want. Raj mostly makes noise when I talk to him."

Raj was about the size of a large Rottweiler. He looked a lot like a dog in some ways, except his front legs were actually arms, though he walked on his knuckles instead of upright on two feet. With leathery gray skin, he was all muscle, and while most gargoyles had wings, Raj had suffered their loss at the hands of the demon who first owned him. Raven won the gargoyle away from the demon in a poker game and had used a spell to make Raj forget the pain he had suffered with the demon, and with that, he seemed to have forgotten he had ever had wings.

He was a good sort, guarding Raven's house and her, and she loved him like I loved Mr. Rumblebutt. He left her ferrets alone, which was surprising given that gargoyles were highly carnivorous, though Raj had developed a taste for human food.

"Is chili even *good* for him?" Herne asked, wrinkling his nose.

"Well, he eats just about anything he finds around. I've discovered the hard way that pineapple and citrus fruits make him sick to his stomach, but otherwise, it doesn't seem to have hurt him in any way." Raven paused, staring out the window. "There are ghosts walking by the side of the road. I can see them. You were right in saying this area is haunted. I've never been over here."

"It's filled with ghosts. Also odd creatures and beings that hide in the forests over here."

"Bigfoot," she said. "I've seen him once, elsewhere. Sasquatch is a freaking scary-ass creature and he doesn't like anybody intruding in on his space. I had to run for my life to get away from him."

I frowned. "You mean he went after you? You're one of the Ante-Fae."

"I doubt he even knows what the Ante-Fae are. To be honest, I don't think his kind are from this planet. As far as I can tell, they're interdimensional beings." She paused. "Just like the creatures who create crop circles. They're a form of earth elemental. People keep talking about aliens doing it, and while I believe there are creatures from other planets here, there are plenty of ways to reach this planet other than linear space. Crossing through dimensions isn't that difficult, but you have to make sure you know where you're headed."

Herne cleared his throat. "You're correct in that. There are so many natural portals. Get the wrong one and you may never make it back here. As for Sasquatch, he's nothing to mess around with. And there are different races within the species—high up in the cold mountains, they're known as yeti."

I nodded. "I've often wondered what it would be like

to go dimension hopping, but even a trip to Annwn makes me nervous. Though there's part of me that wonders about the great lands of TirNaNog and Navane across the Great Sea. Do they despise my type there? Or is it only in their namesake cities here that I'm pariah?"

Herne slowed, turning right onto a long drive. "The great Fae lands over the Great Sea are glorious and beautiful, and terrifying. If you think the skirmishes here between the Light and Dark are bad, over there it's been a full-scale war since the cities were first built. And yet, they never seek to fully destroy the other—both sides know they need the other to exist. But it's like the battle between light and shadow—too much light and it burns the eyes, too much shadow and the cobwebs grow. Together, they make the whole—the balance."

"I have a question," I said, glancing at the wooded thicket we were passing through. This was obviously a private lot, but the driveway was a long, compacted dirt road. The snow was swirling, coming down harder now, and there was about a five-inch accumulation on the ground.

"Save it for later, unless it relates to the case, because we're here." Herne pulled through the end of the driveway into a clearing. The drive ended in a large parking area in front of a single-story house that overlooked Puget Sound. The yard spread to the side and around the back of the house, but even from here, I could tell the view from inside must be spectacular.

There was a pickup parked in the driveway—one that looked more utilitarian than for show—and Herne parked to the side. A moment later, Viktor pulled in behind us. As we got out of the car, the chill of the air and the fall of snow made me shiver. Angel looked around nervously, while Raj bounded around in the snow, snuffling as he kicked it up with his hands.

Raven took a step toward the yard, staring out at the water. "There's something unnatural about this snow," she said.

Angel nodded. "Something feels off. Even I can tell that."

Viktor, Yutani, and Talia crossed over to stand beside us as the front door opened and a bear of a man came bounding out. He crossed to Herne, clasping his hand. The men hugged, patting each other's backs, and then stood back.

"Angus Lesley, you look better than ever," Herne said. "Meet my crew," he added, pointing to each of us in turn. "This is Ember, who also happens to be my girlfriend. Angel, Viktor, Talia, and Yutani. And this is Raven BoneTalker."

Angus stood well over six feet tall, and he had long red hair down to his shoulders and a braided beard that reached his chest. He was burly and looked like he could easily win a log-tossing contest. His eyes were glittering green, and a pale nimbus surrounded him, probably from the fact that he was one of the magic-born.

He shook hands with each of us in turn. He stared at Raven for a moment. "Ante-Fae, are you? We have a number of Ante-Fae over here."

Raven nodded. "My kind tend to congregate in wild areas."

"Right. Well, come in, all of you. Get out of the snow." Angus led us up the steps. "Is this everyone?"

"Rafé should be here any moment. Technically he's not

part of the Wild Hunt, but he's doing us a big favor. He's Angel's beau." Herne wrapped his arm around my waist and we started to follow Angus. At that moment, Rafé pulled up. He joined us and Herne introduced him to Angus as we crowded into the house.

Angus's house was rustic-chic. It had the feel of a log cabin, but was fully functional. A woodstove was roaring, heating the air nicely, and a tea kettle sat on top, steaming away. The living room was painted a pale green, and lace sheers covered the windows, while heavy drapes trailed to the floor on each side. The floors were hardwood, and the furniture was sturdy oak, with a leather sofa and loveseat taking center stage. I didn't see a television, but a computer sat to one side on a desk, a tablet beside it. The living room led into a large eat-in kitchen, and a hallway to the left had several doors along either side. A door to the right of the living room probably led into the garage, from what I could tell by the outside of the house. All in all, it felt cozy and sheltered from the elements.

In the kitchen, a large sliding glass door by the table overlooked the backyard, and there was the view I had expected. We could see straight out over the sound. The backyard stretched for a good hundred feet before dropping off over the cliff's edge. I crossed to the window, staring at the boiling clouds that were letting loose with snow.

"The weather's getting worse." I said, turning back. "This is quite the storm." I was still feeling unsettled from my leap over the side of the ferry.

"That's one of my concerns," Angus said. "Fiona won't be home till early evening. Would you like some lunch?

I've got stew on the stove and biscuits in the oven." He glanced at Raj. "I'm not sure what your gargoyle eats."

"Raj will eat anything we can, except citrus. He's partial to meat, but he's not picky." Raven gave Angus a gracious smile, but I could tell she was uneasy. There was a look that Raven got when she was unsettled, a shifty, jittery look that I was beginning to recognize.

"Then it's settled. Lunch it is," Angus said, opening a cupboard. He gathered bowls and bread-and-butter plates and carried them over to the table. "Do you mind if I put Raj's food in a metal bowl? Fiona would have my head if I fed a gargoyle off the good china. Nothing against him, but we've had this set since we first arrived over here, and she's partial to it."

"Raj can be clumsy, so that's probably a good idea." Raven crossed over to the sliding glass door, staring outside.

"Is there anything I can do to help?" Angel asked.

"You can take the biscuits out of the oven," Angus said. "The oven mitts are to the side of the stove. There's a basket for them on the counter."

Before long, we were gathered around the massive oak table and Angus was dishing out the stew. Everything smelled incredible, with the scent of beef and tomatoes and gravy wafting up. I cut open one of the biscuits and slathered it with butter, digging in. Hot cider completed the meal, and we set to, eating quietly while Herne and Angus chatted. I had the feeling that in this house, at least, serious conversation waited till after the meal.

After we were done, Rafé moved aside with Angel, where they talked in low tones. The look on her face said everything. This might be the last time she would see him, if things went bad. We all knew Rafé was taking a big chance, but he was our best hope for now.

I turned away to find Herne watching them. He motioned for me to follow him and we crossed over to the sliding glass doors, staring out at the tumultuous waves.

"It's his choice, Ember," Herne said. "He made the offer, and we have to allow him this chance to do his part. Rafé knows that he's walking into danger. You have to let people do their part, to have their moments of courage. We can't protect him from everything just because he and Angel are an item."

"You keep telling me that and I keep telling you I know. I think you're trying to convince yourself, Herne." I glanced at Angel. "I think she's falling in love. I know what you're saying is true, but damn it, why couldn't Morgana find someone to go in his stead? Someone who's trained for this sort of danger?"

"Morgana and I talked about this. She said that sometimes, fate hands you what you need, regardless whether you think it's the correct choice. She said to let Rafé go." He slid his arms around my shoulders. "When you jumped over the railing on the ferry, my first inclination was to follow you and bring you back aboard. But I knew you were doing what you felt you needed to, and I respected that. Respect Rafé's desire to help us out."

I looked away for a moment. "I just don't want to see Angel get hurt."

"I know, and neither do I. But we're here, and we have to take this opportunity. Come on, let's see Rafé off with a brave face. He needs to know that we believe in him." He turned, walking me over to where Angel was tearily pressed against Rafé's shoulder.

"I hate to interrupt, but…" Herne said.

Rafé nodded. "I need to get a move on. Everything's set, and I have the location where I'm supposed to meet them. Then…well…let's hope this works." He tipped Angel's face up, kissing her tears. "I'll be back. Trust me, I have no desire to stretch this out longer than I have to."

She nodded, wiping her nose with a tissue. "Come back in one piece."

Raven joined us then. "You're my blood-oath brother. You take care of yourself." She paused, then let out a sigh. "Ulstair would be proud of you."

Rafé shivered. "I needed to hear that."

Ulstair had been Raven's fiancé and Rafé's brother. He had vanished and Raven hired us to find him, only to discover that he had been murdered by a psychopath. Rafé had pledged himself to be Raven's brother, to stand in for Ulstair. The pair had looked very much alike, with coppery red hair and lean, muscled bodies. I had thought being around Rafé might be difficult for Raven, reminding her of her lost love, but Rafé's presence seemed to comfort her.

She gave him a long hug, kissing him on the cheek. "Be safe. Come back to Angel and me."

Rafé nodded. "I'd best head out, then. I'll let you know when I reach Port Angeles." He shook Angus's hand. "Thank you for your hospitality," he said, then shook Herne's hand. He waved to the rest of us before heading out the door.

"I hope to hell he makes it back," Yutani said softly.

"Big case?" Angus asked.

Herne gave him a short nod. "Yes, and one I can't talk about. But that man is putting his life on the line. If, by chance, anybody asks, he's never been here, and you've never met him."

"Understood," Angus said. "Shall we sit down so I can tell you about Fiona and why I'm so worried? I'd like to get through the discussion before she comes home or she'll be furious that I was talking behind her back."

He guided us into the living room, where we settled ourselves. I glanced out the window overlooking the driveway. Rafé was gone, and the snow was still falling.

"The truth is, I *know* something's wrong with Fiona. She seems distant and abrupt, and before you say anything, Herne, I mean more than usual. She's become secretive, and goes out without telling me where she's going or when she'll be home. When I ask, she tells me to mind my own business." A hurt look crossed Angus's face. "We've always been close, but lately, I feel like I don't know her anymore. I'm not sure what's going on, but I think…I truly think that something's possessed her."

"Could there be some other cause? I don't mean to bring up suspicions, but that sort of behavior goes hand in hand when one partner's having an affair," Talia said.

"I agree, which is why I tailed her a couple times. She's headed out into the woods, and then…it's like she vanishes. I will be trailing her and the next moment, she's nowhere in sight. Now, both she and I know these woods like the back of our hands, and we're familiar with all the denizens of the dark living out there. I can track with the best of them, but Fiona…it's as though she's learned a teleportation spell or something of that sort. Yet, I know she hasn't."

"When did this start?" Herne asked.

Angus leaned forward, his elbows propped on his knees. He clasped his hands together. "This didn't start until about ten days ago. Until then, everything was as usual."

"What happened around that time? What might have triggered this off? Can you think of anything unusual that occurred in the past couple of weeks?" Herne frowned, his brow in furrowed lines.

"Not really. Things have been fairly normal." Angus paused as his phone rang. "Excuse me," he said, glancing at the screen. "It's Fiona. I'll be right back."

I kept staring out the window. "There's something going on out there. I can feel it."

"So can I," Angel said. "Why don't we take a walk to see if we can key in on whatever it is?"

"Is that all right?" I asked Herne. "Do we need to be here?"

He let out a sigh. "Go ahead, but take Viktor with you. I will tell you this. Angus isn't a man given to hyperbole. He doesn't exaggerate. If he's worried about Fiona, something's amiss. So be cautious and watch your step. With the number of spirits walking the land over here, possession is definitely on the list of possibilities."

As Angel, Viktor, and I made our way outside, a sudden gust of wind blustered past, sending strands of my hair flying as I braced against it.

"I don't like the way the wind feels," Viktor said. "I feel like we're being watched."

"I think we are," I said, shivering. "This storm's alive and aware. And I think that it knows we're here."

With that, we headed toward the woods on the right,

the trees looming like dark sentinels in the gloom of the afternoon. The snow continued to fall, and it was all I could do to force myself toward the trail leading into the woods. Something was watching us, all right, and waiting, and it felt like whatever was there was weaving a web in which to snare us.

"Whatever this is, it doesn't like us, or trust us," Angel said.

Nodding, I silently plunged into the undergrowth as we entered the forest.

CHAPTER FIVE

*W*e were standing on the edge of the woodlands surrounding Angus's house. The copse was thick, but the snow created a counter-balance to the dark of the wood. The flakes were thicker now, wet and sticking. I zipped up my jacket and pulled on a pair of gloves. Angel followed suit, while Viktor blew on his hands and stuck them in his pockets.

"I hope Rafé makes it to Port Angeles without any problem," Angel said. "The highway can be treacherous in the rain, let alone the snow. Maybe if it's too thick, he won't be able to go wherever they're going to take him," she said optimistically.

"I still don't like that we have no idea *where* they plan to sweep him off to. I hope they don't intend to head into the backwoods. The Olympic National Park isn't any place to meddle with if you don't know what you're doing," Viktor grumbled.

I paused, my thoughts turning from Rafé as I heard a

noise that sounded like icicles crashing down. It came from within the woodland.

"Did you hear that?" I asked, looking around. "There's something out here!"

"It could be a fox," Angel said, her voice trembling.

"That's no fox." Viktor glanced around. "Not in this weather."

"Sub-Fae?" I asked.

He squinted, staring at the trees in front of us. "Could be. Over here, it doesn't matter whether you're in town or out, creatures are watching. Some are sub-Fae, others—well, others are right out of somebody's nightmare. You think the Cascades are haunted with ghosts and creatures? The Olympic Peninsula is older and deadlier…and it has an alluring energy to it. I grew up on tales of the woods around here."

"I sense treachery," Angel said, closing her eyes.

I stared at her. "Do you really think you ought to be reaching out, given how strong of an empath you are?"

She ignored me, staring at a narrow trail that led into the thicket. Seconds later, she began to walk into the copse of trees.

"Angel? Angel!" I started toward her, concerned, but she began to jog through the snow, ignoring me. I quickened my pace, following her, and Viktor chugging along behind. "Angel, where are you going?"

She didn't answer, just rounded a curve in the thicket. I poured on the speed, following her, but as I rounded the bend behind her, I skidded to a halt. Angel was nowhere to be seen. I spun a one-eighty, frantic, looking for her, but then noticed that Viktor wasn't behind me, either. Where the hell had they gone?

"Viktor! Angel? Where are you?" I turned to retrace my steps but the path had vanished. Instead, I was faced with a thick patch of undergrowth, heavy with snow. The snowbank sparkled, mesmerizing me, and I moved toward it. The next moment, the snow exploded as a creature leaped out to confront me.

I stumbled back, trying to take in what I was seeing.

He was like a frog, and yet...*not*. As tall as me, he stood on hind legs that folded the wrong way at the knee—at least for a human. His wide, fat feet were flippered, and his hands were webbed. He was the color of holly leaves, a shiny green mottled with olive splotches. His head was both human-like and yet that of a frog's, as if the product of some horrible genetic mashup. His eyes bulged out, glassy and bulbous, and they flickered with a tangerine light that gave him a cunning look. His tongue lolled out of his mouth and he licked the rim of his open maw, drool splashing over the edges of his lips.

"What the fuck are you?" The words escaped my mouth before I realized I was speaking. I stumbled back, wishing I had brought my crossbow with me. I had my dagger, strapped to my right leg, but I'd left all my other weapons in the car.

The creature lurched forward, springing on those great flippered feet to land in front of me, his tongue whipping out to coil around my right arm. Immediately, I felt a burning sensation as the drool began to sizzle against my jacket.

"Crap! Acid!" I couldn't free my arm to grab my dagger and I couldn't twist to gain hold of it with my left, so I moved in closer and thrust my knee up, catching the underside of his massive head. He let out a whistling noise and reached for my other arm with his other hand. I brought my arm up to block him, then swept around his arm and pulled hard, yanking it out of the socket.

At that moment, I heard Angel scream. Startled, I glanced to the side to see her near me, caught by vines that were thrusting their way out of a snowbank—they were tendrils of glistening ice that seemed to be as flexible as plants. Viktor raced out from behind a large cedar and caught hold of her arm, pulling her out of the clasp of the vines.

The frog-creature's drool was eating through my jacket now, but I finally managed to twist around and grab my dagger with my left hand. I brought my blade down across the length of his oily-pink tongue, slicing it in half. The creature fell back, shrieking, drool frothing from the stump of his tongue and boiling out of his mouth.

I stumbled to the side as Viktor pulled out a throwing dagger and launched it toward the creature's head. The frog-creature screamed again as the blade pierced his skull, but instead of falling, he just limped away, vanishing through the undergrowth, still sporting Victor's dagger like some kind of crazy hat.

Angel crouched down, her hands on the ground, breathing heavily. "What the hell just happened?"

"I don't know," I said. "I have no clue what that thing was, or what those vines were. Viktor, do you think it was Ante-Fae?"

He shook his head. "No. But, whatever it was, we need to get the hell out of here. This woodland is full of deadly creatures and I don't feel like encountering any more of them." He glanced around, shivering as the snow continued to fall silently around us. "Where are we? Where's the path?"

I realized then I had no clue how we'd gotten to this part of the forest. "The last thing I remember was watching Angel head toward the trail into the thicket. Then she vanished, and you vanished and then I was facing that creature and… What do *you* remember?" I asked Angel.

Angel frowned. "Someone called my name—that's why I headed into the trees. Yes, I remember now, somebody was calling me." She glanced around. "I have no idea who it was. But I couldn't ignore the voice." Shivering, she looked around. "Viktor's right. We need to get out of here. There's danger everywhere out here. It feels like one giant trap."

"Where's the trail?" Viktor said, looking around. Then, pointing to a huckleberry bush, he added, "There. I remember passing that bush." He strode over to the bush and pushed behind it. "I was right. Here's the trail. Hurry up!"

Angel and I hustled over to him. He was right, the path was right there, in plain sight now. I wondered why I hadn't been able to see it before, but regardless of the reason, I was relieved to see it now. We hustled our asses along it, and in a few moments, we were back in Angus's yard.

"Come on, let's get the hell inside," I said, running toward the door. With Viktor and Angel behind me, we raced up the steps, bursting through the front door, to safety.

HERNE AND ANGUS WERE SITTING BY THE FIREPLACE. Yutani was poring over his computer. Raj was asleep by the fire, and Raven was nowhere to be seen. Talia was standing at the sliding glass doors, staring out into the snowstorm. She turned as we skidded into the house, panting.

"What's wrong?" Herne asked, slowly standing.

"Angus, I don't know just who your neighbors are, but trust me, they're not the friendly type. Whatever the hell's living out in that patch of trees is dangerous."

I pulled off my boots, setting them beneath the bench near the front door, then shrugged off my jacket. I examined the sleeve where the frog-creature had drooled on me. The acidic liquid had burned clean through the leather, stopping only as it reached the lining. Any more and it would have eaten into my arm. I carried it over to show Herne and Angus.

"I got in a fight with a human frog," I said, handing my jacket to them, pointing out the hole on the sleeve. "My new leather jacket isn't much protection against frog acid, apparently."

"You said a frog-creature?" Angus asked, a grave expression on his face.

I nodded. "Yeah, and something that looked like ice tendrils tried to grab hold of Angel and pull her into a snowbank. It also lured her into the forest. Viktor and I didn't hear anything, but she did."

"I heard someone calling my name," Angel said.

"I was wondering if the frog-creature was one of the Ante-Fae," I added.

"No, it's not Ante-Fae, but I know what they are. I've seen them before," Raven said, emerging from the kitchen.

"They're known as *grigits*." She pronounced the second "g" hard, rhyming the word with *bigot*. "They're a form of malevolent nature sprite."

"You mean they're sub-Fae?" I asked.

"No, these aren't considered sub-Fae," she said, wiping her hands on a dishtowel. "There's a huge classification of nature-spirits that don't belong to the Fae world. They have their own realm, and as a collective whole they're known as the *padurmonstris*."

"Padurmonstris? I've never heard of them," I said, frowning.

"The Ante-Fae tend to have the most interaction with them, because they seldom emerge when humans—or Fae—are around. They fear the Ante-Fae, and so they try to make nice with us," she added, a faint grin on her face. "The snow tendrils are probably from a *schnee-hexe*. A snow witch. In their natural form, they're made up of snow, but they can take on an illusion of an old woman dressed in white and silver. Schnee-hexes can get inside of an empath's head, especially one who hasn't built up strong shields. Angel, don't you know how to ward yourself?"

Angel shook her head, blushing. "Nobody ever taught me."

Raven turned to Herne. "She's part of your team. I would think you'd teach her some basic protection."

Herne reddened and ducked his head. "You're right. I've been remiss, and for that I apologize, Angel. I can't expect to bring you along on these trips without assigning you a teacher who can help you learn how to protect yourself."

"Padurmonstris? I think I've actually encountered a

few in the past, but I always assumed they were just part of the sub-Fae." I paused, then asked, "Would that thing—the grigit—would he have killed me?"

"He might have, but whether he killed you now or later, he would have devoured you. They sometimes eat their meals alive, a much more unpleasant option." Raven sounded cheery enough, like she was talking about a new dress or pair of shoes. "They often respond to bargains—the padurmonstris in general, that is. Like crows and ravens, they love bright, shiny things. Sometimes you can make a deal with them if you can't see any other way out. And not all of them look like frogs—those are only the grigits. If the padurmonstris inhabit the woods over here, we'll really have to be cautious."

"Do they understand English?" I asked.

"They can understand just about any language, if they choose to. Therein lies the problem. If they don't want to listen, they'll pretend not to understand what you're saying. If that happens, run like hell if you can because chances are, they're hungry and looking for a meal." Raven sat down on the rug next to Raj, lightly stroking his back.

Angus let out a slow breath. "The lass is right. These woods are filled with strange creatures and beings. You have to be careful treading the backwoods."

"*Lass?*" Raven asked, giving him a long look.

"You may be Ante-Fae, but you're still a lass. I'm far older than you." Angus flashed her a bright smile, and Raven laughed.

"You've got me there."

"So what do we do about them? I wounded the…grigit. But what about the schnee-hex that was targeting Angel?

Shouldn't we form a party and hunt them down?" It seemed like a bad idea to leave them out in the forest, to attempt to trap someone else.

But Angus shook his head, and Herne followed suit.

"No, those of us who live out here have learned where to go and where not to," Angus said. "I would have warned you if I knew you were actually going into the woods, so I take responsibility. The trees that form the barrier between my neighbor's house and mine are home for the —as Raven said—padurmonstris. We leave them alone and they don't sneak out of the woods to kill us in our beds. Although now, having wounded one, that may upset the balance."

I felt an odd mix of guilt and anger. What did he expect me to do? Let it eat my face off? And yet I knew that Angus wasn't blaming me.

"So we just let them go?"

"Aye, you let them go and leave them be, and it will smooth out." Angus must have caught my expression of disbelief because he gave a little shrug and grinned. "We can't be killing off every creature that threatens us. If we intrude on their territory, we have to expect they will push back. You got away, you're unharmed, and that's as good as we can hope for with one of these unexpected encounters."

Feeling grumpy, I joined Raven by the fire, settling on the rug. I glanced up at Angel, and she gave me a *what can we do about it* look as she pulled out a chair next to Talia. Viktor, on the other hand, glanced at the pile of wood next to the hearth.

"Your wood's getting low. I'll be happy to bring in an

armful if you'd like." He found a pair of gloves in his pack and slid them on.

"Thank you. I'd appreciate it. I'll go with you and we can bring back a load and stack it on the porch." Angus turned to the rest of us. "Make yourself at home for now. Fiona will be home in a few hours, so I'll start dinner when I'm done with the wood."

As Viktor and Angus trooped out the door, I turned to Herne.

"Did you know about the padurmonstris?" I asked.

"You mean that they're over here in the woods? I knew they congregated in wild places, and that the peninsula has plenty of room for them to spread out. But did I know that Angus had them near his house? No." Herne paused, then added, "One thing to remember. Over here, we're out of familiar territory. Even the gods are cautious in areas like this. The creatures of the forest can be terrifying and powerful, and we don't take them lightly. Angus should have warned us, but perhaps he thought we already knew. At least no one got hurt, and now we know to keep our eyes open."

"Well, my new leather jacket got hurt," I muttered, staring at the penny-sized hole the grigit had burned into it.

"The agency will reimburse you. Put in an expense voucher when we get back and buy a new jacket," Herne said, snorting.

I glanced at Raven. She was stretched out on the rug next to Raj, her head on his belly. They were both asleep. Wishing I could fall asleep that easily, I crossed to where Herne was sitting on the sofa. I sat down beside him as Talia joined us, a worried look on her face.

"The fact that the little monsters—the padurmonstris —come so close to habitations is worrisome, though. I'm wondering how Rafé will fare out in the forest. I know that he volunteered for this mission, but with all that's happened today alone, I have to say that I'm concerned," she said. "Maybe Angus's problem is not our fight?"

"I promised Angus we'd help, and we can't let Rafé just go off on his own. Cernunnos and Morgana were specific that we're to do whatever we can to infiltrate the Tuathan Brotherhood and shut it down." Herne shrugged. "They're in charge. We accept what orders they give us."

Talia was about to add something when the door opened and Angus and Viktor returned, carrying armfuls of wood for the fire. They stacked them in the woodbin next to the woodstove.

"It's blowing up a gale out there," Angus said. "I told you, the storms don't feel natural."

"And you can't remember anything abnormal happening around the time they started?"

"No, not really," he said. "I'll start dinner. Would anyone like to give me a hand?"

Angel jumped up. "I will. I love to cook."

"If she cooks, you'll never want her to leave," I warned the burly Scotsman.

He laughed. "I've heard from Herne about her cooking, and I welcome the help."

As they entered the kitchen, I turned to Talia. Herne was at the table, glancing over Yutani's shoulder, as Viktor warmed his hands by the fire. Raven and Raj were still snoring lightly.

"Tell me more about this premonition of yours," I said, keeping my voice low. Herne had already made his feelings clear, but at this point, I felt that we should pay attention to every omen and sign we encountered. Starting with the feel of the storm, then the car going off the ferry, and now, the grigit in the woods, I was thoroughly spooked.

Talia seemed to feel the same, because she glanced at Herne, then nodded for me to follow her over to the sliding doors that overlooked the backyard and the sound. We stood there for a moment before she softly began to talk.

"I honestly don't know how to explain this, but I'll try. When I lost my powers, I still retained some of my natural instincts. One of those instincts is that I can sense when there are other predators in the area. And I'm sensing that in a big way, right now. Not the grigit—though that was disconcerting," Talia said, smoothing silver strands away from her face, "but something bigger. Something ancient. I'm surprised Herne doesn't feel it, too, given he's a god, but I'm chalking that up to the worry over Rafé, because trust me, child, he's a bundle of nerves about the subject right now."

"He seems to feel Rafé's up to the job," I said.

"He's good at wearing a mask when he doesn't want to alarm others, Ember. That's one thing you need to learn before your relationship goes any further. Herne never wants to worry anybody he cares for, and right now, he's concerned about worrying Angel and you…and Raven, given Rafé's her blood-oath brother." Talia paused for a moment.

"Testosterone strikes again," I said.

"It's more than a male–female thing. Herne's a fixer. He likes to fix things, and when he can't, he gets frustrated. And he doesn't want to admit it when he needs help or when things feel out of control. So rather than admit that we're running blind on this—that we have no idea what Rafé's getting himself into—he'll pretend everything's hunky-dory." She sighed. "I've known Herne for longer than I've known anybody else except my family. I can recognize the signs."

"Wonderful. So he'd rather minimize the danger than admit that we're in over our heads."

"You can't blame him altogether. Cernunnos and Morgana expect him to take care of this, and disappointing your parents—especially when they're gods? Not an easy thing."

"Right." I rubbed my head. "So what do we do?"

"There's not much we *can* do, I suppose. We do have a job. Herne has—*the Wild Hunt has*—our orders. I suppose my best advice is regardless of what Herne says, don't allow yourself to get overconfident. Don't assume we've got a leg up on this, because we don't. Keep your eyes and ears open at all times. Watch what you say to others— including Angus. I will tell you this much, and I know it as well as I know my own name, that whatever he's worried about, he's had a hand in creating. He's responsible for this, even though he claims to have no knowledge of what's going on. *I know it*, Ember."

At that moment, a crash outside made us all jump as the power flickered. But the lights held, and Angus barreled out of the kitchen and pushed open the sliding glass doors. Talia and I followed him onto the patio. As he flipped on the outside light, we saw that one of the smaller fir trees had toppled over, barely missing the corner of the house.

Angus groaned. "Great. Well, if that's the least of the damage, we'll be lucky. I'm going to prepare the generator, just in case we lose power. Why don't you and Ember head back inside," he added, seeing the two of us standing there, gawking at the downed tree. "I'll just run around out front and go in through the garage that way."

As he vanished, Talia and I returned to the living room and shut the slider. Herne was standing there, a concerned look on his face as we entered the room. Angel was finishing up dinner—a macaroni and cheese casserole, garlic bread, and salad.

"What was it?" Herne asked.

"A tree fell." I sniffed the aroma of the food that was wafting out of the kitchen. "Herne, did Angus tell you anything more about the situation with Fiona?"

He shook his head. "No. I think we'll have to wait to talk to her. I wonder, though…" He paused.

I knew that look. It meant that he had thought of some possibility. "What?"

"Nothing. Never mind." He gave me a kiss.

"Are you sure?" I tried to dig a little deeper, but he shook his head. Finally, realizing I wasn't going to get anywhere, I wandered into the kitchen and, together with Yutani, set the table. Angus came in as we set the food out and, after washing his hands, he joined us.

"Thanks, Angel. I appreciate you taking over for me like that." He shivered. "It's colder than a witch's tit out there, and I speak from experience. But the generator is ready in case the power goes out, and we have wood for the stove. We'll be fine. Fiona and I don't have that many spare bedrooms, so I suggest the women take the two guest rooms, and the men can bunk out here, if that's fine

69

with you. We have a queen bed in each spare room. I put your luggage in there."

As I dished up the mac 'n cheese, which had a crispy golden topping on it, and accepted a piece of garlic bread, I wondered how many storms the house had weathered.

"How long have you lived here on the peninsula?" I asked.

"About forty years. We originally bought the land and had the house custom built. We started out in Maine, and one of our sons still lives there. Gregory owns a magic shop. Our son Thomas was killed on a fishing boat about ten years before we moved out here. He went down in a nasty storm. And our daughter, Colleen—our oldest— moved back to Scotland. She teaches at a school for the magic-born, and has a brood of her own."

"Herne says you almost shot him when you met," Angel said.

Angus laughed, turning red. "Yes, indeed. I saw the most gorgeous stag in the forest, and I would not have tried to bring him down, save for Fiona and the little ones were hungry and it had been a harsh winter. Herne stayed my hand—and he helped us out. After that, we kept in touch." He handed Yutani the salad, and Yutani served himself then handed it on.

"You're lucky," Raven said. "Some of the gods would have turned you to stone or struck you down when they realized what was going on."

"Oh, I consider it luck, yes. But you know what they say—the harder I work, the luckier I get. I was hunting to feed my family, and good fortune prevailed." At that moment, the front door opened. Angus shot to his feet.

There, in the foyer, was a woman as striking as Angus

was. She was tiny, compared to the giant of a man, but there was a strength about her that chilled me to the core. She, too, had brilliant red hair, and she was dressed in a long white gown, with a thick fur cloak around her shoulders. She shrugged it off, staring at us, each in turn, with unsmiling eyes. Then, her gaze fell on Herne and she blinked, looking startled.

"Fiona Lesley, it's been too long," Herne said, standing.

A pale smile spread across her face as she moved forward, smoothly draping her cape over the back of the sofa.

"As I live and breathe, it's Herne the Hunter, come to visit!" She turned to Angus. "Don't dawdle, bring me a plate. I'm starving." And then she stopped to gaze at us. "You've brought friends with you," she started to say, but paused as her gaze fell on me. The smile slipped away, and she took a step back. "Why don't you introduce us?" she said, but I could swear that meeting the rest of us was the last thing she wanted to do.

CHAPTER SIX

*F*iona Lesley was a striking woman, and her magical energy was impossible to ignore. In fact, she felt supercharged compared to her husband, and I wondered what kind of magic she practiced. But it would be bad form to ask.

"Dear heart, meet Ember, Herne's girlfriend, and his friends Angel, Viktor, Talia, and Yutani. And this," Angus motioned to Raven, "is Raven BoneTalker, one of the—"

"*Ante-Fae*. I can tell," Fiona said, glowering. "I never expected to have one of the ancient ones *gracing* our home." Her words were short and clipped.

I had that uneasy feeling that you get when somebody takes an instant dislike to you and you don't know what you did.

But the next moment, Fiona turned to Herne, a smile plastered on her face. "So, Reilly vanished and now Ember takes her place? How lovely for you."

I blinked, feeling as though I had just been slapped.

Angus blushed again. Flustered, he stuttered out, "Dear, really, is that the way—"

"Never mind me," Fiona said, glancing at Angus with all the affection of a horse seeing a mosquito. It made me wonder just how close their relationship could be, and if this had always been the norm, how had they managed to stay together this long?

Herne seemed as taken aback as Angus did. He blinked, then cleared his throat. "It's good to see you again, Fiona."

Angel tapped me on the arm. "Ember, can I see you in the guest room a moment? I think I might have left my meds at home, and wanted to see if they got packed in your suitcase by mistake."

Frowning—Angel wasn't on any medication that I knew of—I excused myself and followed her into the guest room. Angel shut the door behind us, after peeking down the hall. Keeping her voice low, she leaned close.

"You remember I told you that I sensed something huge—something big?"

"Yeah."

"Whatever it is, Fiona's carrying it on her back, so to speak. I think Angus is right. I think something is piggybacking on her. She's dangerous, and she's—" She froze as the door opened and Fiona popped her head in.

"Is everything all right?" she asked, glancing at our suitcases, which were sitting on the floor, unopened. "Did you find your medication, Angel?"

"I was just going to check," Angel said. "Ember, do you mind if I go through your suitcase?"

I shook my head. "Be my guest."

As I lifted my suitcase onto the bed, Fiona continued

to stand by the door, a canny look on her face. She knew we were lying. I wasn't sure how, but she knew.

"If it's something important, you should probably go home for it. You don't want to chance being trapped over here without the supplies meant to keep you alive."

That was an odd choice of words. I unlocked my suitcase, turning so that I blocked Angel from Fiona's sight. Angel ruffled through my clothes, ostensibly looking for medication.

"I can't find them," Angel said, popping out from behind me. "But I can stop at a pharmacy in town. They should have my prescription on file from the branch in Seattle."

"Excuse me," Fiona said. "I've something to talk to Angus about." Abruptly, she turned and headed down the hallway.

I let out a long breath, my shoulders slumping as I closed the door again. "I don't know what the hell's going on, but she scares me."

"She scares me too. To be honest, I don't like the idea of sleeping here." Angel glanced around. "I don't trust her to not poison our food."

Pressing my lips together, I thought about the creatures out in the woods. They had been deadly, too, but in a different way. Cunning, deceitful, but they didn't feel like a giant hand waiting to crush us.

"I think maybe it's best if we talked Herne into staying in town tonight. Let's go see what she's up to now." I headed toward the door.

Angel's mention of poison had set me off and now all I could think about was we'd be sleeping under the roof of a woman who obviously didn't like us. What could happen if she really *was* possessed? And if she wasn't, then she had either snapped or had a dramatic personality shift, given Herne's kind words about her before. We returned to the living room, to find Angus apologizing to Herne.

"I'm sorry—I had no idea she'd react like that. Please don't mind her. She'll come around."

"What happened?" I glanced at Herne.

He was scowling. "Fiona has requested that we spend the night elsewhere. She says you and Angel were rude to her."

"What the hell? Where is she? We weren't—"

"I know you weren't," Herne said. "As for where Fiona is, she went out for a walk in the snow." He turned to Angus. "I think we'd better stay at a hotel."

"I think we should too," I said. "For what it's worth, Angel thinks Fiona is carrying someone on her back."

"You mean, possessed?" Angus asked. "Like I thought?"

"Quite possibly," Angel said. "But the thing is, I don't sense a spirit hanging around her. Not a ghost. But there's something else. What about you, Raven?" Angel motioned for Raven to join us. "You deal in the spirit world. Is Fiona possessed?"

"That's no *spirit* attached to her," Raven said. "At least, not in the usual terms. But something powerful and angry has hold of her, and whoever it is, it sees us as a threat. Probably because we can sense that Fiona's not herself, so to speak. I concur with removing ourselves to a different location. We aren't safe here."

"What about me?" Angus said. "Am I safe?"

"As long as you don't tell her that you invited us, I think you'll be all right for now." Herne glanced at the door, then back to Angus. "You need to think about anything that happened over the past few weeks. *Anything*. We'll talk tomorrow, but it better be at the hotel since Fiona doesn't want us here. Meanwhile, before the snow gets worse, we'll head to a hotel in town. Talia, find us a hotel, if you would. Yutani and Viktor, take our bags back out to the cars."

As they jumped to do as he bade, Herne's phone went off. He glanced at the screen. "Text from Rafé. He made it to Port Angeles and is checked in at a hotel for the night."

"The Anchor Inn is on Oak Bay Road, just past Breaker Lane. It's near the Port Ludlow Village Market. I'll call and see if they have rooms available. How many do we need?" Talia held up her fingers, counting. "Three men, four women. Four rooms? One for you, Herne, one for Yutani and Viktor, and two for the women?"

"That works," Herne said.

When we were out on a case, he and I didn't share a room. It was one of our ways of separating business and pleasure.

I glanced at Raven. "Are you willing to double up with Talia?"

She nodded. "That's fine with me."

Talia moved to the side as she called the inn. Viktor and Yutani returned from stowing our luggage back in the car.

"The snow's coming down thick and if we don't get out of here soon, we'll be stuck," Viktor said.

"Well, we're in luck," Talia said. "The inn has enough room for us, and it's not that far away. We should get a move on."

"Aren't you worried about Fiona being out in this weather?" I asked.

"Yeah, but she says she loves it. She's never been particularly fond of winter before, but she's taken to going on long walks through the woods. I tell her it's dangerous, and she should know by now, after living here forty years, but she just blows me off." Angus stared at the floor, shaking his head. "I'm at a loss. Please, if you can think of anything… Meanwhile, I'll search my memory. Something had to precipitate this."

"Tell Fiona we're sorry we imposed on you—that we should have called first. We do *not* want her thinking you invited us. Keep your guard up, though, because whatever has hold of her is dangerous." Herne and Angus clasped hands, and Herne pulled him in for a quick hug.

As we gathered the rest of our things and headed out the door, I glanced at the thicket where we had met the grigit and the schnee-hexe. The woods were illuminated, with something deep within the trees glowing with a faint blue light. It occurred to me that it was Fiona, and given the energy I had felt off her, the padurmonstris would do well to hide when she came near.

THE DRIVE TO THE ANCHOR INN WAS PRECARIOUS AT BEST, even with Herne's SUV. Luckily, both he and Viktor managed to navigate the quickly freezing roads and we pulled into the parking lot about twenty minutes later. If the roads had been clear, it would have taken us perhaps half that time, but the snow was falling on black ice, and everything was tinged with that glacial shade of blue from the snow and ice.

The Anchor Inn was three stories tall, built of stone and polished wood. It was a pleasant change from the pseudo-Victoriana that seemed so prevalent over here on the peninsula. The warm lights glowing from within, along with the massive tree tucked into the side of the door, decked out in shimmering ornaments and lights, gave a cozy, welcoming feel to the lobby. The reception counter was made of the same polished cherrywood that adorned the trim on the outside of the inn.

I found myself breathing a sigh of relief, grateful that we were well away from Angus's house. Fiona had scared the crap out of me. We checked in and took the elevator up to the second floor, where the four rooms were side by side. As we entered our room, Angel gave a little squeak when she peeked in the bathroom.

"A jetted tub!" A grin sprawled across her face. "I call dibs on the first bath."

"You've got it," I said, examining the rest of the room. There were two queen beds with a nightstand between them. A TV sat on the dresser, and the closet had enough space for all our clothes and our suitcases. To the left of the bathroom door, a stand held a microwave, a coffee maker, and several mugs. The stand had a built-in mini-fridge in it, as well as the guest bar. All in all, the room was comfortable and looked clean.

I drew open the curtains and we found ourselves over-looking Oak Bay Road. Directly across the road was a patch of trees, and I thought I could see lights from within the thicket.

"I thought the wild places in Seattle were teeming with

life. Look." I nodded to the shimmering lights that seemed to bob and weave across the road.

Angel stared at them for a moment. "I'm glad we're here, to be honest. Even if Fiona had seemed happy to see us, I think we're safer here."

"Yeah, I know what you mean. Tell me, did Fiona seem…" I tried to find the words. "I'm not sure exactly what I'm trying to say. She felt…*not human* to me."

"She's not, really. The magic-born aren't fully human." Angel frowned. "Sometimes I wonder about my own background. I'm an incredible empath—I know that. And Mama J. could read the cards like nobody else. I never knew my daddy, he died shortly after Mama J. got pregnant with me. She loved him so much, and he loved her, but she never told me much about him. For all I know, he could have been one of the magic-born, or he could have been human."

"Is there a way you can find out? What about your relatives back east?"

She shook her head. "No, they fell out with my mother when she took up with DJ's father. They really don't like shifters and were pissed at Mama J. for having DJ."

"Speaking of, have you heard from DeWayne again?"

Angel shrugged. "No. But I expect to, if he's anything like he used to be. He'll be sniffing around, trying to find out about DJ and whether he inherited any money. It almost makes me happy there wasn't anything left after all the bills were paid. When he finds that out, if he loses interest, then we'll know he was just looking for a free ride all along. But DJ doesn't need to know about this until I've figured out just what DeWayne wants. I won't get his hopes up only to see them be dashed by that creep."

It hurt me to hear the crack in Angel's voice. Mama J. had been one of the most loving women alive, and she had taken me in when I was fifteen and my own parents were murdered. Angel and I had already been best friends, but Mama J. treated me like her own daughter, and I'd never forget her kindness.

"Don't sweat it for now. We'll figure it out when we get back home. If he calls again before then, just send him to voice mail." I sat down on the bed. The mattress was comfortable, and I yawned. "It's been a long day. Hell, I'm still wiped out from saving the woman on the ferry."

"At least you managed to save *someone* today. As to your question about Fiona, I'm not sure what to say. There's so much power built up in that woman, and it can't all be from her heritage. The magic-born are strong, but this…" Angel paused. "I don't know what to say, except the woman scared me spitless."

We finished unpacking and then met in Herne's room. It was almost ten P.M. and everybody was dragging ass. I cuddled up beside him as he wrapped his arm around me. I leaned my head on his shoulder as we took a few minutes to let the energy settle around us.

"Well, let's take stock of the day, shall we?" Herne cleared his throat and, with his free hand, ticked off points. "One: the ferry. I think it's safe to say this storm was behind the car that scuttled itself off the ferry. Two: Angus has been worried about the storms. Three: Rafé's in Port Angeles, and he's ready for tomorrow. Yutani, I want you to activate the trace as soon as possible. Four: Angus and Fiona…there really is a problem and she's piggybacking something that has control of her. As to who and why, we don't know."

I cleared my throat. "Let's add another thing. Five: the padurmonstris in the woods. We have to be wary. Which leads me to the question: Does the Tuathan Brotherhood live in territory where the padurmonstris roam, and if so, how do they keep them at bay?"

"Good addition to our list," Herne said.

I shrugged. "As far as Fiona goes, Angel and I were just talking about her. There's something about Fiona's energy that reminds me of something, though I can't quite put my finger on it—" I paused as a gust of wind shook the windows. "Cripes, this is a strong storm. Wait—" I blinked. "That's what Fiona reminds me of! A storm waiting to break. She feels like a pent-up storm. Like weather magic gone awry."

"That's an interesting thought. But what…" Herne froze, a look of understanding spreading across his face. "Crap. I need to call Angus."

"Now? Isn't it a little late?" Talia asked.

Herne glanced at the clock on the nightstand. "I suppose I should wait until tomorrow." Turning to Yutani, he asked, "Pull up the Encyclopedia Mythatopia. Look up the name 'Murray Lesley.'"

Yutani plugged the name into his laptop, then gave Herne a quizzical look. "*Really*? You knew this and didn't think it was important to tell us?"

"Depends on what it says. Read it." Herne leaned back against the pillows, pulling me with him so we were half-propped on the bed.

"Murray Lesley, the Keeper of the Corryvreckan Stone of the Cailleach. 1541–2018."

At that, Herne paled and bolted upright. "Oh hell. Oh, hell in a handbasket."

"What is it?" I asked.

"Angus's father died last year. I didn't know that. It explains a lot. Murray Lesley is—or rather, was—the keeper of the Corryvreckan Stone of the Cailleach."

"Just what is the *Corry*…whatever stone?" Angel asked.

"Corryvreckan is a gulf in Scotland. There's a massive maelstrom there, creating a whirlpool that tops out as the third largest in the world. And in ancient times, the Cailleach used to wash her tartan in the whirlpool, which brought on the long winters."

"Who's the Cailleach?" I asked. "A goddess?"

He shook his head. "No, not in the sense that I'm a god or my mother's a goddess, but she's…a *Luo'henkah*. A spirit who makes up one of the forces of nature. She ushered in the ice ages, and she was forever trying to intrude into spring. One day the goddess Brighid decided to fight back. She takes over the season from Imbolc to Ostara, you know."

"What did she do?" Talia asked.

"Brighid gifted a champion—Fearden Lesley—with a magical stone that acted like a genie's bottle. He went up against the Cailleach and managed to capture her when she wasn't paying attention. He trapped her within the stone and sealed it. But to make certain she never got free again, Brighid set him the task of watching over the stone, and it became the legacy for his family. The eldest is always given the task of taking up the vigil once the stone keeper dies. Now that Murray is dead, it's up to Angus."

"You think he has the stone with him?" I asked.

"I think that's a good bet, and that in itself would be a serious problem. I am thinking that stone was never meant to leave the shelter Brighid created for it."

Angel paled. "Then has the Cailleach somehow escaped and latched on to Fiona?"

"Given the Cailleach is female, and probably furious at the Lesley family for keeping her imprisoned, my guess is that's just what happened. I'll call Angus in the morning. I have the feeling that if I got hold of him tonight, Fiona would somehow sense it, and she might take it into her head to kill Angus." He paused. "If my guess is right, we're facing a vengeful spirit of nature, who won't hesitate to destroy anybody in her way."

"Then we'd better be very careful to not tip her off," Talia said.

And with that, we said good night. Angel and I wandered back to our room, with Raven and Talia behind us. Raj was trotting along obediently, and now he let out a loud fart and the hallway filled with a stench that smelled like rotten eggs.

"Dude, that's nasty," I said, turning to Raj.

If he would have been human, I would have sworn he was blushing. But he just burped and let out a low grunt.

"It's okay, Raj-raj, I know you can't help it. It's the strange food." Raven knelt down. "He's very sensitive about matters like body odors and stomach grumbles," she said, glancing up at me.

It was my turn to blush. "I'm sorry, Raj. I keep forgetting he's smarter than a dog. I didn't mean anything by it." I leaned over and patted his head. "You're really a wonderful boy, you know?"

His tongue lolled out and he reached up with one finger and poked my nose very gently, smiling at me. I met his gaze, and in his eyes I saw genuine affection, and something more. For the first time since I'd known him, I had the feeling Raj understood what I said, and that he was giving me a pass on being a jerk. I leaned in and hugged him, gently wrapping my arms around his neck, and he let out a surprised snuffle, then patted the back of my head.

As I stood, he went back to all fours, resting on his knuckles and back feet. Raven gave me a long look, then smiled and nodded, and that was all we needed to say.

Angel and I peeled off into our room, and as we changed for bed, she stopped, holding her nightshirt half over her head. "What's the Cailleach? I know what Herne said, but what is she?"

"I can't give you a real answer, because I don't know myself. But I have the uncomfortable feeling that by the end of this trip, we're going to know far more than we want to about her."

"Tomorrow Rafé heads into the heart of the Tuathan Brotherhood." Angel turned on the alarm on her phone. I could hear the fear in her voice.

"He'll be all right. He'll do his job and get out of there and we'll take him home safe and sound. Just have faith." But inside, I wasn't sure I believed what I was saying. So far, the trip had been one clusterfuck of stumbles.

Yawning, I crawled into bed, wishing we were at home, with Mr. Rumblebutt. I checked my texts to find that Ronnie had sent me a picture of him playing with a feather toy. With that small comfort, I closed my eyes and tried to sleep but it was a long time before I managed to slip into my dreams, and when I did, they were uneasy, vague shapes hiding in a snowy woodland, and looming over the picture was a stark figure made of ice and snow, bringing her anger with her like a growing storm cloud.

CHAPTER SEVEN

*I*t was amazing how much difference a heavy snow could bring to an area. When I woke, the world was beautiful and clean outside, everything wrapped up in a magical package. It was so picture-perfect that I expected to hear "Winter Wonderland" playing in the background. I opened the window and the cool air came rushing in. The sky was hazy with silver clouds, but there were a few places where the sun had broken through, and everywhere the light touched sparkled like a thousand diamonds had been scattered over the ground.

I took a heady breath of the cold air. Then, as the chill hurt my nostrils, I leaned back in and shut the window. As I turned, Angel yawned and rubbed her eyes, sitting up to squint at the morning light.

"Can you shut the curtains until my eyes adjust?"

I obliged, then moved to the coffee maker and carried the carafe into the bathroom to rinse out and fill with water. After opening one of the packets of coffee grounds and shaking them into the filter, I started the machine and it began sputtering out coffee.

"Do you want to shower first?" I pointed to the bathroom. "Be my guest."

She carried her toothpaste and brush to the bathroom. "Thanks. I feel like I barely slept, even though I know I did. It felt like my head was ringing all night."

As she headed for the shower, I poured myself a cup of coffee and carried it over to the chair by the window, where I curled up to watch the cars pass by, their tires spraying a mist of snow behind them. My phone let out a ding and I glanced at it. Herne was texting me.

ARE YOU UP?

YES, BUT NEED TO SHOWER. ANGEL'S IN THE SHOWER NOW.

THEN MEET US FOR BREAKFAST IN HALF AN HOUR, DOWN IN THE RESTAURANT OF THE INN. LOVE YOU.

WILL DO. LOVE YOU TOO.

I lingered over my coffee until Angel emerged from the bathroom, then stood and stretched.

"I'll take a quick shower and we'll meet the others for breakfast in the restaurant of the hotel." I grinned. "Leave me any hot water?"

"Ha! You wish!" She snapped her towel at me as I passed by.

After I showered and dressed, and we both fixed our makeup, we headed down to the restaurant on the main floor of the inn. It was small but cozy, with a breakfast buffet. The others were already gathered around a table, so Angel and I filled our plates before joining them.

I stared at my plate, my stomach rumbling. I had chosen sausages, two waffles, eggs, and fruit salad. "This is turning out to be a better morning than I thought it would be."

Angel pulled out her phone, glancing at the screen. After a moment, she raised her head, her expression bleak. "Rafé's waiting in a parking lot of the hotel for the Tuathan Brotherhood to pick him up."

"He'll be all right," I said, stroking her arm. "He knows exactly what to do, and Ferosyn gave him a drug to counter the effects of the Ropynalahol they give their recruits."

"Yeah, but what if it doesn't work right? What if…"

"What if you eat your breakfast and have a little faith? Rafé knows what he's doing and we need to give him the credit he deserves," Talia said, her voice gentle but firm.

Angel shrugged, but focused on her breakfast. I leaned back in my chair, feeling my own phone vibrate. As I glanced at the texts I saw one from Rafé and one from Ronnie. Ronnie's was simply a series of pictures of Mr. Rumblebutt—sprawled out on his back, eating his breakfast, and playing with a feather toy. Rafé, on the other hand, had asked me to watch after Angel for him, and to keep her spirits up.

"Who's texting you?" Angel asked, glancing at me.

I decided she didn't need to know about Rafé's text—it would only worry her more—so I just said, "Ronnie. Pics of Mr. Rumblebutt to show me how little he minds us being gone."

"How about we discuss what we're going to do this morning? Angus can meet us at eleven, and he'll come here. But I thought we could also take this chance to get a look inside Nalcops's office," Herne said, calling us to order.

"How do we do that? We need to make certain he's not onto us, at least for the moment." Yutani speared a sausage on his fork and took a big bite out of it.

"I thought we could have Angel go to his office and ask whether he's taking new clients. She's the least visible of us, and could pose as someone who just moved to Port Ludlow." Herne tapped the butt of his knife on the table. "We *know* he's not accepting new clients, but maybe she can get her foot in the door by asking for recommendations when he tells her no."

Angel blinked. "*Me*? You want me to actually go out on an investigation?" She sounded surprised. As the receptionist for the agency, she didn't often get to do field work.

"Yeah, why not? You and Talia are the one who's seldom out in the field. If there's a chance Nalcops knows about the Wild Hunt, then he'll be most familiar with Viktor, Yutani, Ember, and me." Herne winked at her. "Time to get your feet wet. Unless you'd rather not. I won't push you to do it, but I think this would be a good time to utilize your talents as an empath as well. You can get a good read on him and perhaps pick up something we don't know yet."

Angel paused, setting down her fork and knife. She stared at her plate for a moment, then nodded. "All right. I wouldn't mind having more to do than just sit at the hotel, logging notes. And you're right in that I'm probably the least recognizable of the group. So what do I do?"

"After breakfast, we'll rent you a car and you drive

down to his office. Viktor will tail you, hanging back a ways, and he'll park nearby, but out of sight. That way, if you need help, you'll have backup. I'd like to fit your purse with a bug, so Viktor can tell if you need help." Herne stood. "Excuse me, I want another doughnut and more sausages."

As he crossed to the buffet, I turned to Angel.

"You're sure about this?"

She nodded. "It's time I broke out of the box a little bit. This is a good way to start. If Rafé is willing to go into danger, then I can do this." She held my gaze, a glint of determination in her eyes. "I'm tired of being afraid. When we get home, I want to start training with you. I work out, but I want to take some formal training."

Raven finished off the last of her breakfast and said, "You'll be one dangerous woman once you learn how to fight dirty." She glanced over at Herne. "I hate to tell him, but I did some research last night. If he's right in what he's thinking—and I know what it is—his friend Angus is in for more heartache than he can dream of."

I was about to ask what she meant when Herne returned.

"It's ten-thirty now. Viktor and Angel, head out for Port Gamble in fifteen minutes. Yutani can fit you with a bug before you go. The rest of us will meet with Angus."

Angel nodded, finishing her breakfast. "All right. If I'm going to do this, let's get going."

"You know what to do," Herne said to Viktor, as the half-ogre stood.

"Yep. Come on, you two." He motioned to Angel and Yutani, and they left the cafeteria.

"Is Angus coming to the dining room?" I asked.

"No, he'll meet us up at my room. Go ahead and gather whatever you need. Meet me there in ten minutes. I'll pay the check." Herne motioned for us to head off. I gave him a brief kiss, then followed Talia and Raven toward the elevator.

"What did you mean back there, about Angus being heartbroken?" I asked, once we were clear of the restaurant.

"Just that Angus's father was keeper of the Cailleach. If she's broken free of the stone and taken over his wife, I'm pretty sure Fiona's lost." Raven glanced over her shoulder as we entered the restaurant. "The Cailleach doesn't have a heart or a conscience."

"You mean, we might not be able to pull Fiona out of this?" Talia asked.

"I mean, there might not be anything left of Fiona to retrieve," Raven said. "These forces of nature…they're beyond understanding even of the Ante-Fae. The gods can't kill them. They belong to the planet, and any resemblance to human kind is illusory."

"Are they elementals?" Talia asked.

Raven shook her head. "Think of it this way. The Forces are to elementals what the Ante-Fae are to the Fae. Each one is unique, and they predate the elementals. They *created* the elementals."

"Then can we even hope to stop her?" I asked.

"Yes, there are ways to trap her, like she was trapped the first time, but it's not easy. I just don't want you to get your hopes up about being able to put the entire situation to rights." Raven shrugged. She was carrying a takeout box that I assumed was full of breakfast for Raj. "There are some events in this world that simply cannot be fixed. There are some breaks that nothing can mend."

I liked Angus, and the thought that we might not be able to help Fiona hurt my heart. "I hope you're wrong. I'm not saying you are, but I hope so for Angus's sake."

"I do too, Ember," Raven said, stopping in front of the door to her room.

"We'll meet you at Herne's room in a moment," Talia said, following Raven in.

I gathered my tablet and my portfolio where I kept various handwritten notes, and then, after a glance in the mirror to make sure everything was in order, I took a deep breath and headed for Herne's room. I felt far more somber than I had when I had woken up.

HERNE WAS WAITING FOR US, AND SHORTLY AFTER RAVEN, Talia, and I joined him, Yutani ducked into the room.

"She's wired up, and she and Viktor are on their way," he said. There was something different about him—something that I couldn't quite pinpoint. He seemed...*lighter*... was the only way to describe it.

We settled in to wait for Angus, who arrived about ten minutes later. He looked harried and tired, as though he had barely slept.

"How goes it, brother?" Herne asked, motioning for him to take a seat on one of the spare chairs. Raven and I were sitting on the second queen bed, while Herne and Yutani were on Herne's bed, and Talia was sitting in another wing chair.

"Not good. Fiona was furious after you left. I've never

seen her so angry, and she was downright brutal. It's as though she didn't remember you at all, Herne, and she took such a dislike to Ember and Angel that I can't fathom what happened." Angus lowered his gaze to the floor, looking both embarrassed and bewildered.

"Angus, you didn't tell me your father died," Herne said.

Angus jerked his head up, frowning. "How did you know? And no, I was so worried about Fiona that I forgot to mention it. He died last year."

"What happened to him?" Herne leaned back in his chair, crossing his right leg over his left knee.

Angus paused for a moment, then said, "Nobody's quite sure. My father had a heart attack, that much we know, but he had been in the best of health and nobody's sure just why it happened."

Herne asked, "What happened to the stone?"

Angus paled. "You mean the Cailleach stone? I have it with me. I set it up where I could watch over it in the woods near my house. I didn't feel comfortable keeping it indoors, but it's my duty to guard over it, so I put it in a sheltered area."

"You *know* the history of the stone, correct?" Yutani asked.

Angus frowned. "Well, supposedly it's the stone where the Cailleach was trapped, but we know that those old tales…" He paused, staring at Herne, then he looked around at each one of us in turn. "The stone is *real*? It's not just an artifact?"

"Come on, man. Don't play coy," Herne said, his expression darkening.

I stared at Angus. "You can't possibly expect us to

believe that you thought that it was just a symbol? What did your father tell you?"

Angus let out a tremulous sigh. "He said never take the stone from Corryvreckan, that our family must watch over the Cailleach. But I couldn't just up and move back there when he died, so I had it sent here. I didn't think anything of it." He paused, then inhaled sharply. "Do you honestly believe that I unleased something by bringing the stone here?"

"There's one way to tell. We need to see that stone. Is Fiona around your house right now?" Herne asked.

Angus shook his head. "No, she's off somewhere. She wouldn't tell me where she was going."

"I have to stay here to watch over Viktor and Angel's transmissions," Herne said. "Ember, you and Yutani go with Angus and find that stone. Bring it here when you get hold of it."

Once again, Angus caught his breath. "Is that what's going on with Fiona? Has the stone captured her?"

"Not the stone," I said softly. "We think the Cailleach may be controlling her." I jumped up. "I'll get my coat. Meet me downstairs."

Yutani headed for his room as well. We met in the lobby and Angus joined us, the look on his face giving away every fear he was feeling. Yutani had the keys to Herne's Expedition and I rode shotgun, while Angus led us there in his truck. The snow had been plowed, but it was still coming down and I kept quiet to allow Yutani to focus on the road.

Raven's warning kept playing through my head. What if we couldn't save Fiona? What if it was too late? Tired of the loop of worry, I pushed the thoughts out of my mind and tried to focus on how we were going to stop the Cailleach.

Angus pulled into the driveway. There were no other cars around, so Fiona probably wasn't home, which amounted to a blessing for us. As Yutani and I joined him near the edge of the driveway, Angus led us over toward the thicket of trees where Angel and I had met the padur-monstris the day before.

"Are you sure we're headed in the right direction? Those creatures yesterday weren't easy to escape." I didn't want to have to face them again.

"Don't worry," Angus said. "I set up wards along the path to keep them away. They won't bother us."

As we followed him into the thicket, I spied spell bundles tied around trees at regular intervals. Angus's wards, no doubt. I began to breathe easier. I could sense the creatures watching us, but along the trail, snowed over though it may be, we were free of their interference. There was a subtle difference, but the wards were defi-nitely giving off a protective energy that seemed to keep them at bay.

We wound our way through snow-covered fern and bracken, beneath the tall timber that stretched toward the heavens, their boughs thick with snow. Every now and then the wind would gust past, sending a spray of snow off the branches to shower over us, but other than that, the only sounds were the soft crunch of our foot-steps and the light fall of new snow over old. It was peaceful, and I found myself focusing on the feel of the land around me. But then, a soft click startled me and I froze.

"What's wrong?" Angus said, looking back.

Yutani was frowning and he cocked his head, scanning the forest. "What did you hear?"

"I heard a click. There's something here. I'm not sure where it was coming from, but I know the sound when someone cocks a crossbow."

I paused, stretching out with my senses, trying to find out who might have a bead on us. A moment later, I heard the slight shift of a footstep on the snow, and instinct kicked in. I whirled, knocking Yutani to the ground as an arrow came flying his way. Angus dropped to the ground beside us.

"What? Who?" Yutani let out a snarl.

"Stay here," I whispered. I began to crawl through the undergrowth as silently as I could. I felt a sense of curiosity drifting past, as if the archer was wondering whether he had missed. Good. Whoever was targeting us wasn't sure if he had landed a hit. That gave us some wiggle room.

As I crept low, through the snow and ice, I began to hear breathing. Whoever was watching us was nervous. I could sense their worry and hesitation, and I found myself falling into hunter mode. I hadn't brought my bow, but I was armed with two daggers, and I could do plenty of damage with them from the right angle.

As I drew close to the bowman, I paused and peeked through the undergrowth. It was a kobynok and he was peering in our direction, holding a bow and arrow. One of the sub-Fae, the kobynok was a winter goblin of sorts, shorter than regular goblins. He stood about three and a half feet, but his kind were crack shots with the bow, and they had no scruples. They'd happily kill a child as well as an adult.

The kobynok had a dagger hanging by his belt—and he *was* male, that I could see too clearly. But his attention was focused on the last place he had seen us. Kobynoks had good hearing, but since the Cruharach I moved much more quietly.

A bush stood to the right, behind the kobynok, and I slowly began to creep toward it, skirting him as I went. As I rounded the corner in back of him, I realized that I had one good shot to kill him outright. If I missed, he'd have a chance to grab his dagger.

Flipping the snap on both daggers, I eased them out of their sheaths as silently as possible. Then, gathering myself, I let out a soft breath and leaped out behind him, simultaneously plunging both daggers into his sides. I jacked them firmly into the flesh, twisting them to do the most damage I possibly could.

The kobynok didn't even have the chance to let out a shriek. He just stiffened, and then fell to the ground. I quickly slid my daggers out of his side, cutting his throat for good measure. I pulled the bow and quiver of arrows away from his body and, just as with his goblin-cousins, within moments the kobynok began to melt, dissolving as though acid was eating his flesh. Five minutes later, there was a bubbling pile of goo left where he had been laying.

I glanced around, checking to see if there was anybody else, but caught sight of no one. Once I was reasonably sure we were secure, I stood up and trudged my way back through the snow to Yutani and Angus.

"Kobynok. What are the winter goblins doing around here?" I turned to Angus. "Have you seen any others in the area?"

He shook his head. "They never come down out of the

mountains. Or at least, I thought they didn't." He paused
as I handed him the bow and arrow. "Were these his?"

I nodded. "The bow's made of birch, and the arrowheads are polished bone. That's pretty unusual for sub-
Fae. They're usually equipped with rudimentary weapons.
Birchwood bows are expensive and bone arrowheads
require skill to make."

Angus shouldered the bow and quiver, and led us on.
Another ten minutes and we entered a clearing. A circle
of boulders surrounded a tree stump, and on the tree
stump was a stone that stood about a foot tall and six
inches wide. It was carved from a dark rock, though there
was something oddly familiar about it and was covered
with sigils and symbols.

"So you think the Cailleach has broken out of the
stone and taken over Fiona?" Angus knelt down beside
the rock, staring at it like he'd never before seen it.

"Yeah, that's what we're saying," I said. "And Angus, I'll
be honest, I think you knew she was in there. But regardless of whether that's true, the stone's empty." I held my
hands out to the rock, and the hum of energy almost
made me pull away. There was great power here, but it
felt dormant. It also reminded me of the energy I had
sensed from Fiona. "The stone's waiting—I think we can
trap the Cailleach back in the stone, but it's not going to
be easy."

"Should we take it?" Yutani glanced over at me.

I nodded. "If we leave it, we give Fiona the opportunity
to destroy the stone, which she will if she thinks we're on
to her. She'll know for certain once we take it, but maybe
we can put a crimp in her plans. Angus, what can you
remember your father telling you about this stone?"

Angus crouched in the snow by the stone, staring at it. "I remember him telling me the tales when I was little. I know you think I'm lying, but they seemed just like tall tales out of legend and lore. My father was serious about it, but you know how it is…I grew up believing that being keeper of the stone was an honorary position." He shook his head. "In all that time, my father never mentioned anything about any danger attached to it."

"Your father had to know—" I began, but Yutani shook his head.

"Don't jump to conclusions," he said. "Does the legend mention the last time the Cailleach was free? It may have been before Murray's time."

"I don't know," Angus said.

Yutani crossed his arms, shaking his head to shake off the snow on his hair. He suddenly stopped. "Someone's coming."

"Fiona," I whispered. "She can't find us here."

"I'll take care of this," Yutani said. He stood back and began shedding his clothing. I was used to this and gathered them up as he stripped. Angus was staring at us, but said nothing. When he was naked, Yutani turned to us.

"When I take off, grab the stone and get back to the car. I'll find my way back to the hotel. Trust me on this." He began to shimmer, transforming into his coyote shape, and before we could say a word, he darted out of sight.

"Crap. Herne's going to kill me for this. Grab the stone and do as Yutani said." I began to retrace our steps, hoping we could manage to escape before Fiona caught us.

As we swung around a curve in the path, I held up one hand. There, in a patch of woods ahead, was Fiona. She was wearing a long white dress, with an icy headdress atop her copper locks. She was looking for something, and I could only hope that Yutani had managed to catch her attention. I motioned for Angus to follow me and we silently sped by, keeping to ourselves, as the snow continued to fall.

CHAPTER EIGHT

*W*e slipped out of the thicket and raced over to the car, Angus tucking the stone into the crook of his arm. There was another vehicle in the driveway. I turned to Angus.

"Hers?" I pointed to the SUV.

He nodded. "Yeah."

"Get in." I fumbled through Yutani's pockets and found the keys to Herne's Expedition, unlocking the doors as we raced toward it. As worried as I was about Yutani, I was more worried about Fiona catching us.

I yanked open the driver's door and jumped into the seat, tossing Yutani's things in the back. I prayed that he could evade her long enough to get away. I fumbled with the keys, finally managing to turn the ignition. As the car started, I fastened my seatbelt. Angus was staring at the trees, looking like he was about to cry.

"Hold on tight," I said, backing out of the driveway and turning abruptly onto the road. I wasn't used to driving on snow, but I'd better learn fast.

Behind us there was a sudden burst of thunder, and the snow began pouring down so fast that even the window wipers weren't able to keep up with it. I bit my lip as I navigated through the sudden whiteout, hitting the gas and praying for the best. I could feel her anger behind us, roiling along with the clouds.

"What about Yutani?" Angus finally managed to say.

"We'll have to hope he can get out," I said, trying to avoid thinking about him. I had to focus on driving, or we'd be in deep shit if I spun out. Fiona was after us—or rather, the Cailleach was—and I wasn't sure just what she could do.

Finally, we shot off of Olympus Boulevard onto Oak Bay Road, and a few minutes later, I was pulling into the parking lot at the hotel. I leaned back in my seat, staring at the snow that was falling so hard that I could barely see.

"Come on. Let's get inside. Herne needs to know what Yutani did. We may have to mount a rescue mission." As we stumbled out of the car, I took a deep breath. We had made it, but how safe would we be here? As I hustled Angus toward the hotel, a blast of wind gusted past us and I thought I could hear something howling on it.

As we entered the hotel, I dashed for the stairs, Angus on my heels. I didn't want to wait for the elevator, and it had occurred to me that the Cailleach could summon up a storm strong enough to bring down the power lines. I didn't want to get caught in the elevator, not just for one flight of stairs. As we headed down the hall toward Herne's room, I was grateful that I had made the decision as the lights flickered and died.

"Crap. The power." I pulled out the flashlight that I'd attached to my key chain. It was a narrow beam, but strong. As we came to Herne's door, I rapped on it. A moment later, he opened it, letting me in.

"Where's Yutani? What's going on?" he asked.

Angus set the stone on the desk and stood back. "Fiona knows," he said, his voice a whisper. "Here's the stone."

"Where's Yutani?" Herne glanced around.

"I don't know," I said, feeling weak-kneed. "He shifted form to distract Fiona so we could get away." I glanced out the window. "I'm pretty sure the Cailleach is driving the storm that took out the power. I could hear her on the wind."

Herne paled in the beam of my flashlight. "Stay here. I'll be back." He grabbed on his coat and headed out the door. "Talia, call Viktor and ask him what's going down. We can't track Angel without power."

As the door shut behind him, Talia called Viktor. Meanwhile, I sat down by the stone, staring at it. "I wonder if she can track where it is."

"What are Fiona's chances?" Angus asked, sitting beside me. His face was a mask of pain.

I shook my head. "I can't answer that, Angus. The Cailleach is a force like none I've dealt with. You'd have to ask Herne, but I'm not even sure if he knows."

Talia joined us, staring at her phone. "Viktor texted Angel to get the hell out of Nalcops's office and he's waiting on her now." She gazed at the stone. "So, this is what's caused all the fuss. Angus, did it never occur to you that there was something to the old legends? I'm not trying to needle you, boy, but did you really think your father watched over this stone day and night simply because it was tradition?"

Angus started to answer, then paused. After a moment,

his shoulders slumped as he said, "All right. Truth? I didn't want to leave here. I didn't want to give up my life here and go back to Scotland. Over the years, as my father grew ill, I convinced myself that I could watch over the stone from here, and that what he said about never moving it was simply his way of trying to bring me home. He wasn't happy when Fiona and I moved over here."

"Then you *knew* this was a bad idea," Herne said from the door as he opened it. Yutani was following him, naked with just Herne's jacket draped around his midsection. "You know the Cailleach is real. You just chose to cover your ears and sing 'La-la-la-la' and put everyone in danger rather than do your duty. Is that what you're saying?"

From where he was standing, Herne's eyes glittered in the reflection of his flashlight, and the strength of his voice made me shiver. He was furious. I was grateful that I wasn't in Angus's shoes right now, though I did feel sorry for the man. He had chosen to try to alter his destiny and it hadn't turned out right.

Yutani raised his hand to me, nodding. "I'll be back in a moment. I need to dress."

"I have your clothes right here," I said, holding up the sack in which I'd put them.

"Thanks." He took it and headed for the bathroom.

Angus looked miserable. He swallowed as Herne just stared at him.

"Did you get hold of Viktor?" Herne asked Talia without looking away from Angus.

Talia was watching the two men carefully. "Yes. The power outage didn't hit Port Gamble. Viktor's close enough to see the front door. The power going out took us offline, though, and so he can't tie in to the tracking app that Yutani created. He's waiting for her to come out. I told him if she's in there too long, use his judgment on when to go after her."

"Viktor's got a good head on his shoulders. He'll make the right decision." Herne glanced out the window. The snow had reached whiteout conditions and it was almost impossible to see the road.

"Herne, I didn't mean for any of this to happen," Angus said. "Please believe me, if I thought that this would have happened, I'd never had asked them to ship the stone over here. I suppose there was a part of me that truly believed that nothing would happen. My family has watched over the stone since…I don't know how many generations. Nothing has ever happened."

Herne crossed his arms, still looking irate. "Perhaps that's because all of the previous keepers followed instructions."

I didn't want to interfere, but the anguish on Angus's face was apparent and I couldn't help but feel sorry for him.

"I think Angus realizes what he's done," I ventured, keeping my voice neutral.

Without missing a beat, Herne said, "As well he should. But now the entire town—if not the entire peninsula—is in danger. In fact, the Cailleach is a force that the entire world should fear. She can usher in ice ages."

Angus hesitated for a moment, then asked, "Does this mean I'm on my own with this?"

Herne let out a long sigh. "No. It does not. Although it would serve you right. But there are innocent people in danger due to your poor choices. We can't just leave them on their own. And you and I…we have a long history, Angus Lesley. I gave you my word. But for now, you get yourself a room in the inn and you stay put. Don't go home. She'll kill you for sure if you do. We need to plan what to do, but right now, I want you out of my sight until I calm down. Do not disobey me on this."

Angus stood, reaching for the stone but Herne stayed his hand. "Leave that here."

"Aye, Herne. I'll get myself a room." With that, he left without another word.

Yutani came out of the bathroom, using the flashlight app on his phone. "Thank gods there was still hot water in the tank."

"You took a shower in the dark?" I asked.

"A shower's a shower, in the dark or the light." He glanced around. "Where's Angus?"

"Don't ask," Herne said, turning back to the stone. "The question is, how do we deal with this? What can stop the Cailleach? We need power so we can do some research—" Even as he spoke, the lights flickered and came back on. "Well, that helps."

Yutani headed for the table. "I'll man my laptop."

"Hold on there," Herne said. "What were you thinking, running off like that? You could have been killed."

"You know that's how we work in some situations. The bitch was coming for all of us. I gave Ember and Angus the chance to get away with the stone. That's how we roll, dude." Yutani shrugged, sitting down in one of the wing chairs, leaning his head back.

"Yeah, I know. And you probably saved their lives. I'm just angry that Angus put us in this spot to begin with." Herne paced the room, stopping to stare at the stone.

"I know you're angry with him, but don't let this destroy your friendship." Talia voiced what I had been thinking. "Angus made a terrible error in judgment, but don't for the moment think he meant for this to happen."

At that moment, Raven tapped on the door, peeked in, and entered. She yawned, stretching. "Sorry. I felt the need for a nap."

Yutani jumped up, offering her his seat, but she graciously refused, coming over to sit by me. For the past month or so, he had been badgering her to go out with him, and she had told him no several times, but he was like a moth to a flame. I wondered if we were going to have to talk to Herne about this as well. All in all, Yutani had been acting up like a two-year-old, though after he helped to save my life today, I was less inclined to be bitchy toward him.

Herne frowned, staring at Yutani for a moment, before he turned back to Talia. "I hear you. I do. But this isn't just a minor slipup. However, we'll help him, and then I'll decide what to do. I'm not at all sure how to proceed. Yutani, can you run down to the restaurant and order coffee and pastries? I don't want to bother with room service right now."

The coyote shifter nodded, then vanished out the door. When he was gone, Herne turned to Raven. "Still bothering you?"

She blushed. "How did you know? I didn't tell you." Her jaw dropped and she gave me a quick look. "Did you tell him?"

"No, I didn't. But I think you guys better finish your conversation before he gets back," I said.

Raven gave Herne a nod. "Yeah. He's still sniffing after

me, but Ember's right. This is neither the time nor the place to address it."

It wasn't long before Yutani entered the room again, a waiter behind him who was carrying a tray of coffee and various pastries. Yutani slid into his seat in front of his laptop and booted it up, quickly typing orders as soon as the screen lit up. A moment later he wiped his mouth and leaned back.

"Got the tracking system back for Angel."

Herne pulled out his phone and quickly texted out a message. Another moment and he looked up. "Viktor says Angel's still inside with Nalcops. Should I text her?"

"I wouldn't," Yutani said. "At least not now. How long has she been in there?"

"I'll ask." He typed out the text. In another moment, he said, "Ten minutes. I'll give her another ten minutes, then I'm telling Viktor to go in. Things aren't going the way we want them to and, color me superstitious, but the last thing I want is for Angel to get herself in trouble."

We waited, anxious, staring at Yutani's laptop. Five minutes later and Herne let out a long breath. "She's out and returning to the car. Viktor says she doesn't look in a hurry, so maybe she got away with it." A moment later and he visibly relaxed. "They're on their way back. Angel told Viktor that Nalcops didn't seem on to her at all."

"Now that that's over, what do you want me to look up?" Yutani asked.

"Right," Herne said. "See what you can find on the stone. Specifically, how can we destroy the Cailleach? Or rather, how can we trap her again?" He glanced at the clock. "Have we heard from Rafé since this morning? He should be on the road with them now."

"He wouldn't be able to text us," I said. "They have a moratorium on outside contacts. I think they keep a sharp eye on the recruits."

"True, but we also have the trace on him. Yutani, pull him up and see where he's at." Herne leaned over his shoulder.

Yutani's fingers flew across the keyboard, but then he straightened, looking confused. "I know the storm didn't knock out everything but…" He paused, then again, focused on entering something. I held my breath. Something felt off.

"What's going on?" Herne asked.

"The trace appears to be off-line. Maybe the storm took out satellite communications or maybe something's malfunctioning with my program. Let me debug it and see if I can find out why it's not showing him."

"Oh hell. When Angel gets back here, don't mention this to her until we know what's going on." I turned to the Cailleach stone. "Meanwhile, where should I put this? We can't just leave it sitting around."

"Leave it here, in my room," Herne said, the expression on his face far from reassuring.

"Hey." I tapped him on the shoulder. "Come on, walk with me while Yutani works on the program."

I led him back to my room and pulled him down on the bed, leaning in to give him a gentle kiss. "I know you're worried, but what's going on? You seem really upset. I know Angus fucked up, but I don't think he meant to put everyone in jeopardy, I can't believe that of him."

Herne stiffened, then—letting out a long breath —relaxed.

"I know he didn't, but damn it, he was such a fool.

Such an incredible fool. He knows the power of the ancient ones. He knows what forces exist in this world. He was selfish, not wanting to accept what destiny had in store for him." Herne groaned, lying flat across my bed.

"Couldn't the Cailleach have gotten loose over there as well? Otherwise, why have someone watching her at all? This could have happened anywhere."

He shook his head, drawing one arm across his eyes. "This did not happen under Murray's watch. He was true to his calling. True to his word. He didn't shirk his duties."

"Angus didn't ask to have his life disrupted. He built a life over here with Fiona. He didn't want to give that up." I didn't like playing devil's advocate, but it seemed like Herne was being incredibly harsh on the man.

"Angus was trained in his duty from the time he was a bairn. He knew that one day he would take his father's place, and he understood all that entailed. He can't lie to me and tell me he didn't believe the story was real." Herne shot up, grunting. "The man was *hoping* that nothing would happen. That's a far cry from *believing* that nothing would go wrong. He might as well have just crossed his fingers."

I brought my feet up on the bed, wrapping my arms around my knees. "So, you've never made any mistakes when your father told you to do something? You've never made any mistakes that accidentally hurt somebody or had far-reaching repercussions?"

Glaring at me, Herne crossed his arms and pressed his lips together, staring at the floor. But after a moment, he sighed again, dropping his arms to his sides.

"I'll admit, I have. More than once. But damn it, nothing quite like this. Why couldn't Angus have just accepted the charge in his care and done what he was told to do?"

I scooted close to him. "Maybe he didn't want to live the rest of his life chained to a stone in Scotland? Maybe he loves it here so much it would break his heart to move? Maybe part of him truly didn't believe the stone was important. If you've never seen a tiger strike, it looks just like a big kitten. Maybe Angus doesn't really believe in the magic of the past? Sure, he's one of the magic-born, but they're just like everybody else in so many ways. And Angus lives in a world filled with science and technology."

"And with gods and magic. Just because science has a good grasp on how the cosmos works doesn't mean that it knows how *magic* works. Just because you have more computing power in your cell phone than the Pentagon used to have in an entire building doesn't mean that your spells don't work. You can't just ignore the past when it's still alive and thriving in the present." Herne pulled me to him and wrapped his arm around my waist as I straddled his lap.

"I know you're trying to help, but you aren't. Angus and I will be all right. It's just going to take some time. He could have gotten both you and Yutani killed today. He could have gotten himself killed today. He knows that the Cailleach has possession of Fiona and I think he's been afraid of that all along. He just wanted us to come over here and reassure him that he was wrong."

I leaned my head against his shoulder and he kissed me, then, slow and tender, his lips warm against mine, growing deeper with every passing moment. He stroked my face, touching my lips with his fingers, caressing my cheek.

"I wish we had time to make love, but right now, we have to make certain Angel's all right, and we have to figure out what happened to Rafé. Everything will be all right, love. I'll talk to Angus and we'll get past this."

"Good, because I'd hate to see you break up your friendship over this. It's going to be bad enough if we have to destroy Fiona." I stopped, not wanting to hear Herne's answer.

He stared at me for a moment, then kissed me again. "Let's cross that bridge when we come to it," he said. "We can't know for sure, yet. The only thing to do is keep hoping. Fiona's a lovely woman. I'd hate to think we've lost her for good." He glanced at the clock on the night-stand. "Come on, let's get back to work. It's nearly time for dinner. Once Angel and Viktor get back, we'll order room service and see what we can figure out."

Clinging to the hope that we'd be able to save Fiona, I followed Herne back to his room. Sometimes, it just didn't pay to get up in the morning.

CHAPTER NINE

*A*ngel and Viktor returned shortly and once again, we gathered in Herne's room. Talia called for room service and they sent up three large pizzas, all homemade and smelling absolutely mouthwatering. They also sent up several sides—mozzarella sticks, tomato soup, and breadsticks. It was a carb-fest but a delightful one.

Angel was looking a little like Bambi-in-the-headlights. She shivered as she joined me on the bed, sitting cross-legged.

"I think I need to leave the investigations up to you guys. I was terrified the entire time. I don't know how you do it, because I felt so awkward and worried that I was sure I was giving myself away." She paused as Herne passed her a mug of the soup. "Thank you. I need something hot. The storm is giving me a headache. It's as though I can hear someone shouting through it and don't know how to tune it out."

"We'll teach you to ward off intrusions as soon as we get back to Seattle," Talia said. "We should have thought of it earlier, but honestly, I guess we just assumed you knew how."

Angel shook her head. "Mama never knew how. I know, because she'd get a splitting headache after some of the readings she gave. I think she just thought it was part of having the gift of sight." She took a long sip of the soup, letting out a contented sigh as she closed her eyes.

"Do you feel up to discussing what went on in Nalcops's office?" Herne asked.

"Yeah, I'm fine." She paused to bite into a slice of pizza. After swallowing, she said, "First, it didn't look like any doctor's office that I've seen. Of course, I didn't go into the back rooms. I asked him if he was taking on new patients when he opened the door, and all I got was a curt 'No,' but before he could shut the door, I begged him for a reference to a doctor who was. He let me in, though I felt like he was watching me every minute."

"He's Fae, if I remember right." Yutani asked.

"Right. I wonder if he was drugged, as well, to make him comply with their demands." She shook her head. "Why would a doctor hurt his patients, otherwise?"

"I suspect we're dealing with a WYSIWYG situation here." Yutani crossed his legs, staring at the computer.

" 'WYSIWYG'?" Angel asked.

" 'What you see is what you get,' " Raven interjected. "Often used to reference editing software. Ulstair used enough tech jargon around me that I learned by osmosis."

Yutani glanced at her, a faint smile on his face. "Right," he said. "There are bad apples in every profession and, if you remember right, Nalcops was drummed out of TirNaNog for using questionable healing methods that left his patients maimed. He's just a rotten person at heart."

"Anyway," Angel continued, "he let me in and told me to have a seat in the waiting room while he checked through his references. He asked me what was wrong so he could know what kind of doctor to recommend. I told him I needed an OB/GYN right away, so he came up with a couple names. I'd be interested to know if they actually know him and are somehow involved in the situation, or if they were just names he pulled off of Recced.com."

Recced.com was an internet review site for personal service providers.

She held out a piece of paper with two names on them. They had been written on a prescription pad. Nalcops's handwriting was oddly legible for a doctor's, and extremely rigid. I wondered if it reflected his personality.

"What did he say?" Herne asked.

"Not much, just wrote the names down and handed them to me. I was hoping he'd have to leave the room so I could peek behind the other doors—there were three of them—but he didn't. For a waiting room it had an extremely homey feel, not cozy but…like a parlor. It was also dusty, and I got the feeling he doesn't use the room very often."

"Did you see anything else?" Talia asked. "Any books… magazines…anything that might relate to the Tuathan Brotherhood?"

Angel thought for a moment, then shook her head. "No. I recall thinking there wasn't anything remarkable about the place at all, except for how unremarkable it was.

Very little personality to the room. The reception desk wasn't the professional kind, but more of a slap-together table for execs who never actually do any work that requires drawers. There was a computer behind it on a side table, but it looked old."

"I guess that's a dead end, then." Herne sighed and tossed his notebook on the table. "Everybody, eat your dinner. We're getting nowhere fast with this."

"But Rafé will pull through for us, what with infiltrating the group, right?" Angel asked, forcing a cheerful smile to her face.

I almost choked on my pizza and shot a warning glance at Herne. Under no circumstances did I want her worried about Rafé any more than she already was.

Herne's eyes widened, but then gave an offhanded shrug and picked up a breadstick. "Sure, but that will take a little time. Meanwhile, I suppose I should call my father about the Cailleach and ask him what we can do to trap her in the stone again."

"Did you find out what's going on with Angus?" Angel asked.

"I suppose so, if you want to put it that way." While Herne headed into the bathroom to call his father, we filled Angel and Viktor in on what had happened that morning.

"So Angus knew what the danger was but he still brought the stone here and decided that it wouldn't do any harm? No wonder Herne is so upset," Angel said after we finished telling her about the storm. "And you're thinking Fiona's in trouble because the Cailleach has her hooks in her?"

"Pretty much, though I hope I'm wrong." I glanced over at Raven. "What do you think?"

"What I think is that Angus needs his backside horse-whipped. But you're right, Ember. I hold out little hope for Fiona. And even less hope that both of them will emerge from this unscathed. The forces of nature are nothing to reckon with, especially the spirits of the storms. Borealis is dangerous as hell—the Force of the north wind. I wish I'd known what we were dealing with before I agreed to come. I thought it was a simple posses-sion, but there's nothing I can do in this situation."

"What? You don't relish a little vay-cay from your everyday routine?" Talia asked, laughing.

Raven winked at her. "Honey, my everyday routine is a whole lot safer than running around trying to clean up messes that humans and others get themselves into."

"What about that case you had recently? That was no walk in the woods," Angel said with a snort.

Raven grimaced. "Don't remind me. On second thought, maybe a little vacation is good for the soul, after all."

At that moment, Herne returned, looking even more dour. "Well, that was an unpleasant conversation. Cernunnos is pissed out of his mind at Angus." He paused, his glance lighting on Angel. "But I do know what will stop the Cailleach. The only thing that will put her back in that stone is to shoot her with one of the Fiery Arrows."

"A fiery arrow? But you're a great shot," I said. "That shouldn't be difficult."

"You would think so, except for the fact that the Fiery Arrows I'm speaking about come from one place only: the goddess Brighid. She has to approve the use of them. My father will visit her and ask on our behalf. She was involved in trapping the Cailleach in the stone to begin with. Cernunnos said that when she does find out what Angus has done, she's going to blow her stack. I'm just glad it's not me going to be on the receiving end of her wrath, but you can be sure Angus will hear an earful."

"Do you think she'll give us one of her arrows?" Viktor asked.

"Cernunnos seems certain of it. The last thing the world needs is for the Cailleach to be loose again. Apparently, she's even more unpleasant than we surmised, and she has little use for humankind, the Fae, the gods, or anybody else. She's all about returning the world to a frozen wasteland. Given the emissions problems and global warming we've been suffering from, some of her energy might not be a bad thing, except that she's an all-or-nothing kind of force." He grimaced.

"All right, so while we wait on the arrow, I suppose we have to avoid Fiona."

"*Ding*, right again! Thank you for playing." Herne shook his head.

"Have we heard from Rafé?" Angel asked.

Herne cleared his throat. "You look worn out. Why don't you go take a nap?"

Angel gave him a long look. "Herne, you know I'm an empath, right?"

He nodded. "Right. Why?"

"And you realize that even though you're a god, I can read your energy?"

At that, he closed his eyes for a moment. "I suppose I forgot about that."

"Well, I just reminded you. And let me add on top of

that, you're a horrendous liar, especially to me. What are you trying to hide from me? Is it about Rafé?" Angel leaned forward, hands on her hips.

"You might as well tell her," I said. "We're not going to be able to hide it, and Angel's an adult." I hated that she was going to find out Rafé's trace had disappeared, but she had to find out sometime.

Herne grimaced. "Right. All right, you want the truth, here it is. Rafé disappeared off the tracking screen and we have no idea where he is. I was waiting for Yutani to see if we could pick up anything on him before mentioning it to you, but the cat's out of the bag."

Angel let out a soft cry, pressing her fingers to her lips. She gnawed on one knuckle before turning to Yutani. "Have you found any other signs of him?"

Yutani shook his head. "Not since he last checked in. The trace vanished from the screen and I haven't been able to pick him up again."

"What does that mean? What could cause it?" Angel asked.

"Several things. One could simply be that the implant stopped working. Or the signal is being blocked, and given the terrain around here, that's not out of the question. I'd say that's the best guess. However, there is the chance that they found out he was wired and forcibly removed the trace."

"Wouldn't it still show on the screen, though?" Talia asked.

Yutani nodded. "Yes, it would, and since it doesn't, I'm thinking somehow it was either defective, or somebody destroyed it."

"Destroyed it! Doesn't that mean they'd have to hurt him?" Angel was halfway standing now.

"Not necessarily," Yutani said. "They could have just taken it out of his arm, which would require a surgical cut but not more than a few centimeters."

"But that would mean that they have him hostage. And that means when they find out what they want to know, they'll probably kill him."

I was surprised Angel wasn't crying, but she straightened her shoulders, the same bleak expression on her face that she had the night she found out that Mama J. was dead.

She hadn't cried then, either, not until all the arrangements were made and we were alone after the funeral. She had held it together for the undertaker and the funeral parlor and the aunts and uncles who had called but never bothered to come out for the ceremony. She had kept her head high for DJ and all of Mama J.'s customers from the diner, and the hundred or so homeless who showed up to pay their respects because of the soup kitchen. Angel had held it together until after Mama J. was buried, and then, when we got back to her apartment and I put DJ to bed, she had broken down and silently cried until she passed out.

I knew better than to reach out. Right now, she was processing the odds that Rafé was still alive. At that moment, her phone rang. Startled, she glanced at the screen and murmured something that sounded very akin to "Oh, fuck," which was unusual, because while Angel swore, it usually didn't involve the F-bomb.

"I'll be right back. I have to take this. Ember, will you come with me? I want a witness to listen in." She led me back to our room, where she punched the speakerphone. "Go ahead. What do you want, DeWayne?"

Great. DeWayne again.

"You promised to tell me who my kid is. I tried calling your mother over the years, but she never answered my calls. I know she was pregnant when I left—but I want to know. Who the hell is my kid? And what did Nina leave him or her? I ought to know about my kid. I have a right to know!" His words were slurred and it was obvious he was drunk.

Angel glared at the screen, shaking her head. She looked up at me and anger filled her eyes, replacing the fear from a moment before. Finally, she let out an exasperated sigh.

"You know what, DeWayne? My mother didn't answer you because you aren't the father. She told me so years ago. She met somebody else before you left. *He* was the father. And Mama J. told me she was glad you left because it saved her the trouble of breaking up with you. As to who my sibling is, you don't need to know. Your sperm didn't do a damn thing but hop around, unloved and unwanted. And in case you might be sniffing around for money, think again. I sold Mama's restaurant to pay her debts. What little was left ended up incinerated by a house fire this year. So don't call me again." She punched the end talk button and then brought up his number and blocked it.

I stared at her. "Is that true? He wasn't DJ's father?"

"Of course it's not true. But DeWayne doesn't know that. And what he doesn't know won't hurt him. All he wants is cash or stuff he can pawn. As for DJ, well, Cooper's been more of a father than DeWayne could ever hope to be. So no, I didn't tell him the truth and I'm not sorry."

She dropped to her bed, holding her head in her hands. "I have a splitting headache."

I sat beside her, gently placing an arm around her shoulders.

"I know. It's the storm," I said. The storm that was bringing her headache was actually the storm going on inside of her, but I didn't say anything about it. "You did the right thing. DeWayne would have disrupted everything and he would have left DJ confused."

"Right. I'm not going to let DJ be used by his creep of a father." Angel shook her head, covering her eyes."

I rubbed her shoulders, murmuring soft sounds. While I knew she was upset over DeWayne's calls, I also knew she was upset over Rafé, but I wasn't going to approach that subject until she was ready to talk about it. She could deflect her anger and fear onto DeWayne for the moment and safely feel it without facing the fear that Rafé was in trouble or dead.

"You know what gets me?" she asked after a moment.

"What?"

"DeWayne...the first time I met him, I told Mama J. he was trouble. And she nodded and said, *I know, child. I know. But something good's going to come out of this, you wait and see.*" She paused. "Do you think she was talking about DJ?"

"I think that's likely. Who knows what that brainy little brother of yours is going to grow up to do? He's brilliant, and he's such a good kid. He might end up saving the world." I rubbed her shoulders another moment, then pulled away and leaned back to stare at the ceiling.

"Do you think Rafé's alive?" Angel asked softly after a few seconds.

"I don't know, but my gut tells me yes. So let's listen to that until we find out otherwise, all right?" I hadn't even realized that I *did* believe he was still alive until right then, but as I answered her, it felt right—it felt true in my core.

"All right. I'll pull myself together and we'll go back in. I just hate not knowing. I hate having to wait. It's the worst thing in the world." Angel crossed to the bathroom, where she washed her face.

There was a tap on the door and Raven peeked in.

"Can I come in?" she asked.

I motioned for her to enter. "Sure. We're getting ready to rejoin the others."

"You might want to give it a couple minutes. Kipa just arrived and he and Herne are hashing out something." She raised her eyebrows. "They're apparently arguing over how to proceed from here."

"Lovely," I said. "Just what we need. More testosterone wars."

"Tell me a little about Kipa. He's gorgeous," Raven said, and I caught an undercurrent in her voice that I doubted she was aware of.

I cocked my head, staring at her for a few seconds. "Well, Kipa is Herne's…you might call him a distant cousin. He's Lord of the Wolves. An elemental god of the wolves or something like that, from Finland. He was banished from Mielikki's Arrow—an agency like the Wild Hunt run by the goddess Mielikki—for putting the moves on her. He also stole Herne's fiancée, a long, long time ago. But he's a good guy, basically, a bit more chaotic than is good for anybody, but he's saved our asses a couple of times."

Raven's eyes flickered. "He's incredibly hot."

Hot was an understatement. Kipa was darker, with a Mediterranean skin tone. He had long dreads that were a dark brown and eyes the color of melted chocolate. He was muscled and strong and had a sly smile that made it easy to want to lick him up. Kipa—whose full name was Kuippana—had five earrings on each ear, tiny hoops that banded the lobes, and he had a dolphin bite piercing on the center of his lip—the two rings that ran vertically were silver.

"Yeah, Kipa's gorgeous, I'll say that much for him." I watched her for a moment. Since Ulstair had been murdered, she hadn't shown any interest in men but now, I sensed a spark. "He's single, you know."

"How is that possible?" Raven laughed, then as if she caught her thoughts wandering in a direction that made her uncomfortable, she shook her head. "Anyway, the men are arguing, Talia and Yutani are searching for Rafé's signal, and Viktor is cleaning up the remains of lunch."

Angel returned at that moment. "What did I miss?"

"Kipa showed up. As usual, the *tree twins* are arguing." Recently, during a tipsy evening, Angel and I had come up with the name for Kipa and Herne. Neither one of them had seen the humor in it, but we decided that it bore remembering.

"Oh, lovely. One more thing to add to our list. But Kipa might just come in handy. He can track like nobody's business—hell, between Herne and him, they own the woods. Maybe they can think of a way to track down

Rafé." A glint in her eye told me she had caught hold of a slender ray of hope.

"Good idea. Let's go in and see if we can get them to stop bitching at each other and actually get something done. Coming?" I asked Raven.

She blinked. "I wouldn't miss it for the world," she said.

And right then, I knew that she was clawing her way out of her own melancholy, whether or not she realized it.

CHAPTER TEN

The first thing I noticed when we entered the room was that Yutani wasn't around. Talia and Viktor were sitting at the desk that served as a table, watching as Kipa and Herne stood in the corner, grumbling at one another. Whatever argument they'd been embroiled in seemed to have calmed down. Angel wiggled her fingers at Kipa and I gave him a smile and nod. I was cautious with how much I interacted with him because Herne had a jealous streak, and given the background between the two men, I didn't like bringing up bad memories. As we sat down, I glanced at Raven, who was staring at Kipa with a calculating look on her face.

"Hey, Kipa, how goes it?" I said. "You haven't met Raven yet, have you?"

Kipa flashed her a quick look, then did a double take. He blinked and a slow smile spread over his face. "Well, well, if it isn't one of the Ante-Fae? And aren't you just a welcome sight for sore eyes?"

She paused for a moment before answering. "And just

how sore are your eyes, Wolf?" She held his gaze in a way I couldn't have managed—firmly, without blinking, with a sly smile to match his. "So, Ember tells me that you're the Lord of the Wolves? I've no doubt of that."

Kipa slowly approached the table where we were sitting. He stopped near me, but faced Raven. "How now, you're a necromancer, aren't you?"

"I'm known as the Daughter of Bones among my own people, and yes, I'm a bone witch." She straightened, lifting her chin just enough to tell me that she could sense his interest. Hell, everybody in the room should be able to, I thought. He was sniffing around her skirts like a wolf on the prowl.

"You work with the dead under the moon, don't you, O Ancient One? Yet, you seem very young compared to most of the Ante-Fae." He leaned toward her ever so slightly and I scooted my chair back, feeling like I was in the middle of a pair of magnets. "So, what line do you descend from?"

Raven cleared her throat. "My mother is Phasmoria, one of the Bean Sidhe, and my father hails from the Hanging Hills—Curikan, the Black Dog." She paused, then asked, "You are Herne's cousin, Ember tells me?"

Kipa nodded. "I am that, in a distant manner, milady. I hearken from Finland." And with that, he held out his hand and she stared at it for a moment before placing her own in his palm. He lifted it to his lips. "It's an honor to meet you, daughter of death."

I glanced over at Herne, who was suppressing a smile. After a moment, he said, "If introductions are done, we should get down to business. If my *cousin* doesn't mind."

Raven, as if suddenly aware she and Kipa had been

exchanging more than pleasantries, shook her head and blushed. "I'm sorry. I didn't mean to hold up the meeting."

"Don't apologize. Herne just likes to hear himself talk," Kipa said, winking at Raven.

At that moment, Yutani returned to Herne's room, carrying his laptop. "I've tried time and again but…" He paused, glancing from Raven to Kipa, back to Raven. I realized that he could smell their pheromones. The smile slipped off his face, but he stoically placed his laptop on the table and cleared his throat.

"As I said, I've tried several times, but I can't seem to bring up Rafé's signal. I'm not sure what's going on, or what we should do next." He turned to Herne. "I can think of one thing, but I'm not sure you'd like it."

Herne looked at him steadily. After a moment, he said, "I have a feeling I know what you're going to say. And it may be the only way. I don't like the thought of it, but with what we're facing, and the pressure from Cernunnos, I think it's our only choice right now."

I glanced at Yutani, then back at Herne. "You're both being extremely cryptic. What are you talking about?"

"If Yutani is thinking along the same lines I am, it means we're going to kidnap Nalcops and get the truth out of him as to where the Tuathan Brotherhood makes its headquarters." He gave me a veiled look, and I could see his father in his eyes. Once in a while, Herne had a way of reminding me he was a god, and that he didn't mind doing things that most people would shy away from.

I suppressed an automatic *We can't do that*, forcing myself to think it through logically. Nalcops was our only connection to the group at this point, and Rafé's life depended on finding them. When I thought about it that way, the idea made a lot of sense.

"I think you're right," I said, glancing at Angel and Raven.

Raven nodded. "You can't just leave your man in there. Just who is this Nalcops? And what kind of powers does he have?"

"He's Dark Fae, as far as I could tell," Angel said. "As to powers, I have no clue. I tried to shake his hand but he avoided me, and I couldn't get a read on anything about him other than that."

Herne turned to Viktor. "Best way of going about this?"

Viktor thought about it for a moment, then said, "I think we head over there this evening after dark. We render him unconscious and smuggle him back somewhere private. We don't want to stay at his house, but we should search it while we're there to see if we can find anything important. The question becomes, what do we do with him afterward? We can't free him. The first thing he'd do is contact the brotherhood. Also, once we find out what we can, we better get our asses up to Port Angeles, to find Rafé. The moment they discover Nalcops is missing, they're going to know something's wrong and they'll probably suspect Rafé."

"Good points, all of them. All right, next question is, how do we knock out Nalcops without raising any sort of alarm? We can do it the old-fashioned way, but we run the risk of accidentally killing him, and then we'd be out of luck. We need him alive long enough to find out where the headquarters are. As to what we do with him afterward, I suggest we take him to Cernunnos."

"But do you have a contact around here able to send him through to Annwn? If there isn't a portal handy, we can't just lug him around with us," Talia said. "I'm afraid that I have to opt on the side of getting rid of him. Then again, what do we do with the body? We need to make him just disappear."

"I can handle that," Kipa said. "There are enough of my children around that I can call on them to devour him. All I need is a patch of woods, and there's no lack of that around here."

Angel was sitting there silently, her expression blank. I knew she had a hard time with decisions like this.

"Are you all right?" I asked.

She nodded, surprising me. "Rafé's life is in danger. Nalcops has been party to killing numerous people. I have no problem with what's being discussed."

"Then I suggest we stop by Nalcops's house and grab him. We can question him on the way to Port Angeles, and stop off in the woods to let Kipa do his work." Herne leaned back, a dark gleam in his eye.

"What about Angus and the Cailleach? We can't just leave him in the lurch, can we?" Yutani shut his laptop, pushing back on the table.

"We'll have to take care of that situation after we've found Rafé. I'm afraid the Cailleach will just have to run amok for a while. I'll tell Angus to hide out until we return. In fact, he can come with us if he wants." Herne stood and stretched. "I'm going down and pay our bill through tomorrow. That way, we can leave when we need to. Meanwhile, get your gear packed. Viktor, you and Talia come up with a way to knock out Nalcops without harming him. We'll also need rope and a good gag. All right, let's get busy. We've got a long night ahead of us."

And with that, the meeting was adjourned.

IT WASN'T LONG UNTIL DARK. ONCE WE WERE PACKED, WE carried our stuff out to our cars. Kipa would be riding with Viktor, Yutani, and Talia. As Herne and I arranged the suitcases and bags in the back of the Expedition, he jostled me in the ribs with his elbow.

"Was I imagining, or did you sense a spark between Raven and Kipa?" He sounded hopeful.

I nodded, handing him Angel's suitcase. "Yeah. I doubt if Raven would admit it, but there was definitely something there. I think they'd suit each other, to be honest. I'm surprised Ulstair was able to keep up with her, but he apparently had a courage and fortitude that we never got to see." I paused, then I just had to needle him a little bit. "Are you still worried that I find Kipa attractive?"

"I can see the appeal," Herne said, grumbling.

"All right, listen to me. *For the final time*, Kipa is a gorgeous man. God. Elemental spirit. Whatever you want to call him. But the thought of trying to deal with his personality fills me with as much dread as it would if I were considering Raven for a lover. I consider both of them friends, and they both have good hearts. But I pity the fool who gets involved with either one of them. On the other hand, given their natures, I think they'd make good foils for one another. Are you at peace with this now?"

Herne straightened up, sighing. "I'm sorry. I am, and I

won't bring it up again. I know in my heart that you aren't interested in Kipa, and while I won't ever trust him fully again, he does seem to have changed. So I'll give him the benefit of the doubt and say that I don't think he's out to get you. I just… Ember, I love you so much, but I know I have baggage. A lot of it. I suppose I'm afraid that you'll get tired of dealing with the crap coming out from my past. You've been wonderful about Danielle, more so than I had a right to expect."

"Danielle is your daughter. You didn't even know she existed. She's happy now, and we seem to have made our peace. As far as your past lovers, unless one of them returns, sniffing around and wanting to dig her claws into you again, well… We all have our own baggage. I've got several boyfriends in my past. And then there's Ray." I grimaced, wishing I had never met Ray Fontaine.

"All right. I promise, I'll stop worrying about you and Kipa. I won't mention it again." He pulled me into his arms, leaning down to place his lips against mine for a long, luxurious kiss. "Are you ready for what we're facing next?"

I shook my head, snuggling in against his chest, secure in the warmth of his embrace.

"I don't know if I'll ever be ready for this sort of thing. But I understand the necessity. So, I suppose the answer is yes. I just hope Talia and Viktor figured out some way to knock him out so that nobody notices."

"You and me both, love. You and me both."

By the time we reached Nalcops's house, it was dark.

The days were growing shorter, heading toward midwinter, and sunset came early. Angus had opted to stay at the hotel, and he promised he wouldn't go home until we contacted him. In a way, I was relieved. The fewer people we had in on this, the fewer chances we had of somebody going off kilter.

Yutani had fashioned a smoke bomb with a sedative in the gas. He had also managed to procure a gas mask from somewhere, and he volunteered to take the lead. There was nobody parked around the house once we got Port Gamble, and the lack of people actually inhabiting the town made it much easier.

Both Herne and Viktor parked in front of Nalcops's house, and we watched as Yutani headed up the front sidewalk. The moment the door opened, he slammed down the gas mask and lobbed the bomb in through the open door, shoving Nalcops back inside. He slammed the door behind him, and I held my breath until I sputtered, realizing I still needed to breathe. We waited until Yutani texted all of us in a group text.

I'M IN AND HE'S OUT. I'M GOING TO TIE HIM UP AND THEN I'LL SEARCH THE HOUSE. VIKTOR, COME GET HIM. DON'T COME INSIDE, THOUGH, JUST RAP THREE TIMES ON THE DOOR.

Viktor headed toward the house. He had more room in the back of his SUV, so we had agreed in advance that he would transport Nalcops to the place where we were going to interrogate him. I was still fuzzy on where we were headed, but apparently Herne and Viktor and Kipa had agreed on a location.

As we watched, Viktor knocked on the door. Yutani opened the door, handing Viktor a large, heavy plastic bag, which he slung over his shoulder. The door shut again, and I surmised that Yutani was still searching the place. Viktor headed back to his car and stowed Nalcops in the back. A few minutes later, Yutani came out the house, locking the door behind him. He was carrying a sack and what looked like a laptop. Probably Nalcops's. He jumped in the front seat of Viktor's vehicle, and silently, Herne pulled away from the curb, followed by Viktor.

We drove over the Hood Canal Bridge, slow and steady as the snow continued to fall. I had the feeling the bridge would be closed before long, given the storm's strength. Shortly after we reached the other side, we took a right onto Paradise Bay Road, then an immediate right onto the Shine Tidelands State Park Road. There was nobody around at this time of night, especially on a stormy evening, so we drove down to the turnout facing the water, where we could park. We had the entire place to ourselves.

Herne glanced at me, then back at Raven and Angel. Raj was sitting patiently between them, looking bored.

"Ember, come with me. The three of you, stay here. And don't stink up the car." He looked expressly at Raj.

"I'll try to keep him from farting," Raven said, a grin on her face.

I zipped up my leather jacket, wishing I had brought a hat. As I pulled on my gloves and slipped out of the car, I dreaded what was coming. I knew that Herne and Viktor were used to applying force to get what they needed, but it still made me squeamish.

We headed toward the water, toward a couple of long drift logs that acted as benches. They were covered with mounds of snow, but I could still see the ends peeking out. Viktor and Kipa joined us, Nalcops over Viktor's shoulder, still in the bag. Viktor laid him down on the snow, carefully opening up the bag. He lifted Nalcops out, and sat him on one of the logs, beside Herne.

"I doubt if he's going to cooperate, so I suggest that you let Ember use her Leannan Sidhe powers to get information out of him." Viktor stared at me, as though challenging me to object.

I blinked. I hadn't even considered that line of action. In fact, it had never crossed my mind. But the truth was, I knew I could do it. And then, I realized something else. I could take care of Nalcops. I could suck the life out of him and no one would ever know what happened. We could dump him in the water, and he wouldn't be found for some time. In fact, if I contacted some of the elementals in the sound, they could take him into the deep to where he'd never be found.

The weight of what I was capable of rested heavily on my shoulders. But I also knew the stakes, and I knew what Nalcops had been party to.

"You knew this when we came here, didn't you?" I looked at Herne. "You knew the easiest solution lay in my hands."

He gave a little shrug. "Yeah, I knew. I didn't know if you had thought it through or not. If you aren't comfortable with this, if you feel you cannot do it, we'll find another way. This is your choice, Ember. Just remember what's at stake."

I stood there, staring at Nalcops as he began to wake up. The look of fear in his eyes chilled me, but then, I remembered the explosion, and being blown off my feet as a hail of glass turned me into a pincushion. And I remembered the pictures of the dead. There was so much at stake, and so many lives had already been lost.

"I'll do it. There's no other choice. Not really, not when I think of it."

THE MEN MOVED BACK, GIVING ME ROOM TO WORK. I yanked off the duct tape covering Nalcops's mouth. He said nothing, merely staring up at me, bound and trussed tighter than a Thanksgiving Day turkey. His jaw was set, and there was no compassion in his eyes. He knew what the score was, he just didn't know who he was playing with.

I took a step back toward the water and closed my eyes, staring up into the snow falling down into my face. Fine flakes landed in my hair, on my shoulders, all around me. They were small, almost the size of dust specks, but they kept coming, hundreds of thousands of them, building into a blanket of white carpeting the grass and the shore. The road was silent, and the only cars here were those belonging to us. The water lapped behind me, the wind whipping the waves toward shore, frothing them up into icy-cold sea foam.

I went inward, actively seeking that part of myself who continually hungered. I could feel her there, all the time, but she usually kept quiet. Ever since the Cruharach, the barrier cutting me off from both sides of my lineage had vanished, and I had created my own barricades to keep them in check. Both sides of my bloodline were preda-tory, and I could feel the urge to hunt, the urge to conquer, pushing at the boundaries continually. I had managed to create a balance, but now I needed to let that balance drop for moment.

I summoned the Leannan Sidhe out of the corner. I summoned up the hunger, keeping in mind my goal. And then, as it rose, churning within me, I turned back to Nalcops, and began to walk toward him.

His eyes grew wide. When I allowed this side of myself out, I looked different—not in appearance, but in stature. In energy.

"What do you want?" he asked. His voice was oddly high. I had expected it to be deeper for some reason.

"I want to know where the Tuathan Brotherhood's headquarters are. And you are going to tell me." I straddled him on the log, my knees on either side of his lap.

He began to sweat, even in the cold. "I can't tell you. They'll kill me. Please don't make me tell you."

I pressed against him, and I could fill him harden beneath me. But the look of fear in his eyes was what really turned me on, the knowledge that he understood just how powerful I was, and what I could do to him. I ran my hand through his hair, smoothing it back away from his face. Taking hold of his glasses, I tossed them in the snow behind me.

"You're going to tell me what I want to know. I can make this easy and pleasant, or I can make it more painful than anything you've ever experienced in your life. It's your choice. Now I'm asking you once more, where can we find the headquarters of the Tuathan Brotherhood? Tell me the truth, and I won't hurt you." I stared down into his face, feeding on the fear that ran through his eyes.

His lust didn't touch me, but the fear? It was an aphrodisiac.

"Up off Hurricane Ridge. Shortly before the visitor center, you'll see a red graffiti painting on the rock face next to the road. It's shaped like the Bendaryi rune. On the other side of the road, you'll find an access road into the woods, leading downhill. The road is big enough for one vehicle and it's roped off, but the rope is easy to untie. Take that access road about a mile in, and you'll find another road turning off to the left. It's not really a road, but it's been carved out, and a good vehicle can travel on it. There's an illusion across it, so you'll have to look carefully for two huckleberry bushes on either side, and there are red runes on their trunks."

"How do we dispel the illusion?"

"You don't have to. You can just drive through it. It's set up to disguise the opening. Only a powerful witch can dispel the actual illusion." He was sweating now, shaking under my touch.

"Who's in charge of the brotherhood? Tell me." I leaned down to stare in his eyes, compelling him to speak. My lips were close to his and I could feel the energy escaping on his breath. It stirred my hunger and I had to force myself to wait.

He stuttered a moment, then said, "Nuanda. That's the only name I know for him."

"Tell me about him. Who is he? What does he want?"

Nalcops was practically ready to explode. His pulse was racing, and he was so hard that I expected him to burst at any moment. I was grateful that I was wearing a pair of jeans, and that he had pants on. Because despite my hunger, I didn't want to touch him.

"I don't know his history. He never told me when he hired me. Everything was done over the phone. All I know is that he's descended from Lugh the Long Handed. He hired me when nobody else would, after I got out of prison."

"What were you in prison for?" I asked.

"Insurance fraud. I just got my license back three years ago, but I have had a rocky go of it."

Of course you have, I thought. "Why did Nuanda form the brotherhood? What's the ultimate goal and where can we find him?"

Nalcops began to stutter. "I don't know why he's doing what he's doing, and I don't make inquiries. I know what happens to people who ask questions."

"What else can you tell me? Anything at all?"

Nalcops shook his head, spraying sweat against my face. I grimaced, wiping the beads of perspiration off of my nose. He looked absolutely terrified and I was beginning to feel repulsed. I liked my meals to crave me. Fear was good, but I wanted them to crave my touch and Nalcops was far too crude for that.

"I don't know anything else. I just prescribe what he tells me to, to the people he tells me to. None of this is my fault."

I glanced over at Herne. He gave me a slow nod.

"That's where you're wrong, my dear. You know exactly what you're doing and you know what you're part of. And the fact that you don't ask questions means you know there's something wrong. So, I think it's time to hang the out-of-business sign, don't you?"

I placed my hands on either side of his head, holding him firmly. He struggled a little, but gave up as I placed my lips on his.

As I began to suck the breath out of his body, the energy flowed through me, seeping through my soul like food to a starving man. I breathed in every drop of his essence, every breath that made him who he was. As the life force swirled through my veins, shoring me up and strengthening me, Nalcops began to collapse. One more breath, and I let him go.

He fell backward into the snow as I slowly stood and backed away from his body. I felt triumphant, and yet somehow tainted. I didn't like the taste of his energy, I didn't like the feel of his breath. For a moment, I considered finding another source to take away the taste, but then I caught myself and forced the hunger back.

We've had enough, I told myself. *Go back to sleep until I need you again.*

And the Leannan Sidhe quietly crept back in her corner, and I soothed her to sleep, thanking her for being part of me, and promising her that I would let her out again when I could.

I turned to Herne.

"Are you all right?" he asked.

I nodded. "I think so. At least we know where to look. You guys carry him into the water and I'll ask the elementals to take him."

They silently obeyed, and I knelt in the freezing water, calling out to any elementals who might be near. One swam up next to me and I formed the picture of Nalcops in my mind, visualizing him sinking to the bottom of the sound forever. The elemental washed over me with a soft, liquid hand, as if sensing how raw my nerves were. Then, it coiled around his body and swept him out into the darkness, into the depths.

I turned back to the others. "I'm going to walk along the shore for a moment."

As I walked in the swirling snow, the chill of the flakes calmed me, soothing the heat of the hunger within. I had never expected to be like this. But this was who I was, this was what the Cruharach left in its wake. This was my destiny, and I wouldn't make the same mistake Angus had. I was learning to accept my fate.

I stared at the water as it thrashed against the shore, wondering where all this would take me. I had barely begun to plumb the depths of my nature. Who would I be in ten years? Twenty years? But for now, I would take it one day at a time. I inhaled a deep breath, then let it out slowly. Yes, I was getting to know myself all over again. One day at a time.

CHAPTER ELEVEN

*T*he ride to Port Angeles was hair-raising, at best. All the curves and turns along the road were fraught with ice, and the snow made it hard to see. It took us twice as long to get to Port Townsend as it should, and we thought about staying there for the night until morning. But with Nalcops out of the way, it seemed prudent to be ready by first light.

The highway that ran along the peninsula was often closed for landslides, and snow and ice made it that much worse. Luckily, it was still navigable at this point, but I hoped we wouldn't get stuck in Port Angeles. It would take time for the plows to get out and clear the highway. At least we were all together, except for Rafé and Angus.

Normally, it would take about two hours to drive from Port Gamble to Port Angeles, but the storm slowed us down so much that it took us nearly twice that long. In some places, we were creeping along at twenty miles per hour, the snow was coming down so hard. By the time we inched into the town, it was nearing midnight, and to our relief, we found the hotel that Angel had called ahead to. It was the same hotel that Rafé had checked into—the Comfort Choice Hotel.

All of us seemed to be feeling weary as we hauled our suitcases out of the cars and carried them into the cozy, well-lit hotel. Herne and Talia took care of checking everybody in while the rest of us sat in the lobby's waiting area, sinking into the plush microfiber sofa and chairs.

I felt wrung out, exhausted from the interaction with Nalcops. It was taking everything I had to keep my eyes open.

"Are you all right?" Angel asked, leaning toward me.

I shrugged. "I'm not sure," I said. "I feel like every fiber of my being is electrified, like I grabbed hold of a live wire. I think it's partially emotional, given what we just went through." I glanced around, not wanting to talk too much in case somebody was eavesdropping.

Angel nodded. "I can imagine. Well, I can't, but it sounded horrible. I'm sorry you had to do that."

I held my finger to my lips, shaking my head. "Later, when we're alone we can talk about it. Here comes Talia with the keys."

Raven dragged herself to her feet. Even she looked tired.

"Come on," she said. "I'll go get a dolly for the luggage. I know we don't have a lot, but we might as well make use of any help we can get." She glanced at Talia. "Did they say Raj could stay here?"

"I told them he was a dog and they said all right. You might want to throw a blanket over him or something so they don't question exactly what he is when they see him."

Raven arched her eyebrows. "Oh, I'm sure he's going

to love that." She turned to Herne. "I need the keys to get Raj out of the car."

"I'll help you," Herne said.

I had the feeling he didn't trust giving his keys over to Raven. Come to think of it, given her nature, I wasn't sure I'd want her driving my vehicle either. As the rest of us piled our luggage onto the dolly and headed for the elevator, Herne and Raven exited the building. I made a quick stop by the reception desk.

"I suppose room service is closed for the evening?"

The clerk nodded. "I'm sorry, yes it is. But we have a wide variety of vending machines over in the alcove across the lobby."

I glanced around at the nook she was pointing to. True enough, there were at least ten different vending machines in the crowded space. I motioned for the others to hold up.

"Anybody want any snacks?"

Everybody mumbled in the affirmative, so I held out my tote bag and went to work with a bunch of dollar bills from my back pocket. I filled the bag with various packages of chips, candy bars, packaged doughnuts, cheese and crackers, and other goodies. Adding a half-dozen cans of soda, I finally wandered back to the elevator just in time for Herne and Raven to return from the car. Raj was wearing a throw over his back, and Herne was leading him so that his head was shielded from the reception desk. It wasn't the best disguise, but the clerk glanced up briefly, then went back at her work, and we all headed into the elevator that Talia was holding for us. As we scrunched in together, along with the dolly and suitcases, Raj let out a whimper and looked up at Raven. She patted him on the head.

"I know you're hungry. I'll see what we have when we get up to the room. I'll find something for you." She sounded so loving that I couldn't help but think about Mr. Rumblebutt.

I pulled out my phone and texted Ronnie, and she responded immediately.

EVERYTHING IS FINE. I WOULD HAVE SENT YOU A PICTURE THIS MORNING BUT I FORGOT. HERE'S ONE FROM TONIGHT.

As the picture came through, I smiled. Mr. Rumblebutt was staring up at the camera with a disgusted look on his face. He was wearing a bow on his head and standing over what looked like an entire bag of cat treats. I bit my lip, wishing I was home with him now. I nudged Angel and showed her the picture, and she laughed.

"I miss that purr butt." She glanced at me, then put her hand on my arm. "He's fine. Ronnie dotes on him."

"Yes, she does," Talia said. "She sends me pictures of Roxy and Rema, and they always seem happy when I get home, but they do love her."

Raven glanced at Talia, and then at me. "Do you think that she would consider pet sitting a gargoyle?"

I glanced at Talia, who shrugged.

"I suppose," I said. "Raj isn't any more trouble than any other pet, if you can call him that."

"He straddles the line between pet and companion. But he's like a pet in that I can't leave him alone or he frets and gets into mischief. He's not very good at feeding himself either." Raven glanced down at Raj. "We have to get you comfortable with her first, but that might be an option instead of me having to bring you along every time

I go out of town." She raised her eyes to meet mine. "Raj doesn't like to travel. It makes him nervous. He always thinks I'm going to abandon him. He feels safe at home, and I like to keep him in that space whenever possible."

As the elevator doors opened and we spilled out onto the fourth floor, Herne handed out the keys. Once again we had four rooms, pairing off like we had before, only this time Kipa would be sharing Herne's room. The rooms were all together, which was a blessing, and we sorted out our luggage as I divided the snacks between everybody. Nobody was fussy, so I handed them out at random, although I made sure to give Raven a sandwich that I had managed to find for Raj.

We were all too tired to talk, so we peeled off to our various rooms. I stopped for a moment in Herne's room, closing the door behind me. Kipa excused himself into the bathroom to give us some privacy.

"I miss having us time," I said. "How long do you think this will take us?"

He shook his head. "I don't know, to tell you the truth. And while I didn't say it in front of the others, the truth is I'm worried about Rafé. Tomorrow we'll head up to Hurricane Ridge to see if we can find him. And we're going to see if we can find Nuanda as well."

"Do you think the Cailleach is behind the storm?"

"I don't know the answer to that either, although it does feel magical in origin. The Olympic National Forest gets plenty of snow. But there's something different about this." He pulled me into his arms, holding me tightly. "I'm so sorry we had to ask you to take care of Nalcops, but it was the easiest way. And it was the only way I could think of to find out the truth."

"I know. I didn't like it, but I know how necessary it was. In a sense, I've become a weapon in my own right since the Cruharach. It's an odd feeling. I worry about losing my sense of humanity."

"I don't think you ever have to worry about that, Ember. I think your sense of what's right and wrong will never be something you lose." He stroked my face, searching my eyes as he leaned close. "Kiss me, and then I think we better get some sleep."

I wanted to do more than kiss him, I wanted to run my hands over his chest, and feel him caress every inch of my body. I leaned up, placing my lips against his, and lingered in the long, luxurious kiss. He made me feel warm and safe as he held me, and I rested my head against his shoulder for a moment, sinking into his embrace. Finally, I pulled away.

"Good night, love." He opened the door, escorting me gently to my room. As I shut the door behind me, Angel glanced up, smiling.

"You guys are doing really well, aren't you?" she asked.

I nodded. "I have something with Herne that I never thought I'd find. Only it scares me sometimes."

"Why?"

"Because when you have something this strong, then you have something to lose. And I haven't been in that space in a long, long time."

We undressed in silence, taking quick showers to warm up. As I crawled into bed, I tried to forget what had happened with Nalcops. I tried to forget the storm swirling outside. Instead, I held tight to the feeling of Herne holding me in his arms, keeping me safe. I carried that feeling into my dreams, and luckily, my slumber was peaceful, without nightmares.

COME MORNING, WE GATHERED IN THE HOTEL DINING ROOM for breakfast. Everyone was antsy, especially when Yutani mentioned that he had gone outside early and found Rafé's car.

"Did you, by chance, break into it?" Herne asked, buttering a piece of toast to go with his bacon and eggs. He had also ordered a huge side of hash browns and fruit. I opted for waffles and bacon, as had Angel and Raven. Talia was having steak and eggs, and Viktor, Kipa, and Yutani were diving into the massive buffet.

Yutani nodded, scooping up a spoonful of the porridge and raisins. "Wasn't that hard. I found his phone," he added, placing the phone on the table. "But I didn't find his keys. Nothing else looked awry. And I found no sign of the trace." He glanced over at Angel. "He carries a picture of you dangling from his rearview mirror." He smiled at her. The coyote shifter was usually edgy, but at times he really seemed to have a heart.

Angel stared down at her food, pressing her lips together, but she said nothing.

Herne reached across the table to place his hand on hers. "We will do everything in our power to find him and bring him home safety. Don't lose hope. There's always hope, at least until you find out otherwise. Don't borrow trouble."

"Mama J. used to say that." She raised her gaze to meet his. "I know you'll do what you can to find him. And I know he did this voluntarily—don't think I'm blaming you. I'm just worried and no matter what I do, that worry doesn't want to go away."

Raven ordered twelve sausages to go, along with a big bowl of oatmeal. "Raj loves oatmeal," she said.

"We should head out as soon as breakfast is over. Talia and Angel, you two are staying here. Raven—" Herne started to say, but she raised her hand.

"You might want to take me along with you, given how many Ante-Fae are in the area. I can be a good go-between, especially with some of the more peculiar beings who live in the woods. But I don't guarantee to help you if we meet Sasquatch."

"You made that abundantly clear earlier." Herne laughed, and in fact the entire table laughed, including Angel. "Finish breakfast. We should order some sand-wiches to take with us. In fact, raid the vending machines as well. We don't know how long we're going to be stuck up there. We need snowshoes, so Kipa, as soon as we're done with breakfast, I want you to go find several pair. Seven to be precise, in case we find Rafé. Everybody, pack a light bag. Bring extra clothing, at least one set, wrapped in plastic so that it doesn't get wet. Dress in layers. Viktor, make sure we have a survival kit. I'll gas up the car. Meet back at my room in half an hour. Talia and Angel, see what you can find out about the conditions up on Hurri-cane Ridge. See if we can still drive up there."

As we scattered, Raven taking her doggy bags up to Raj, I thought of our coming trek. I dreaded the thought of hiking out into the snow, but this was our job, and one of our own was missing. So we did what we had to do, regardless of the circumstances.

FORTY-FIVE MINUTES LATER, WE WERE ON THE ROAD, leaving Angel and Talia behind at the hotel. Raven convinced Raj to stay with them, promising him she'd be back as soon as possible. Raj didn't look happy, but neither would he be happy tromping through the snow with us. Herne had put chains on his tires, which would give us an added advantage.

The ridge was seventeen miles in, and it rose to an elevation of over five thousand feet. The road was two lanes, and while snow didn't usually linger in the lower elevations, now it was sticking. Herne was a good driver, though, and with chains and a heavy all-wheel drive, it made our trip a little easier. Raven and I were sitting in the second row of seats, with Viktor and Kipa in the back. Yutani sat up front with Herne, reading the map.

On either side of the road, the forest began to thicken as we went along, the tall tree branches laden with snow. The landscape was picturesque and beautiful in a way that only winter can bring, but there was a silence that went beyond hearing, that enveloped us as we drove deeper into the park. In some patches, our side of the road gave way, diving into deep ravines where the trees along the side hid the bottom.

We were barely into the park when I felt eyes on us, watching as we passed by. I wondered if we lit up the sky like a blue light special—after all, we had two gods, a half-ogre, a coyote shifter, one of the Ante-Fae, and me—a full-blooded Fae — all cooped up in one little vehicle. The contained energy in Herne's SUV could have powered the entire state.

"Can you feel them watching us? Who is it?" I was sitting by the window, and I stared out nervously.

"I can feel them," Raven said. "This park is rife with creatures and wild places." Even she sounded nervous.

Kipa leaned up between the seats to stare at both of us. "It isn't safe to walk abroad here. Herne and I can, but I wouldn't advise it for anybody else. At least not without a group. I'm guessing that the number of people who vanish within the national park system would surprise you."

Yutani quickly tapped away on his tablet. "Interesting. There's no national database of how many people disappear in the national parks, but there have been at least a thousand over the years. People disappear in one area and show up in another without knowing how they got there, people vanish for good, people are found dead with no apparent reason for their deaths. All sorts of strange things happen out here." He glanced back, his gaze darting to Kipa and then to Raven.

"There are many things in this world of which people remain unaware," Herne said from his seat, keeping his eyes on the road. "I've spent most of my life out in the forest, and I've seen things that would make your hair curl. I've had several run-ins with Sasquatch over the years, and I don't care to repeat them. I may be a god, but Sasquatch is a freak of nature. And I'm not talking natural as in endemic to this place."

"I met him once," Raven said. "As I mentioned to you before, I had to run for my life to get away from him. He chased me through a graveyard, and the only way I managed to escape was to hide inside of a crypt. The inhabitants of the crypt weren't too happy with me once they realized I could see them. Actually, they weren't too happy with anybody, I got the feeling."

"Where was this?" Yutani asked.

"It was down in Gig Harbor," Raven said. "I was visiting a friend there, and she's kind of obsessed with trying to attract creatures like that. She thinks they're all like the space brothers all the new-agers used to go on about, or some such nonsense. So she sets up magical grids on her property to try to encourage them in. Oh, they were attracted, all right. Now she can't get rid of them and she realizes just how insane the idea was. She keeps asking me for help, but I don't know what to tell her at this point. I deal with the dead, not the denizens of the dark, so to speak. Give me a spirit any day over Bigfoot. Or any of his ilk."

I snorted. It wasn't so much what she said, but the way she said it. Raven had a way of making the most peculiar things sound absolutely normal.

"I'm guessing that not all spirits are that easy to deal with, either."

She shrugged. "No, but I'm pretty good at zapping them back into their grave if they don't behave. At least most of them. There are some that I don't involve myself with, if at all possible. Like the one I had to deal with in October."

I was about to comment—she had been on one hell of a case and Angel and I had heard about the aftermath— when Yutani interrupted.

"We just passed the Heart O the Hills campground and entrance. Things are going to get a little more dicey now." He glanced out the window. "The road's slicker. I'm sure as hell glad you put chains on this vehicle."

Herne nodded, keeping his eyes on the road. "Unless it's important, I'd appreciate it if you didn't talk too much. I want to focus on driving because we are starting to pick up elevation and the road is getting more dangerous. I'm surprised they haven't set up a roadblock to turn people around. I'm betting they will before dark."

"They're probably going to close it down by then. We'd better be off the road and hidden so they don't chase us out." Yutani leaned against the window, staring out.

As we continued on to the visitor center, Raven and Kipa kept their eyes on the left side of the road, looking for the red graffiti rune. The Bendaryi rune was difficult to mix up with others. It was a Fae rune, meaning solidarity. If Nalcops was right, we would hopefully be able to see it given it was daytime, but with the snow coming down, it might not be difficult to miss.

Two cars passed us on the way down. One of them looked to be a park service vehicle. There didn't seem to be many people out today, and I had my doubts whether we would run into many hikers, given the weather.

The road was treacherous in some places, the guard railing looking over the edge of a ravine that ran so deep it was difficult to tell where the bottom was. A sea of green and white splayed out in front of us, the conifers covered with mounds of snow. I wasn't sure how long we had been driving, but after a while Kipa exclaimed from the backseat.

"There—just up ahead. That looks like runes to me." He pressed his face against the window.

"I think you're right," Raven said. "See it, Herne?"

Herne slowed, checking behind us to make sure that we weren't being followed. The last thing we needed to do was to cause an accident by parking in the middle of the road. He idled the Expedition, peering to the side, toward where they were indicating.

"That's it, all right. That means we should be close to an access road on the right. Ember, Yutani, do you see anything?"

Yutani shook his head. "I don't see a road."

"Hold on," I said, unbuckling my seatbelt and slipping out of the car. I heard Herne yelling behind me, but I ignored him as I approached a roped-off section of the guard railing. Sure enough, beyond it a steep road led down into the ravine. I unhooked the rope, and motioned for Herne to ease the car off the main road, onto the path. He cautiously turned, guiding the car over the edge onto the bumpy snow-covered path. Once the car was fully on the access road, I roped it off again, then climbed back in my seat and closed the door.

"Fasten your seatbelts," Herne said. "It's going to be quite a bumpy ride."

"Yes, Bette," I joked.

"Huh?" He flashed me a confused look.

"Bette Davis—*All About Eve?*" At the lack of comprehension on his face, I shrugged. "Never mind. If I have to explain it, it's not funny."

"Right," Herne said, snorting. "Back to business. The road looks steep, but I think we can make it without flipping. My SUV isn't all that top-heavy."

"It's not like you're driving a Hummer," Yutani said.

I made certain that I was strapped in securely and glanced over my shoulder. "Everybody belted in?"

Kipa nodded. "We're ready."

Herne cautiously began to ease the car down the slope,

trying to stay on the road. Because of the snow, there were points where it was difficult to see where the road ended and the ravine took off. Finally, he shook his head and stopped.

"Yutani, I need you to get out there and play air traffic controller. Do you think you can do that?"

"Not a problem, boss." Yutani didn't look happy, but he pulled on a pair of gloves, jammed a ski hat over his ears, then scrambled out of the car. He slid along the path, staying off the immediate road in front of us, then began to guide Herne along, pointing to where he should drive. We had a full mile to go, but about one third of the mile in, the access road became clearer, and Herne motioned for Yutani to get back in the car.

"It's cold as fuck out there," Yutani said, shivering.

"Thank you. I don't think I could have navigated the earlier section without you. But the road's more defined here."

As the trees crowded around us, the snow continued to fall. It felt like we were entering another world. If we had an accident, there would be no easy way to call for help. At least the forest buttressed both sides of the road now, so although we were still headed downhill, we couldn't go toppling off the side of the road.

I watched the forest for any signs of life, but I didn't see anyone. We seemed to be the only ones in the world here.

"Everybody sitting on the left side, look for two huck-leberry bushes with the same red runes. We're approaching the area where the hidden access road is supposed to be." Herne put the car in low gear, trying to compensate for the tires spinning on the slick snow.

Ten minutes later, Raven tapped on the window. "There. There are two big bushes. I see a glimpse of red."

Herne stopped the car again and this time, Yutani jumped out without a word and went over to examine the two huckleberry bushes. It looked like they were standing on either side of a giant fern, but Yutani waved his hand through the bush and then glanced back, nodding. He returned to the car.

"The access road starts there, right where the fern is. It's an illusion. I poked my head through and the road is fairly level from there on out. It looks bumpy, but we should be able to navigate it. But I'm going out on a limb here and cautioning that, the moment we break through that illusion, we better be prepared should the brotherhood happen to be out on patrol."

"Good thinking. All right," Herne said. "Hold on, people. We're going in."

As we turned onto the access road, driving through the illusion, I stiffened, wondering what we would find on the other side, and whether we would find Rafé while he was still alive.

CHAPTER TWELVE

As we forged ahead, I was grateful for my seatbelt, as well as the overhead handle grip. Yutani was right, the road was bumpy as hell. I was grateful we left Raj back at the hotel.

Raven seemed to pick up on my thoughts. "I'm glad Raj isn't with us. He can be one hell of a guardian, but he isn't used to being out in the forest. The wilds make him nervous and he does better in the city."

About ten minutes later, Herne suddenly paused, idling the engine. "Yutani, is that a road to the left?"

Yutani frowned, then nodded. "It looks it. Which way do we go?"

"I don't know. Nalcops didn't mention a second road." Herne paused for a moment. "I think we should take this one. We don't want to drive right into the encampment, and my guess is that their headquarters are probably at the end of the main road here. This road looks rougher, so I doubt it's used as much. We can make camp, and then sneak in on foot."

"How far do you think it is to their headquarters?" I wasn't relishing the thought of a long hike through the snow.

"I'm not sure, but we have snowshoes. I just have the feeling that we should take this turnoff and we better make it quick." Herne forged onto the side road and we lumbered through the snow, quickly entering an even thicker patch of woods. A few moments later, he stopped, turning off the engine, and opened the window. He held his fingers to his lips.

Sure enough, we could hear some sort of vehicle back on the main road. I held my breath, hoping they wouldn't see us from the hidden access road, but they continued along and soon the sound of the engine vanished. We couldn't see who they were from here, or what kind of car they were driving, but it had to be some sort of all-wheel drive to make it through the storm.

Herne closed the window, then turned back to us.

"I'm hoping they didn't hear us earlier. I think we may have gotten away with it, but I'm not sure. But that just confirms that we should make camp along this road somewhere, then scout our way back to see what we're dealing with."

Yutani groaned. "I know what the word 'scout' means," he said. "You're going to send me in coyote form, aren't you?"

Herne grinned, then shrugged. "It makes the most sense. But I'll go with you. I can change into my stag form." He glanced back at Kipa and Viktor. "The two of you should stay here with Ember and Raven."

"It makes more sense for me to go," Kipa said. "I can go in as a wolf. Most people can't tell the difference between a coyote and a wolf, which means they might think we're just a couple of wolves out for a run."

Herne frowned, then nodded. "Yeah, that does make sense. All right, the two of you get ready to go. Try to remember where we're at." He paused, then added, "Hold on a moment. Let me pull ahead a little farther. I think there's a clearing ahead."

He pulled ahead, easing the Expedition forward. Sure enough, a moment later we pulled into a clearing. There appeared to be a ranger's cabin there, but it looked abandoned. I breathed a sigh of relief. This meant we wouldn't have to camp outside in the snow.

We got out of the car, and Herne approached the cabin. He opened the door and peeked inside, then waved us in. We joined him and looked around. The cabin itself was a sturdy, two-room affair. The main room held a bunk, a sofa, a table and chairs, and a fireplace. There was also a smaller woodstove that looked like it'd been used to cook on. The second room had a composting toilet in it, and a sink that ran only cold water.

"At least we'll be able to heat up some water," I said.

"Think again," Herne said. "We don't want any smoke rising from the chimney to indicate we're here. We want to take them by complete surprise."

I let out a grunt. "Wonderful. Well, at least we're protected from the storm itself. It's cold, though, so what do you suggest we do to keep warm?"

"Jumping jacks?" Herne asked, a half-assed grin on his face.

"I can help," Raven said. "I can heat up rocks with my hands to a degree. They won't be warm enough to start a fire, but they should be hot enough to heat the air some. If you can find enough pebbles, I can turn them into hand-warmers for your pockets. I can also start fires, but Herne vetoed that idea."

"I didn't know you worked with fire," I said.

"I have a number of secrets you don't know about," she said, smiling. "Yes, I *do* work with fire, as well as death magic. They often go hand in hand. Fire is a cleanser, it purges and destroys, and it comes under the control of bone witches."

"Cool. Good to know," I said. "I'll go outside and start gathering rocks. I'll stay near the cabin, though." As I headed toward the door, Yutani started to strip.

Kipa shook his head. "I'm so glad that the gods don't need to strip in order to shift form."

"I'm not," Raven said, giving him a suggestive look.

Yutani shot her a quick look, then turned and finished taking off his clothes. I paused, admiring his form. He was gorgeous, with a runner's body, muscled and taut.

Kipa arched his eyebrows at Raven, then winked. In the blink of an eye, he changed into a wolf. Yutani changed into his coyote form, and Herne opened the door.

"Don't take any unnecessary chances," he said. "Scout around, see what you can find. But don't give yourselves away. Get back here before dark."

As the pair raced off into the snow, it was hard to believe they were actually our friends. They looked very much like a large fluffy wolf, and a smaller, younger wolf. I knew the difference between coyotes and wolves, but Kipa was right—a lot of people didn't. And whether or not the brotherhood knew the difference, it probably wouldn't matter unless they were pegged as shifters.

I motioned to Viktor. "Come on, help me find some rocks so that Raven can warm us up." As we stepped out into the storm, I felt a presence lurking on the wind. It was the Cailleach. And she was just beginning to vent her rage.

VIKTOR AND I MANAGED TO FIND A GOOD AMOUNT OF stones. Some were smooth and flat, obviously left behind in the great alluvial deposits scattered throughout the Cascades as the glaciers had receded during the last ice age. Other rocks were chunky, broken off from some mountainside.

Raven selected the smooth stones and settled down by the fireplace, placing them inside of it. "It will be easier for me to heat them all at once. This is going to take me a little while, so please don't disturb me."

Herne was sorting through his pack and brought out a map, which he spread out on the table. He began to study it as Viktor unpacked food, piling the sandwiches on a plate that he found in the cupboard. He set out the packages of chips and cookies, and cans of soda that we had brought with us. Pulling out several boxes of ramen cups, he turned to Raven.

"Can you heat up water in a cup?"

"I can," she said.

He filled a teapot that was sitting on the woodstove with water from the sink, and Raven cupped her hands around it. A few moments later, it was steaming and he poured the water into four of the ramen cups, sealing the lids back over them to cook the noodles.

Raven went back to the stones, and by the time the soup was ready, she stood up and arched her back. "They're about as warm as they're going to get for now, without me building a flame to immerse them in. They're pretty toasty, though. I recommend putting them in your pockets." She glanced around. "Soup and sandwiches! Yum."

I slid four of the smaller rocks into my pocket and was surprised by how warm they were. I wrapped my hands around them, almost burning my fingers.

"How long will these stay hot?"

"At least three or four hours. I can trap the heat inside them for quite some time. I do that often when I go out camping. I heat up rocks and take them to bed with me." She scooted over so I could sit next to her and handed me a cup of ramen.

Accepting it, I selected a ham and Swiss sandwich to go with it. "At least we have food and shelter. I wonder how Yutani and Kipa are doing."

Herne glanced up from the map. "I hope they're all right. Not only are we facing the icy weather, but I have a nagging feeling that there are spies in the woods." He shook his head, sitting back in his chair. "Why do I feel like we're walking into a trap?"

"How would anybody know we were coming? Nalcops didn't have a chance to warn anybody, did he?" I finished my sandwich, and spooned the noodle soup into my mouth, shivering as the warmth hit my bloodstream.

"They could have seen us coming in. Maybe they have cameras posted along the way, for all I know. I have a nagging feeling we missed something, or overlooked something, and that they know we're here." Herne was looking concerned enough now that I began to worry. He ran on the cautious side, but he wasn't quick to imagine trouble where there wasn't any.

"I suppose they could have planted cameras around the hidden road." I finished my soup and tapped Herne on the arm. "Eat. Who knows when we might get another chance to."

As he accepted a cup of soup and a sandwich, I thought about the possibilities. Suddenly, a thought sprang to mind that was about as discomforting as it could get.

"Crap, do you think they had a trigger spell set on the illusion that would warn them if it was breached?" The more I thought about it, the more it made sense. Illusions were usually used for deception. If someone broke the illusion, the spell caster would want to know about it.

Herne paled and set his spoon down. He looked sick to his stomach.

"You may be right," he said. "Considering that shortly after we turned onto the hidden road, they sent a car down it. They were probably expecting to find us. That means, they may have watched us the entire way, they probably know we're here, and…I wonder if this cabin is bugged. Oh hell, I could have sent Yutani and Kipa right into a trap."

Viktor immediately began poking through Yutani's bag and pulled out the device Yutani used for detecting magical and electronic bugs. He flipped it on and began slowly skirting through the cabin, staring at the meter on it. Five minutes later, he shook his head.

"The degameter shows no sign of hidden bugs, magical or otherwise. We should be safe with what we talk about inside the cabin, but outside? There may be cameras throughout the woods. There's no way to detect them, either."

"Thank heavens for small favors." Herne let out a sigh as he paced the length of the cabin. "The question is, what do we do now?"

Viktor finished off a package of Cheetos and dusted his hands on his jeans. "Do you want me to go after them?"

Herne shook his head. "Kipa's a god. He can handle an ambush. I just hope Yutani doesn't get hurt. Meanwhile, Viktor, you and I will go out to have a look around. Ember, you and Raven stay inside."

I started to protest, but Raven shook her head at me. As Herne and Viktor headed outside, she leaned close. "All we'd do by being out there is to dilute Herne's focus. He and Viktor would be worried about protecting us. I know it doesn't make sense, but men have that protective nature. Or at least, some of them do. Ulstair did."

I bit my lip, but she was right. "I know, but I want to be out there helping." I paused, then asked, "You're interested in Kipa, aren't you?"

She blushed. "It shows? I don't know—I didn't think I'd find anyone so attractive, not this close to losing Ulstair. But there's something about Kipa that resonates in my core. He feels...*familiar*. That's the best way I can put it. Did you see the look Yutani gave me?"

I nodded. "He's going to have to learn how to let go. I think he's just had so many things happen to him lately that he's not thinking clearly."

I paused as a shout echoed from outside. Raven and I rushed to the door, opening it just in time to see Kipa racing through the woods. He bounded inside the cabin, with Herne and Viktor right after him. I glanced out the door, looking for Yutani, but he was nowhere in sight. Quickly, I slammed the cabin door closed, and turned as Kipa shifted form.

"Where's Yutani?"

"We were separated. There's some sort of creature out there, several of them. I'm not sure what it is, though I know it isn't Sasquatch, and it's not a yeti. But it reminds me of both of them. It seems to be guarding the front of the encampment. I sensed a great deal of magic around it before it attacked us."

"Was Yutani hurt?" I asked, leaning forward.

He shook his head. "No, but Yutani ran one way and I ran the other. It started to chase Yutani, but I doubled back and led it away. I know Yutani managed to escape, but I don't know where he is. I led the creature on a wild chase to draw him off Yutani's scent, and I didn't want to bring him here, so I had to play leapfrog through the forest and wait until I managed to ditch him."

"Where's the encampment?" Herne asked.

Kipa pointed in the direction of the hidden access road. "About a mile and a half down the main road. It's not very large, not nearly as big as I thought it would be. But it's fenced off, and there are guards watching the gate. We got that far before the creature startled us."

"What does the creature look like?" Raven asked.

"At first I thought it was a yeti, because it's large, with white fur and blue eyes. But the yeti doesn't have a lot of magic, and this creature is rife with it."

"I know what it is," Herne said. "A Saumen Kar. I'm surprised the brotherhood's managed to convince one to help them out. You said there are more of them out there?"

"What's a Saumen Kar?" I asked.

"He's a relative of the yeti, but more intelligent. The Saumen Kar are shamanistic in nature. They usually stay out in the wilds, off in the cold lands like Greenland and up in the Arctic." Herne shook his head. "That there's at least one of them down here is strange. Regardless of the reason, it doesn't bode well."

"Are they dangerous?" I asked.

"They can be, especially when angered. My guess is that whoever summoned him—or them—here managed to get some sort of magical control over them. What would it take to do that? I don't know," Herne said.

Raven crossed her arms, shaking her head. "I hate it when people indenture creatures this way. I know a bit about the Saumen Kar, and the only way they would willingly work for someone else is if a loved one was in danger or if they were pressed into servitude."

"Which way did Yutani go?" Herne asked.

"He ran further into the woods. At least he got away. But the snow is falling so steadily that I'll tell you this right now: there's no way we can drive out of here this afternoon. I'm afraid we're stuck," Kipa said.

"Wonderful. We were speculating while you were gone. We think that they know we're here." Herne told Kipa what we had been discussing.

"It makes sense," Kipa said. "We should have thought of it earlier, but regrets are useless. Now we have to figure out what to do."

"First, we find Yutani. We can't have him wandering alone out there." Herne stared out the window, watching as the snow fell in heavy, thick flakes. It was piling up fast.

"Well, it's not like he had a spell cast on him. He knows exactly what is going on, he just may be lost in the woods," Viktor said.

"What's the cell reception like? You know he always keeps his phone with him." I paused, eyeing the pile of clothes on the table. "Never mind. I keep forgetting he has to take off his clothes in order to shift form."

"I'll go look for him," Herne said. "I can run through the snow in my stag form easier than Kipa can as a wolf, mostly because of my height. If I don't find him in half an hour, I'll return. Meanwhile, keep a close eye out for anything or anyone approaching the cabin. Do what you have to do to stay safe." Without another word, he opened the door and slipped out into the storm. A moment later, a silver stag went bounding off into the woods.

While I knew that very little could hurt him, given he was a god, I still worried as I watched him disappear into the forest. There were so many things that could go wrong. And so many things already had. I opened the door, peeking outside. The path to the car was already covered with four more inches of snow. I turned back to the others.

"We should bring in everything we need from the car. We don't want to be stuck having to try to make our way out to it."

Viktor nodded. "Kipa and I'll take care of it. I know what Herne said, but we will need heat. Raven, build a fire."

Kipa let out a sigh. "I concur. If they were watching as we broke through the illusion, they already know we're here. And I have a feeling, with the storm, they're not going to be out traipsing through the woods any more than they need to."

Raven glanced at me, and I nodded. We would need the warmth before long. She might be able to heat up rocks, but it wouldn't keep the air in the cabin warm, and I could see my breath as I spoke.

I turned to Viktor. "While you're outside, see if you can find a woodpile. There's some wood in here, but it's not going to last long." I pointed to the metal wood box sitting next to the stove. "I suggest we just use the wood stove for now. It's probably safer than the fireplace."

As Raven joined me, I examined the stove, finding the damper and opening it. I peeked inside the belly to find a very thin skiff of ashes on the bottom. The stove had been used, yes, but it had also been cleaned out. I arranged kindling at the bottom, then a series of logs propped around it. I knew how to make a campfire, and I could even spark a flame from two sticks, but I was grateful that Raven could take care of that aspect.

Kipa and Viktor disappeared out the door. Raven held out her hands, cupping them around part of the kindling. She closed her eyes and murmured something. A second later, sparks flew from her fingertips, catching hold of the wood shavings, where they set the bundle to crackling. A few seconds later the kindling sparked off the larger pieces, and heat began to warm the air. I adjusted the damper, making sure smoke didn't back into the cabin, and then returned to the table.

"You're worried about Yutani, aren't you?" Raven asked.

I nodded. "I know he can take care of himself, but he's

been in such a mood lately. I don't know what to think. I mean, he can fend for himself as a coyote, yes, but can he defend himself against the Saumen Kar? You said you've dealt with these creatures before. How dangerous are they?"

She sat down beside me, opening up another bag of chips and pushing them between us on the table. "The Saumen Kar are considered relatives to the yeti, but they are very different. They may stem from the same mother race, but the Saumen Kar have magic. They can be helpful when they choose to be. It surprises me to find any of them working for the Tuathan Brotherhood. They seldom work for anybody but themselves. They have their own agendas and usually stick to them. I'm convinced that the Tuathan Brotherhood must have a spell caster who can force them into obeying."

"Is there a way to communicate with them? To find out if we can help them break away? You said they have magical powers." I picked up a potato chip and sucked the salt off. It melted in my mouth and I swallowed it and picked up another.

"There might be, but I'm not keen to chance it without more knowledge. They're dangerous in ways you can't even fathom. I wish my father were here. He knows more about them than I do. When I was very young, we met one in the Woodlands. I don't remember why it was there, but my father and the Saumen Kar had a long talk." She squinted as she stared at the stove.

"What is your father like? Are you still in touch with your parents?" I knew very little about the Ante-Fae or the way their families worked. In fact, my only exposure had been Blackthorn and his son, and they *definitely* hadn't been good role models when it came to family relations.

"My father? He's considered an unlucky omen by humans. To see him once brings good favor into your life. But to see him a second time, well, that portends danger. When you think about it, both my parents are considered unlucky by humans, especially."

"Yeah, given your mother is a Bean Sidhe, I suppose that's true. Does she live in the United States?"

Raven shook her head. "No. She returned to Scotland shortly after I turned twelve. She was called back to her duties by the Morrígan. I stayed with my father, and he brought me up. Usually, I don't talk about him because he is so very misunderstood. I go to see him every few years. We email. But he stays in hiding while I'm out in the world."

"You said he's the Black Dog of Hanging Hills?"

She nodded. "His name is Curikan. He's not always in his dog form. At times he'll walk through the countryside in human form. That's how he and my mother got together. But when he takes the shape of the dog—which is his natural form—the first time he meets people, he brings them joy. Something wonderful happens in their lives. He tries to avoid them after that, but some of them put two and two together and seek him out."

"And it doesn't work out the way they hope it will, right?" I was beginning to get the picture.

"Right. The second time he meets them, tragedy often follows. It's not something he causes deliberately, it just seems to be wedded to his nature. Which means, I will never allow you to meet him more than once. His powers affect Fae and human alike—as well as many other Cryptos. He stays out of sight because he dreads bringing sorrow into people's lives. He's a recluse. Curikan brought me up to take pride in my work and to be strong. He taught me to follow my heart and my instinct."

"Why did you stay with him? Didn't your mother want you with her?"

Raven shook her head. "As I said, my mother is a Bean Sidhe. She's bound to the Morrígan. She lives within the world of spirits, and seldom walks abroad on the earth. She stayed with my father as long as the Morrígan allowed, but when I was old enough, the Morrígan required her to return to her job. Phasmoria had the option to take me with her, but she decided that it wouldn't be a good upbringing, given I'm not a Bean Sidhe. The mix of my mother and father's blood resulted in me being a bone witch."

"Do you miss her?" I stared at the bag of chips. I knew how much I missed my own parents. It was bad enough that they had been murdered. I couldn't imagine what it would feel like to know that your mother voluntarily left you behind.

Raven thought for a moment, then shrugged. "She contacts me every now and then. I've seen her four times since she left, about once every twenty-five years. She brings me a gift, and she always says that we should get together more, but it never happens. I don't think she expected to get pregnant when she slept with my father. Gods know, I doubt if either one of them envisioned a future together. She's nice enough, but she's very focused on her job, and frankly she makes me nervous when I'm around her. I couldn't tell you why, though."

"I miss my parents. They were really good to me,

though sometimes I wonder if they truly thought things over. Both Morgana and Cernunnos hinted that they knew they were going to die. Sometimes I wonder if they just waited around to be murdered, instead of trying to change the future. When I think about that, I get angry at them."

"I would too," Raven said.

At that moment, the door opened and Viktor and Kipa returned, their arms full. They had carried in everything we might possibly be able to use from Herne's car, as well armfuls of wood. As they were stacking the wood by the stove, Raven and I began to sort through the things on the floor. I was just about to place the first-aid kit on the table when the door opened and Herne stamped the snow off his boots and entered the cabin. Behind him, I could see two figures.

Yutani followed him in, naked and shivering, and behind him came a tall dark man. The man had long shimmering black hair, and he was wearing a pair of blue jeans and a flannel shirt, along with a cowboy hat. He was also wearing a necklace of turquoise and silver beads, and centered on his chest, part of the necklace, was a small skull about the size of a large man's fist.

Raven handed Yutani his clothes, then silently backed away, her eyes glued to the man behind him. Kipa bristled, looking wary.

Yutani silently slid into his jeans, then his shirt. As he sat down to put on his shoes, he said, "Ember, Raven, I'd like you to meet my father. Coyote."

CHAPTER THIRTEEN

I froze. That was the last thing I expected to hear. I glanced at Herne, who gave me a single nod. I could tell by the guarded look in his eyes that it would be best to say as little as possible. All I knew about Coyote was that he was a trickster, and extremely unpredictable.

"How do you do," I said, trying to maintain my composure.

Raven murmured something along the same lines, then moved toward the stove, standing near Kipa. Viktor dropped into a chair, shaking his head.

"Trust me, I'm just as startled as you guys are," Yutani said. He sounded guarded, but there seemed to be an excitement bubbling below the surface. At least he had managed to contact Coyote. I just prayed it was the contact he was hoping for.

Coyote glanced around the room, a sly smile on his face. After a moment, he cleared his throat. "I realize that I'm an unexpected guest. I usually am. But when I found my son wandering around in the woods, I had to help him find his way back home." His voice was deep, a rich baritone with a hint of laughter behind it. I had the feeling that Coyote was the life of the party wherever he went.

Herne cleared his throat. "I was looking for Yutani when I came across one of the Saumen Kar. I had a bit of a talk with him, and sure enough, it's as we thought. The Tuathan Brotherhood have them bound to a servitude spell. There's not much we can do about it." He frowned, shaking his head with a disgusted look on his face. "I also found the headquarters. At least, the backside. My guess is that will be the easiest place to infiltrate. I promised the Saumen Kar that we would do what we could to free them, but I made certain they understand it's not a promise. For that, they have given their word that they won't deter us unless a member of the brotherhood is watching."

"Did they by chance tell you how many members of the brotherhood are in there?" Viktor asked.

"Yes, or rather," Herne said, "I got an estimate. Perhaps twenty members or so. I don't know if that includes the current crop of recruits, including Rafé." He looked over at Coyote. "You wouldn't by chance be interested in helping us out, would you?"

Coyote sat down at the table. He opened one of the sandwiches and took a bite out of the roast beef. Wiping his mouth, he said, "Sorry. It's none of my concern." He sounded so nonchalant that it made me angry.

I was going to say something, but Herne shot me a quick look and I shut my mouth.

Yutani walked over to the stove and warmed his hands against the heat. He ducked his head, looking like he wanted to say something, but the tension was so thick that I had the feeling he didn't know where to begin. Hell, I didn't blame him, considering the circumstances.

"What now?" Viktor asked.

Herne glanced from Coyote to Kipa, then let out a sigh.

"All right, all cards on the table. We need to take care of the situation. Coyote, we welcome your presence. My father speaks highly of you, but right now you're a monkey wrench in our plans. I know you need to talk to your son, and the gods know, he needs to talk to you. So I think we'll head out and leave the two of you here. Viktor, stay here in case there's trouble."

Viktor nodded. "Will do."

Herne stood, holding out his hand for a sandwich. "All right, then get ready to head out."

Raven and I began to suit up. I stared at her skirt. That wouldn't be practical at all for maneuvering through the snow.

"Do you have anything else to wear?" I asked.

She arched her eyebrows, smiling. "I'm wearing leggings under the skirt. Since we have snowshoes, I think you'll be surprised by how easy I can cavort on top of the snow. I'm not a *pants* sort of woman." She slid on her jacket, which looked equally unsuited to the weather. At my look, she held out her arm. "Feel."

I ran my hand over the arm. There was a warmth to it that belied the thin fabric. It was radiating some sort of heat. Raven lifted her leg, placing her foot on a chair and pulling up her dress to show off the leggings. I felt them, as well. Again, the warmth radiated through my hand.

"What the hell is that and where can I get it? That would be *so* handy."

"I can charm garments and they act like one of those reflective blankets that you see in the survival kits. My leggings and my jacket use my body warmth to increase the heat factor. I'll stay nice and toasty out there." She paused, then laughed. "I suppose you're going to want me to do this for you? I wish I could do it now, but we'll have to wait till we get home."

"You've got a deal. I'll pay you whatever you want. I'd love to have a couple outfits like this and I know Angel wouldn't mind one either."

Herne and Kipa placed the snowshoes on the floor. As Raven and I stood on them, they fitted our boots in them.

"Have either of you ever used snowshoes before?" Herne asked.

"I have," Raven said.

I shook my head. "Not me. How do I do this?" I stared down at them, wondering how they worked.

"These are a lot easier to use than the old-fashioned kind. Take a wider stance than usual, and pick up your feet. It doesn't take long before you'll get the hang of it, and it's mostly flat ground to the encampment. When going downhill, make sure you step heel first. If you're going up the side of a ravine, lodge the inner side of the snowshoe — the side closest to the hill — onto the snow first. We have snowshoe poles in case you want them, and I suggest that you use them if you've never snowshoed before." Kipa seemed right at home. He motioned for me to follow him outside, where he demonstrated the techniques he was talking about.

After the first few minutes, I found that it wasn't too difficult. Herne and Raven joined us, handing us our backpacks. I slung mine over my back, fastening the belt around my waist. Raven handed me a scarf. As I wrapped it around my neck, I found that it was heated, too, like her jacket and leggings.

"I figure you need this more than I do," she said, winking at me. Herne peeked back inside the cabin as Viktor came out of the door. Viktor shut the door behind him, glancing over his shoulder. He was carrying my pistol grip crossbow with him.

"Oh crap, I almost forgot." I reached out and he handed it to me. "Thanks. What's going on in there?" I nodded at the cabin.

"They're having a long talk. I'm just pretending to mind my own business." Viktor turned to Herne. "Are you sure that you don't want me to come with you?" He looked like he'd rather be anywhere than here at this point.

"No, you stay here. Who knows if Coyote's going to decide to just run off again? I don't want anybody on their own out here. I have my phone with me. I don't know what the reception will be like, but it's worth a shot."

"Do you have your crossbow?" Viktor asked.

Herne nodded, holding up his bow. Viktor let out a sigh, then stood back.

"Be careful then, and don't take any stupid chances."

Herne clapped him on the shoulder. "We'll be okay. Just stay here and wait for us." With that, we headed off, Herne in front, Raven and me coming second, and Kipa flanking our backs.

As we started snowshoeing through the trees, I tried to ignore the whispering I heard on the wind. It was the Cailleach, all right.

I could hear her, feel her around me, sense her everywhere, within every snowflake. I had no clue why I was so aware of her, but then it crossed my mind that snow was simply frozen water. And my connection with water meant that I had a connection with snow as well.

I closed my eyes, tuning in to the landscape surrounding me. She had surrounded us with her power. I began to understand, then. The Cailleach was no god or goddess like Herne or Cernunnos or Morgana. She was truly a force of the land, and therefore she was as far from human as were the rest of the elements. There would be no reasoning with her. There would be no bargaining. She was what she was, and she would reach out and take as much as she was able.

I opened my eyes and realized the others were staring at me. Herne had turned around, and Raven had a worried look on her face.

"What's going on?" Herne asked.

"I was just sensing the Cailleach. She'll bring the storm to bear as long as she can. She feels greedy, almost hungry."

"When the Cailleach is free, the winters are long and fierce." Herne glanced up at the sky, blinking as snow fell on his face. His hair was already covered, and his shoulders. In fact, we all were, except for Raven. The snow melted as it touched her jacket.

"We have to put her back in the stone," I said. "She might be able to overcome global warming, but we can't leave her unattended out here."

"Oh, I concur," Herne said. "But there's nothing we can do about it right now. We'll just have to work around the storm." He glanced back over his shoulder in the direction in which we had been going. "Let's get a move on."

As we went back to trekking through the snow, I wanted to smack Kipa. Snowshoeing might not be complicated, but it certainly wasn't easy on the thighs. I felt like I'd been riding a horse for an hour and I was ever so grateful for my workouts. Wondering how Raven was doing, I glanced at her, but she seemed unperturbed. I was beginning to get the feeling that the Ante-Fae all had some sort of super strength, or something like that.

Another half mile, and Herne slowed, holding up his hand. It was growing dark in the woods, although the snowstorm brought with it a silvery glow that allowed us to see through the gloom.

"We don't have far to go. We're moving cross-country as the crow flies, rather than on the road itself, so we've cut distance off." He pointed toward the right. "I think we need to head that way. It will be easier and safer in the long run if we add a little distance to our trek."

"I disagree," Kipa said. "I think we need to swing around on the road. If we keep going in the direction we're headed, we'll get there after dark. I don't want to be hiking through these woods after the light's faded. It's not safe."

"No. What's *not* safe is approaching from the front. They're more likely to see us." Herne turned to him, tilting his head in a way that I had come to recognize as the *I'm so stubborn and you're not going to budge me* stance. "You can't argue with that logic."

"I most certainly can argue with your logic, especially since it doesn't make any sense. You already said they know we're here. If we keep wandering through the woods, after dark we're going to lose our way. You may *think* you know the way, but I don't trust us not to get turned around after dark." Kipa leaned on his snowshoe poles, glaring at Herne.

"*I'm* the leader of this expedition, and I say we go around the back of the compound. I thought you agreed to this back at the cabin." Herne was getting a little hot under the collar.

As they began to argue in earnest, Raven and I stepped back. I wasn't sure where this was leading, but I sure as hell didn't want to be in the way if it led to a boxing match. I glanced at her and she shook her head. My legs were getting really tired and I started looking around, trying to find a fallen tree or a boulder on which to rest.

"What are you looking for?" she asked, keeping her voice low. I wasn't sure what good it did, given that Herne and Kipa were now engaged in a loud debate.

"A place to sit down. My thighs hurt."

She glanced back at the arguing gods, then nodded for me to follow her. "I think I saw something over here. It looked like a log under the snow."

I thought about letting them know where we were going, but one look at their angry faces and I decided I wasn't going to chance it. There was more going on than just an argument over which direction to go. I had a feeling that Herne and Kipa's long-brewing animosity was coming to a head.

Raven led me toward a large thicket of trees. As the light began to wane, I thought I saw the fallen log she had been talking about. As we approached the log, there was a sudden shift in the ground beneath us, and I began to lose my footing.

"What the hell?" I scrambled, trying to get out of the way, but I couldn't move fast enough on the snowshoes.

Raven was doing the same, and seconds later we both went tumbling into a pit.

"WHAT THE FUCK?" RAVEN SHOUTED, FLAILING AS WE WENT tumbling. Instinctively, I turned in mid-air, trying to land on my stomach rather than my feet so I wouldn't twist an ankle because of the snowshoes. I managed to land on my side and, although I hit hard, I didn't feel any immediate sensation of pain. The fall knocked my breath away, but I was alive.

I looked around, trying to see in the dark. Above us, the faint glimmer of dusk shone overhead, but I couldn't tell how far up the top of the pit was. Then I remembered that Raven had fallen with me.

"Raven? Raven? Are you all right?" I reached in my pocket for the flashlight that I kept hooked on my keychain. I found my keys and pulled them out, flipping the light switch. It was bright, an LED flashlight. The beam would last for a long time on the two lithium batteries that it required. I shined it around, looking for Raven.

A groan led me over to one side of the pit. There, I found Raven trying to sit up. I flashed the light over her, looking for any signs of blood or broken limbs.

"Are you all right?" I kicked off my snowshoes and hurried over to her.

"I think I sprained my ankle," she said, groaning again as she leaned forward, trying to reach her left ankle.

"Stop. Let me look at it first." I knelt, examining her ankle. It was hard to see beneath her leggings and boots, so I gently removed the snowshoe and was about to untie the granny boot when she shook her head.

"If it's sprained, I won't be able to get the boot on again if you take it off. For now it's acting as a compression device. We need to get out of here. I don't like the feel of this place. There's something here, though I don't know what it is."

That got me moving. If Raven was nervous, I wasn't going to sit around and question her.

I stood, cautiously moving my way over to stand beneath the opening to the pit. As I looked up, the best I could gauge was that we were about fifteen to twenty feet down. The shower of broken branches and snow scattered around the ground beneath the opening told me that the pit had been camouflaged by a layer of branches and snow.

"Herne! Herne? Herne!"

While shouting could bring unwanted attention, we weren't getting out of here without help. I might be able to gather enough broken branches to form a pile a few feet tall, but that wouldn't give us enough height to scramble up and out. And with Raven's ankle banged up, there was no way I could stand on her shoulders, or vice versa.

"How far away were we from them when we fell?" I looked back at Raven.

"Maybe ten yards? Maybe a little farther?" She let out another moan, and I flashed my light toward her. She was holding her leg, grimacing.

"Do you think it's broken?"

"I'm not sure," she said. "But the energy I was talking about that made me uneasy? Whatever it is, it's growing in strength. Maybe you should see if there are any other exits down here. Walk around the walls of the pit?"

"Good idea." Using the flashlight to guide me, I made my way over to one wall of the pit. "First, I want to find out how wide it is." Back to the wall, I began to stride forward, trying to keep even steps of about a foot long. By the time I reached the opposite wall, I had gone twenty paces. "Good gods, this pit is twenty feet wide. Who the hell made it?"

"I don't think I want to know," Raven said.

I began to circle the pit, keeping my shoulder against one wall and using the flashlight to search for any openings. Two-thirds of the way around, probably about four yards from where Raven was sitting, I caught sight of a small opening near the floor. I crouched to look at it. The hole was about three feet high and about two feet wide.

"I found something." As I flashed the light into the opening, I heard something scuttling inside. It was loud enough for Raven to hear as well.

She twisted around, leaning back on one hand. "I don't like that," she said, her voice trembling. "That's where the energy is coming from. Be careful, Ember. Whatever's in there is dangerous." She rolled over onto her hands and knees and tried to crawl away from it.

"Raven, you're only going to hurt yourself more—" I started to say, then stopped as the scuttling noise sounded again, louder this time. I backed up, putting myself between Raven and the hole, keeping the light trained on it at all times. Raven scooted back against the other wall, motioning for me to move to the side.

"I don't want any spells I cast to hit you, so get out of the way." She winced, and then pointed toward the hole.

"Train the light back on the opening. It may be the only thing keeping whatever's inside from attacking us."

I turned around, stepping out of the way so she'd have a clear shot if need be, but positioning myself halfway between her and the tunnel. It was then that I realized I didn't have my crossbow with me. It must have flown out of my hand when we fell through the covering of broken branches. I flipped open the snap on my dagger, withdrawing the blade. My stomach was knotted with fear. There was nothing like being trapped in the dark with something hiding in a hole to set the adrenaline pumping.

The beam from the flashlight suddenly flared, as something reflected the light back toward me. I froze, tensing. A massive spider began to slowly emerge from the hole. Or at least it looked like a spider. Fully eighteen inches across and at least a foot high, it scuttled out, followed by yet another. I thought I glimpsed of a third one behind them.

"Holy crap. We're in trouble," Raven said. "*Etho-spiders.* They exist on both the etheric plane, and the physical plane. They phase in and out. And they're deadly."

As she spoke, the front one scuttled toward me, moving faster than I expected it to. I held my dagger ready, hoping to hell that I could hit it before it sank its fangs into me. As it raced forward, there was a sudden rush behind it as five more spiders came racing into the room.

"You aren't kidding. We're in trouble. I hope to hell you have some sort of spell that can help, because I can't move fast enough to kill them all before they get to us."

CHAPTER FOURTEEN

"Do you have a weapon?" I asked, praying she had some sort of dagger. Or maybe a gun. A gun would definitely be good.

"I have a boot knife. Shut up and let me focus on a spell."

I didn't bother looking back and just shut my mouth as I tried flashing the light directly at one of the spiders, hoping I could blind it. The creature scrambled back a step or two, but then began to scuttle forward again.

Running through the magical tricks I knew, I thought that I could try to collect the moisture in the air, but that would just make it rain on us and I didn't think the spiders would care much about getting wet. And if I tried to suck the moisture out of the air, it wouldn't bother the spiders either. They weren't water-based.

Taking a deep breath, I darted forward, plunging my dagger toward the nearest one. It dodged my attack and then lunged toward me. I managed to pull back before its fangs sunk deep into my hand. They were nasty-looking, glistening with some sort of venom.

Raven's voice echoed through the pit.

> *Fire to flame, flame to fire,*
> *build and burn, higher and higher.*
> *Flare to life, take form and strike,*
> *attack now, fiery spike.*

Her words had barely broken the silence when a spike of fire came shooting past me, aimed at one of the spiders. It struck deep, right in the center, exploding the spider into a churning froth of goo. The others skittered back, eyeing their fallen companion.

Impressed, I kept my eyes on our opponents, and called over my shoulder, "How many times can you do that?"

"A few. Unfortunately, it takes me time to prepare. It'll take me a few minutes to build up the energy for another strike. You're going to have to occupy their attention until I'm ready."

"I'll do my best," I muttered, praying it wouldn't take her too long to recharge.

The other etho-spiders were already starting to creep forward again, easing around their fallen comrade. I had to hand it to Raven, though. All that remained were a few charred legs in a big pile of bubbling ooze.

All of a sudden, the etho-spiders froze and began to move to the side, their attention no longer focused on us. A sound echoed from the tunnel as though something was breaking through, tearing rock and soil as it pushed its way along.

"How big do these things get?" I asked, not sure I wanted to hear the answer.

"I think these are babies," Raven said. "We're in a lot of trouble. Where the hell are Herne and Kipa?"

"I don't know, but we can't rely on them to save us."

"What about your Leannan Sidhe side? Anything there?"

"Sorry, but I'm not going to suck face with a spider trying to convince it not to bite us!"

"Good point," Raven said, grabbing her pack and rummaging through it. "I think…"

As she spoke, the entrance of the tunnel began to crumble as two giant legs broke through, followed by six more, and all of those legs were attached to a much larger etho-spider. With a leg span of at least four feet, the damned thing must have been a good six feet long. I backed up, moving toward Raven.

"We're screwed," I whispered, trying to swallow my fear.

Raven shoved something into my hand. I could tell she was gathering her energy. I wanted to ask if her spell could bring down a monster that size, but I didn't want to interrupt her focus. Right now she was our best bet, but something inside warned me that even she wouldn't be able to handle something this big.

I glanced down at what she had given me. It was a small, glittering dagger. I could feel the magic emanating from it, and it was dark and deadly. A wicked-good pulse vibrated through the silver, and my Autumn Stalker side whispered, *The blade has a venomous bite of its own.*

As the spider struggled out of the hole, dirt and rocks caving in behind it, I swallowed hard. I'd have to slide beneath it and strike from there. In other words, pull a *Samwise-on-Shelob* maneuver.

"Get ready," Raven said, and I heard the magic flickering through her voice. "When I cast the spell, go for it. That dagger can kill the beast. Watch out for her children, though."

I caught my breath, stepping out of Raven's path as I prepared myself.

She once again chanted her incantation, and a crackle broke the silence as a fiery spike drove forward, a bullet of flame aiming for the massive spider. I braced myself to run the moment the fire distracted the spider. As it hit, exploding, the spider let out a loud hiss, and I sprang forward, dagger ready.

The younger spiders scattered as Raven's spell hit the mother. As I raced forward, I gauged the distance between us, and—like a baseball player—went skidding beneath the massive stomach. I was at home plate. Now I just had to make sure to touch the base.

I brought Raven's dagger up, point aimed toward the belly of the beast. As the tip of the blade pierced the spider's exoskeleton, I rolled to one side, trying to protect my eyes from the spewing liquid. The dagger bit deep, and I could feel the magic pulse as it envenomated the spider's belly. I yanked the dagger out—Raven would kill me if I left it inside the spider—and rolled away as the creature wavered, hissing and waving its front legs. It reared up with fangs exposed, but it wasn't aiming at me. A howl echoed through the pit as it staggered back.

The baby spiders backed away, watching their mother. As I rolled into a crouch, I decided another hit wouldn't hurt, and so I stabbed at the side of the spider. The dagger once again reverberated in my hand, pulsing with thirst as it delighted in its conquest. I withdrew the blade and backed away, hoping this would be enough to finish her off.

Behind me, Raven sputtered out another spell—a much weaker spiral of fire—at one of the babies that was getting too close. It exploded on contact. I backed up, watching the mother as she writhed in pain, her legs flailing wildly as she listed to the side. She let out another howl and began to waver, her form becoming almost transparent. Another moment, and she slumped to the floor, no longer moving.

At that moment, Herne and Kipa dropped into the pit, between the spider and us. They took one look at the situation, and Herne aimed his crossbow toward the creature, letting fly with an arrow.

"You're late to the party, dude," I said. "We already killed her. Take care of the babies."

I knelt beside Raven, wiping the blade of her dagger on a nearby branch, getting it as clean as I could. I handed it back to her, hilt first. She slid it into a metal sheath, which she affixed back on her belt. I hadn't noticed it under her jacket.

"That's one wicked blade," I said.

"My father gave it to me when I was little. I've taken good care of it, and it's taken good care of me." She winced, gritting her teeth.

"Your ankle?"

She nodded. "I hope I can get the boot off when we get out of here."

"We have to get you back to the cabin. You can't come with us in this shape." I looked over to where Herne and

Kipa were fighting the rest of the baby spiders. They had taken care of most of them, and as we watched, they finished off the last one. I stood up as they shuffled back our way, sheepish grins on their faces.

"So you finally decided to quit arguing and pay attention to the fact that Raven and I were stuck in a pit?" I crossed my arms, glaring at Herne.

He glanced at Kipa. "I told you we were in trouble."

"It's your fault—" Kipa started to say, but stopped as Raven interrupted.

"*Both* of you are to blame. Now how the hell are you going to get me out of here? I sprained my ankle, or maybe I broke it—I don't know—when we fell down into the pit. And we wouldn't be down here in the first place if you guys hadn't been standing around, having a cock-measuring contest. So shut the fuck up and do something."

She sounded so angry even I took a step back.

"I'm sorry," Herne said, staring at the floor.

"Sorry," Kipa added.

"It's a little late for that, given Raven's hurt. Just get us out of here." My own temper wasn't much better than hers right now.

Kipa glanced up at the edge of the pit. "I can climb the wall, but I can't carry anybody with me while I do. But if we fashion a harness and strap you into it, I can lift you out."

I wandered over to the hole from where the spiders had emerged, and shined my light down the tunnel. Even though it was partially caved in, I could see that it grew larger farther on. Brushing away the dirt, I slipped into the tunnel, scouting a few feet ahead. I suddenly found myself in a five-foot-tall metal tube. This was no natural spider burrow. This was man-made. A thought occurred to me, and I turned, hurrying back to the pit.

"That tunnel actually turns into a metal pipe when you get about five or six feet in. The spiders didn't make that. Do you think that runs under the encampment?"

Herne glanced at the opening. "There's only one way to find out." He turned back to Kipa. "If we get Raven up top, can you take her back to the cabin without a problem?"

Kipa nodded. "I know exactly where it is. I promise she'll arrive there safely."

Herne looked at me. "Are you willing to go on with just the two of us?"

"We need to find Rafé. Kipa, take Raven back to the cabin, then you can rejoin us. That way, if somehow we get stuck in the tunnel, you can find us."

"Good idea. And I promise, no more stupid arguments. Herne?" Kipa turned toward Herne.

"I promise as well," Herne said. "You have my word."

Kipa pulled a length of rope out of his pack. Together, he and Herne fastened a secure harness that would hold Raven while they lifted her out of the pit. Kipa scampered up the side of the pit in a way I could only dream of. Once on top, he began to pull up the rope as Herne held Raven steady. A few moments later, Kipa peeked down.

"Safe and sound. I'll run her back to the cabin, and then I'll be back to join you. Be careful."

I turned to Herne. "Are you ready?" I paused, flashing my light around the pit. "I dropped my crossbow when I fell. Help me find it."

We scouted around the pit until he finally found the

bow and my quiver of bolts near the other side of the wall. As he held the light, I examined it. It seemed to be in workable condition, so I notched one of the bolts in it, then sent the arrow singing into the opposite wall. Herne retrieved it, and I put it back in my quiver.

"It works. I guess we're ready. I hope Kipa can get Raven safely back to the cabin."

"He will. Trust me on that. I'm so sorry, love. I can't believe that we didn't notice you were both gone for so long. Our stupidity could have killed you."

I took his hand, gazing into his eyes. "Herne, I love you. You know that. I love you very much, but dude, if you and Kipa don't put your animosity to rest, one day either one of you will end up dead, or you're going to get somebody else killed. *Learn from this*. I'm tired of your whiny-assed macho bitchfests. You guys have got to get your shit together."

He hung his head, a solemn look on his face. "I know you're right. And I'll do everything I can to make peace with him."

It didn't take a genius to realize that if Herne made peace with Kipa, it would partially be the result of Kipa's interest in Raven, but I kept my mouth shut. As long as they could come to some comfortable coexistence, I'd be happy. And they made for a powerful force when combining their strengths.

"You big doofus." I smacked his chest lightly. "I don't like macho men. Alpha? That's another matter. But macho's just going to push me away. Got it?"

"Yeah, I get it. Okay, let's get moving."

Herne entered the tunnel first, and I followed behind him, wishing I still had Raven's dagger with me. That was a handy little blade, and I wondered where I could find one like it.

We crept along, quickly entering the metal tube. It was around five feet tall, so we were walking with hunched shoulders, crouching as we made our way. Up ahead, the tube split into a T. When we came to the juncture, Herne motioned for me to pause while he crept ahead to look. He returned a moment later, having taken a look into both sides.

"To the right, it ends in a natural tunnel. I think that's where the spiders came from. We can't count out that there might be more, so we'll need to be careful."

"What about to the left?" I asked.

"The tube ends about twenty feet to the left. When I flashed my light down there, I saw a ladder attached to the side of the wall. My guess is that we're in an access tube."

"I wonder what they use it for. But my guess is that when they discovered the spiders down below, they decided to make use of them as guardians." I shivered, not wanting to see any more of the beasts. Spiders normally didn't bother me, but these were the grist of nightmares.

"I want you to go in front, just in case there *are* any more spiders that come after us. I can guard the back that way. Come on, let's hurry. We don't want to hang around down here too long or we might attract attention from more of the beasts." He changed places with me, urging me to fit a bolt into my crossbow so I'd be ready. I did so, then took the lead, cautiously turning to the left as we came to the juncture.

The sound of water dripping from somewhere up ahead echoed through the metal pipe. About halfway to the ladder, I noticed a leak to the left. A fine trickle of water was dripping down the sides of the pipe to the metal below our feet. It appeared to be a steady flow, so it couldn't just be coming from snow melt.

I frowned as I flashed the light over the edges of the eroded pipe. The metal looked thin and fragile and seemed to have rusted through, and the water had breached the pipe through a half-inch hole. Around the hole, for about a four-inch diameter section, the pipe looked fragile and the rusty metal was flaking. Without thinking, I pressed my thumb against one of the thinner sections. The metal broke and the flow of water increased.

I glanced back at Herne. The trickle was rapidly becoming a steady stream, as though someone had left the faucet on.

"I have an uneasy feeling that we're either next to or below a stream. If the metal breaks any further, I'm afraid the pipe will flood. Let's get the hell out of here." Herne shook his head, glancing at the flowing water. "Don't touch it again. We don't know how weak the rest of the metal around the leak is and I don't want to find out. If there's enough water on the other side, the pressure could split the welds that hold the tube together. Have you noticed? This isn't one solid tube. We passed through five sections that have been welded together."

I hadn't noticed, but now that he mentioned it I took a closer look and could see what he was talking about. The breach was at one of the welds, and I quickly pulled away from the leak and hurried through the last ten feet toward the ladder.

Herne shined his light up the rungs. They led about twenty feet up, ending at a circular hole against the ceiling, which appeared to be domed. There, a valve about two feet in diameter was attached to the top of the dome. It had to be a trap door, and my guess was that turning the valve would open the top of the tube.

I reached out to grab the first rung and let out an involuntary shout as my fingers began to blister. I pulled away quickly and turned to Herne.

"Iron. The damn thing is cast iron. I don't think the tube is—or at least it's coated because it didn't hurt me when I touched it, but the ladder is going to be a problem. Let me get my gloves and see if it helps." I pulled out my gloves and slid them on over the blistered tips of my fingers.

Herne looked concerned. "Do you think you can climb with your hand injured like that?"

I nodded. "Yeah, it's not going to feel good, but I can climb. When I get up there, should I open the door? There's no way of knowing what's on the other side." I paused as the rushing of the water grew louder.

We turned back to look at the breach in the pipe. There was a pause, and then a large section of the pipe crumbled as a torrent of water began to pour through. The broken section was at least eight inches wide, and the flood showed no sign of stopping.

"Get moving," Herne said. "Now. It's amazing how much water can accumulate from a stream that large."

For a moment I considered whether I could do anything about the water, but unless there was an elemental in it, I didn't think I had much of a chance. I could try to hold it back, but my skills with water magic weren't that refined. Without another word, I swung onto the ladder, grimacing as the iron reverberated through the gloves. I could climb, all right, but it was still uncomfortable. As I hurried up the ladder, Herne swung onto the rungs as soon as there was clearance.

I climbed as quickly as I could, glancing over my shoulder. Water was beginning to accumulate in the bottom of the pipe, and while I knew it had to be running through the tunnel toward the spiders and the pit, there seemed to be plenty more coming. Herne was probably right—we must have tapped into a stream and soon, the entire pipe would be flooded. I glanced up at the top, hoping to hell that I could get that valve open. Otherwise, we'd be trapped.

When I was almost at the top, I paused a couple rungs below. Reaching up, I got as good of a hold as I could on the valve. I began turning it counterclockwise, and while it budged a little, I just didn't have the strength to jar it loose. I looked down at Herne.

"I can't get it open. You need to change places with me."

I flattened myself against the side of the shaft as Herne squeezed up next to me. Then I managed to maneuver myself below him on the ladder.

I glanced down again, shining my light onto the water that was rapidly building up. From what I could tell, the breach had widened and now the water was pouring in. In the distance, I could hear squeaks and hisses, no doubt another bunch of spiders trying to cope with the sudden flood. We still had a little while before the water would climb the shaft around the ladder, but I didn't want to bet on how much. And given the length of the tunnel, we couldn't swim back through to the pit on one breath of air. Oh, Herne probably could, but I sure couldn't, not without help like I had had from the elemental in the sound beneath the ferry.

Herne was struggling with the valve now, and finally, a loud creak told me that he was managing to wedge it open. He pushed, climbing the rungs as he pressed his shoulder against it, and with one last grunt, shoved it open. He scrambled through, and I followed him. We weren't sure where we were headed, but we had no choice. The rising water below ensured that we were committed.

CHAPTER FIFTEEN

*A*s I popped through the opening, Herne reached down and yanked me out, slamming the lid behind me. I shivered as a cold blast of wind railed against us, swirling snow every which way. We were outside, behind what looked like a shed.

I quickly looked around, trying to get my bearings.

Behind us, about two yards away, was a tall chain-link fence. Snow had drifted halfway up the sides. The fence must have been a good ten feet tall. To the left was the back of another building that reminded me of army barracks. To the right was another shed, with a pathway running between the two.

I blinked as my eyes adjusted from the darkness of the tunnel to the dim light of the snowstorm. The shed behind which we were hiding had no windows on the back wall, so nobody could glance out and see us. The snow and the howl of the wind guaranteed that no one had heard the thud of the tunnel door as it slammed shut.

I glanced down to see that the valve on top was almost hidden. The cover was sunk two feet into the ground.

Herne pulled me toward the building, and we huddled against it. "I think we're in the compound. At least we didn't come up inside a building, although that might actually be easier."

I nodded, wrapping Raven's scarf tightly around my mouth to warm my breath. I hoped she and Kipa had made it back to the cabin, but then it occurred to me that Kipa would be headed back down to the pit, which by now was filling up with water.

I was about to say something when Herne pressed his finger to his lips. I froze, hearing the crunch of footsteps nearby. I readied my crossbow and made sure my dagger was easy to access. As we pressed our backs against the building, a figure appeared to the right. Whoever it was, he was tall, with a gun slung over his shoulder. With a quick glance behind the dormitory, and then down our way, the guard turned and vanished, walking slowly. I let out a slow breath, relief flooding over me. The shadows had hidden us, but how long we could stay here without being noticed was another question.

"What do we do?" I whispered to Herne, trying to keep my voice low.

He gnawed on his lip for a moment, then glanced up at the low-hanging eaves of the roof. I knew exactly what he was thinking. We silently moved forward and he knelt, holding out his hands with his fingers interlaced. I placed my boot in his hands and he boosted me up as I grabbed hold of the eaves. He gave me a push and I scrambled up to lie flat in the snow, against the sloped roof. Herne leapt up, swinging one leg up to pull himself over the edge. He motioned for me to climb higher, and so I did, with him following right behind. As we neared the top, I eased up to peek over the ridge.

The compound spread out around me. It was fairly small, surrounded by the chain-link fence that ran around the entire perimeter. I realized we were facing the direction in which the cabin was. But the building directly in front of us was impeding our view of the gate, so it was difficult to tell much more. The compound was dimly lit by a few scattered floodlights, but they seemed more for the benefit of those walking around the encampment rather than to keep an eye out for anyone who might be trying to sneak in—or out.

The yard was empty except for the occasional guard, but a yellowish light spilled from the windows of one of the buildings toward the left front of the compound. All the buildings—from what I could tell there were six or seven—looked to be of modular construction. I squinted, trying to make out the gate, but because of the building between us and the front, couldn't see it very well.

I pulled back. From what I could tell, the Tuathan Brotherhood's headquarters wasn't exactly a jumping place. I frowned. For a group that was targeting victims across the nation, it didn't really make sense. Nobody could run a nationwide hate group from this small of a compound.

"Herne," I whispered. "This can't be the main headquarters."

"What do you mean?"

"Think about it. The TB has become a nationwide group. This place is just too small and quiet to be their primary headquarters. And it doesn't make sense to have all your eggs in one basket. Taking out this compound would disrupt the entire organization, and they aren't going to be that stupid. And given they're working on the Dark Web, chances are they're bigger than we gave them credit for."

Herne stared at me. "Fucking hell, you're probably right." He started to say something else, but then shook his head. "We can't discuss this here."

"Then what do we do next?"

"We find Rafé and get out of here, and regroup. We take this place out if we can."

He held his finger to his lips and scooted over to the corner of the roof. Cautiously, he set his bow on the roof and pulled out a wicked-looking dagger. He motioned for me to get ready and I brought my crossbow to bear.

A moment later, the soft sound of footsteps sounded around the corner, and Herne swung down from the roof, taking the guard down and coming up with his dagger at the man's throat. I grabbed his crossbow and silently joined him.

"Say one word and you're dead." Herne's voice was gravelly. The guard stiffened as I pointed my crossbow at him. Herne held up his dagger. "See this? My blade says you're going to talk to us, and you're going to do so very softly. If I even think that you're about to shout for help, you'll be dead before you can take your next breath. Nod once if you understand."

The man nodded, his eyes wide.

I slipped off my pack and rummaged through it, finding some rope. Quickly, I knotted it around the man's hands and feet, trussing him up like a pig on butchering day. I rolled a handkerchief into an effective gag and held it ready. Herne lowered him to the ground. I knelt on one side as Herne knelt on the other, still keeping his knife to the man's throat.

"Is Nuanda in this encampment?" Herne whispered. "Nod once for yes, shake your head for no. And if you tell us a lie, you die."

The guard shook his head.

"Who's in charge? Give me a name."

Shivering, the guard opened his mouth and whispered, "Cranston."

I took a closer look at the guard. He was a Light Fae from what I could tell. "Is Cranston Fae? Nod yes or no."

The guard nodded.

"How many guards are there here? And how many people in the encampment total?" Herne traced the blade down the man's cheek, poking it just enough to draw blood. The trickle of blood dribbled down the guard's face.

"A dozen guards, six on duty at any time. There are a total of thirty-five people here."

"Does that include new recruits? And do you know a man named Rafé?"

"Yes, there aren't very many of us here. I believe someone by that name was brought in a couple days ago." He paused, then added, "Please don't kill me."

Herne stared at him for a moment. "You help us, and we'll see you get out of this alive and in one piece. If you give us away, you forfeit your life."

I watched Herne for a moment, hoping he was telling the truth. I had come to accept that there were occasions during which we needed to take out our enemies, but I didn't like deceit, even though I recognized that sometimes it was the only means to a necessary end. Herne gave me a soft smile.

"What do you want from me?" the man asked.

"Do you know where they took the man named Rafé? We need to know where he is."

"He's with the new recruits. In that building over there." The guard nodded toward the building that I had thought was a dormitory. "There's a nine P.M. curfew, so he should be in there." He paused, then said, "I signed on for the work because I needed the money. I'm just trying to feed my family."

"What do you know about this organization?" I asked.

"The Tuathan Brotherhood is aimed at making life better for our kind," he said, staring at me. "I didn't realize how oppressed we were until I started talking to some of the members."

I wanted to smack him. The Fae weren't oppressed in anyway, other than having to deal with the Fomorians, and we all had to deal with people we didn't like. There were a great many people who were facing a hell of a lot more resistance and oppression than us.

Herne looked at me. "Gag him."

I did so, making sure the gag was tight but that he could still breathe. I double-checked the ropes, making sure they were still taut.

"Now what?" I asked. "If Rafé is in that dormitory, how are we going to sneak him out without bringing the whole camp down on us? If we still had—" I paused, not wanting to talk too much in front of the man. The fact was, if we still had Kipa and Raven with us, we could have chanced taking on more opponents. But we were two people down, and while Herne probably could escape without being hurt, I wasn't so certain I could.

"Stay here. If anybody comes at you, shoot them. Use your crossbow if possible because of the noise." Herne handed me the man's gun. "But keep this as a backup."

He peeked around the corner, then—crouching low— he dashed toward the dormitory, flattening himself against the back of the building.

I leaned against the back of the shed, holding my crossbow ready. The guard let out a muffled sound behind the gag, but I ignored him. I kept my foot on the rope to keep him from trying to wiggle off. As I watched, Herne approached one of the back windows. No light came from within, and I held my breath as he swung himself up to pry it open and slip through.

I looked down at the guard. "You do realize that you've been fed a bunch of garbage? The Fae are no more oppressed than the status quo. And your fucked-up organization has killed innocent people. Congratulations on winning against the innocent."

As I spoke, the guard jerked his head up to look at me. He frowned.

"Don't play innocent with me. I'm *certain* all the victims of the bank bombing would agree with you— especially the dead. And the people who were beaten to death, and run down. Hell, I'm *ever so glad* to know that you're just trying to help *our kind*, and I'm certain all the shards of glass that impaled my back from that bomb… well, they really helped me out."

He frantically shook his head, but I grabbed hold of his hair to keep him still. I glanced over at the dormitory, wondering what was taking so long. Realistically, it hadn't been that long, but it seemed to be taking forever. A moment later, I heard a commotion coming from the front of the encampment.

Please don't let them have caught Herne.

The noise grew louder, and I wondered what the hell was going on. I glanced at the guard, roughly tilting his head up so that he was looking at me. The dim light that filtered around the compound illuminated the fear on his face.

"Do you know what's going on?" I whispered.

He frantically shook his head.

Wondering whether I should go find out, I glanced back over the dormitory, but there was still no sign of Herne. And the noise didn't seem to be coming from the building.

Biting my lip, I weighed the pros and cons of sneaking out to find out what was happening. I glanced over the back of the shed, looking for anything I could find to tie the rope onto so that the guard couldn't squirm away. Finally, I found a loose board. It wasn't loose enough that he would be able to yank it off, but I could slip the end of the rope around it and tie it firmly. Making sure the ropes were still tight, and the gag was secure, I was reasonably sure he wouldn't be able to get away.

"I'll be back, so don't you try anything." For good measure, I pulled a handkerchief out of my pocket and blindfolded him.

I crept to the opposite edge of the shed, peering around the corner. The shouts were continuing and getting louder from what seemed to be a well-lit place near the front of the compound, to the left of the gate. Another building sat between the shed and the voices.

The building was dark, and the roof was steeply sloped, close enough to the ground where I could actually touch it. A lot of roofs in snow country were slanted so the snow would slide off of them, forestalling collapse. I darted to the back of the building, grabbed the eaves, and swung myself up onto the roof.

Spreading flat against it, I began to inch my way up, hand over hand, using my feet to propel me up the side of the shingles. The snow was thick and cold against my chest, and it made it difficult to ascend, but finally I reached the apex. I eased up, barely peeking over the edge.

Now I could clearly see the gate—and something else, as well. The lights at the front of the compound were focused on what seemed to be a fenced-off enclosure, like a chain-link pen. A group of guards surrounded the pen, and inside were two men. I squinted, trying to make out what was going on, and then I realized the men were fighting, spurred on by the shouts of the guards. From where I was, I could hear grunts and groans, and the thud of flesh against flesh. One of the guards shifted, and I managed to gain an unobstructed view of the men. I caught sight of a shock of coppery-colored hair, and gasped.

Rafé. That had to be Rafé's hair.

I eased back away from the edge, trying to think. The way the men were fighting made it clear that it wasn't in fun. And the guards were egging them on. It was a death match, and given the size of Rafé's opponent, and Rafé's skill at fighting, I wouldn't place my bets on him.

I have to find Herne.

Scrambling down the roof, I tried to be as quiet as I could as I dropped into the snow below. I started to return to the shed when I realized that I could see the line of footprints that I had made wading through the snow. I should have taken the sidewalk, which was compacted down into a thick layer of ice.

Crap, why hadn't I planned this out better? But it looked like a good share of the guards was watching the match, so as long as it continued, there was a chance that they wouldn't notice me or the guard that we had tied up. I hurried back to the shed, swinging around it to find the guard was still there. At that moment I saw Herne returning from the dormitory. I motioned for him to hurry.

"What's going on?" He glanced toward the front of the encampment. "Do you know what's happening up there?"

"Unfortunately, yes. I went to see. Rafé's up there with another man in a chain-link pen. They're fighting, and a lot of the guards are egging them on. I think it's a match to the death. We have to do something."

"I wonder where Kipa is? Of course he couldn't come through the pit, so he's probably out running around the woods looking for the encampment." He pulled out his phone, glancing at it. "No bars out here. At least none that I can pick up. All right, we can create a diversion. Maybe you can slip in and free Rafé while I keep the guards occupied."

"Can you possibly distract all the guards?"

"I have more tricks up my sleeve than you might realize."

I snickered. He was right on that one. Herne had the ability to make vegetation work for him. He could also light fires and a number of other things, including some I didn't know about yet, I was sure.

"I think it's time to warm up one of their cars. That should cause a stir." He froze, glancing at the fence behind us. Very slowly, he brought his crossbow up to bear.

At that moment, Kipa leapt over the top of the fence, landing in a crouch. Herne relaxed, letting out a long sigh.

"I almost shot you," Herne said.

"I couldn't come through the pit because of the water. What on earth did you do to it?"

"That doesn't matter now. Rafé's in a pen with another man, being forced to fight for his life. I'm headed to start a distraction, so Ember can get to him."

"What should I do?" Kipa asked.

"First, drop this guard over the fence. Make sure he's hidden from sight, then help Ember with Rafé. Hurry up. Every second we wait puts him in further danger."

Kipa silently gathered up the guard, swiftly cutting through the rope that I had used to bind him to the shed. Then, he slung him over his shoulder and silently ascended the fence, dropping over the other side to the ground. A moment later he returned, not even winded.

"He's hidden. All right, get moving. Ember and I will rescue Rafé."

Herne nodded, then silently vanished around the edge of the shed. I turned to Kipa, who motioned for me to follow him the other way. We passed in back of the dormitory, then turned right to skirt the edge of the fence toward the front of the encampment. We stopped behind the left front-most building and I peeked around the edge, just long enough to verify that the fight was still on. From here it was easier to see the size and scope of what was happening.

The guards had erected a pen out of chain-link fence

that was about four feet high, eight feet wide, and ten feet long. Inside, Rafé and the other man were still going at each other, but Rafé was definitely getting the worst of it. The other man landed blow after blow on him.

I winced, wanting to run forward screaming for them to stop, but I restrained myself. That wouldn't do any good. As Kipa and I waited for Herne to make his move, I strapped my crossbow to my back, along with the quiver of bolts. Less than thirty seconds later, from the other side of the encampment, a huge fireball illuminated the night as an explosion rocked the camp. When Herne said distraction, he *meant* distraction.

All I could think was that he had opened a gas tank and shot pure flame into it. A shrill alarm pierced the night, shrieking throughout the encampment. The guards around the pen turned as one, racing over to the right, toward the vehicles and the billowing clouds of smoke.

Kipa motioned to me, and we dashed across the clearing to the side of the pen. Nobody seemed to notice us, too focused on what was going on with the cars.

Inside the pen, Rafé was on the ground. Bleeding, his shirt was torn open and bruises were forming all over his body. His nose looked broken and one eye was swollen. One arm stretched out to his side in an unnatural position, and his hair was matted with blood. The other man stood over him, then looked up at us, frowning as he clenched his fists. I held my crossbow trained on him, warning him back.

He was Dark Fae, that much I could tell, and tattooed on his shoulder was the insignia of the Tuathan Brotherhood. I recognized it from the flyer. There was a gleam in his eye, and not a good one. He raced over toward the gate leading into the pen, but I let go with an arrow, hitting him directly in the chest. The man dropped in his tracks. Kipa opened the gate, standing back as I rushed in to kneel by Rafé's side. He was still alive, thank the gods.

"Kipa, we have to get him out of here."

Kipa quickly examined Rafé, then looked up at me. "He's got several broken bones, but we don't have time to splint them. Can you hide? I'll take him through the gate, back to the cabin. I can run faster than you, so if you came with me, you'd end up lost in the woods."

I nodded. "Get him to safety. Get him back to the cabin." I stood as Kipa scooped up Rafé in his arms, then charged out of the pen. He headed for the front gate and I realized that he couldn't both hold Rafé and open the gate, so I floundered along behind him, wishing I still had my snowshoes.

"Hide, damn it!"

"You need somebody to open the gate," I said, my crossbow up and ready to fire at anybody who tried to stop us.

But all the guards were over by the fire at the side of the encampment now, which had spread to another vehicle and was burning out of control. There was another explosion down the line, and more shouts. I ignored the commotion, keeping my focus on the front gate. Just before I reached it, Herne appeared, and he opened the gate, shoulder butting it wide, then dragged me through by my wrist. Kipa followed with Rafé in hand.

"I was about to take him back to the cabin," Kipa said.

"I've got a little surprise they don't expect." Herne turned back to the encampment, lobbing something that he had pulled out of his pocket. Another explosion rocked the night as the front gate went up in flames.

"What about all the men in the dormitory?"

"I'm pretty sure they can cut a hole in the chain-link fence if they need to evacuate. Meanwhile, we'd better get Rafé out of here. With those injuries, the cold could kill him." Kipa paused as we neared the tree line. He lifted his head, and let out a howl that echoed through the night. It was eerie, sending shivers down my back, and it felt like a call to action.

"I'm going to change into my stag form. Fasten Rafé over my back. I can run faster than either of you." Herne stepped to the side, shimmering into his silver stag form. Kipa and I obeyed without question, doing our best to fasten Rafé onto Herne's back without hurting him any more than he was already hurt. Rafé groaned, letting out a pitiful moan. I leaned close, brushing his hair back from his face.

"Don't worry. We're getting you to safety." I kissed his forehead, then stood back as Herne leapt into the forest, darting around tree after tree. He was gone in the blink of an eye, a blurry silver form racing toward the cabin.

I turned back to Kipa, then stopped as four large wolves came out of the forest to surround him. They were larger than normal wolves, and they looked mean and vicious. They turned and raced toward the gate where three of the guards had started toward us.

Kipa turned to me. "That will keep them occupied. Meanwhile, when I shift into my wolf form, get on my back. I can change into a larger wolf than I usually do. Even with you on my back, I'll be faster than you can run, especially without snowshoes, which you seem to have lost along the way."

Without waiting for me to answer, he turned into a large wolf—twice as large as normal. I silently straddled his back, leaning down to put my arms around his neck. With a soft huff, he leapt up and away, and we raced after Herne, into the forest, leaving the burning compound behind us.

CHAPTER SIXTEEN

*R*iding on Kipa's back was quite different than riding on Herne's. For one thing, I was a lot closer to the ground. Kipa was a little bigger than a large St. Bernard. Even though he seemed perfectly capable of carrying me, I was all too aware that I was riding on him. The thought seemed odd. But getting caught by the guards back at the encampment would prove deadly, and *odd* beat *deadly* every day of the week.

We wove in and out of the trees, skimming the snow in a way that bespoke Kipa's nature. No regular wolf could run atop the snow like this. I closed my eyes, bracing myself as we careened through the undergrowth, piles of snow shaking off as we passed by the bushes and trees. Kipa was racing at a blur, but the ride seemed to stretch out far longer than it should, and my thoughts wandered back to the guard we had left tied up. He could easily die of hypothermia if nobody found him.

A few moments later, we burst through the tree line into the driveway surrounding the cabin. Kipa slowed, and I jumped off of his back. As he transformed back into himself, he grabbed me around the waist, brushing my hair back from my face.

I shivered at his touch—he was Lord of the Wolves, and regardless of how much I loved Herne, there was no denying the sensuous energy that followed Kipa like a magnet.

"Are you all right?" he asked. "I tried not to knock you around too much."

I shook my head. "I'm fine," I said, breathless. Then, to take my mind off where it was starting to wander, I added, "What about the guard that we left back there, the one who was tied up?"

"The danger is too great to go back for him. I'm afraid he has to take his chances in the wild." Kipa shook his head, his eyes dark and glowing.

I thought about my promise to the man, that we would let him live. "Is there any way we can help him? He was just doing his job."

"That's what all the soldiers said who belonged to the Nazi Party. That's what soldiers have been saying all throughout history," Kipa added. "If you ask Herne the same question, he'll give you the same answer. Herne and I have been through wars before, we've seen what mankind does to its own when given too much power. Hell, the gods are just as bad."

"I know, but...I promised. Herne promised." My words were almost a whisper, though I knew it was useless.

Kipa gazed at me for a long moment. "All right. I'll double back to see if I can find him. But we're not turning him loose. He'll answer for what he's done. I'll bring him back if I can. He might make a good informant for us. But there's no way in hell that I'll set him free. Do you under-stand?" His eyes glittered with an icy sheen that reminded me of how great a divide there was between mortals and the gods.

I ducked my head. "Don't go if you think you'll put yourself in danger." I was so conflicted. I knew Kipa was right, and yet—and yet, we had *promised* the man. We had given our word. To me that meant something.

"I won't be in danger. But nobody else is coming with me." He paused, then pushed me toward the door. "You go in there and see if Herne is back with Rafé. If he is, give me a wave and I'll attend to the guard. If he's not, then I'm going out in search of them."

I nodded. "Thank you," was all I said as I opened the door to the cabin, hoping that everyone would be all right and intact.

I should have knocked first, because I realized I was facing the point of Herne's crossbow, aimed right at me. Viktor was sitting by the fire while Rafé was laid out on the table. Raven had her foot propped up on a stool, but she was helping Coyote look him over.

"You almost got yourself killed," Herne said as he lowered his bow.

I glanced over my shoulder and waved, then entered the cabin.

"Where's Kipa?" Herne asked.

"He'll be back. He needed to check on something." I entered the cabin and shut the door behind me, deciding that I'd wait until Kipa returned. He could argue with Herne better than I could, and I suddenly realized that Herne would be pissed if he realized Kipa had gone back to check on the guard.

I hurried over to Rafé's side. "How is he?" I looked over at Raven.

She was handing Coyote strips of cloth that looked like they'd been torn from a shirt. Coyote was wrapping a splint around Rafé's arm, trussing it up so he couldn't move it. It looked like he had already bandaged several of Rafé's cuts and wounds, and a makeshift ice bag was strapped to Rafé's nose. Yutani was sorting through his pack, looking for something.

Coyote glanced at me. His eyes were as dark as the night, and I recognized an odd familiarity in his features. Glancing at Yutani, I realized that I could see the resemblance. Both had the same wild, feral look, hidden beneath a beguiling exterior.

"He'll live. He's got some internal injuries, but they should hold until you can get him to medical treatment. He's got a broken arm, a broken nose, and a busted ankle. I think he may have a broken rib or two, so I've wrapped his ribs to keep them stable until you can get him back to your people for treatment."

I was about to say something about the *your people* comment when I realized that Coyote meant the mortal world, not the Fae. "How are we going to get him down to Port Angeles? I don't think we can all fit in Herne's Expedition."

Coyote arched one eyebrow. "I can take care of that. I'll get my pickup. It's got a camper on the back."

I stared at him, then glanced at Yutani, who looked bemused. "You drive a pickup?"

"Your boyfriend drives an SUV," Coyote said.

He had me there. Somehow, I had pictured the Great Coyote as more ethereal than the other gods, as someone who seldom mixed with mortalkind. The fact that he drove a pickup with a camper on it kind of threw a wrench into that image.

"In fact, I've done as much as I can for Rafé, so I'll head out and be back in half an hour with my truck."

"With the road conditions, how are you going to make it here in that time?" I asked, still not functioning on all four cylinders.

Herne snorted. "Chances are he's parked right up at the ridge. Am I right?" He looked at Coyote.

Coyote gave him a nod. "Score one point for you." He turned to Yutani. "Do you want to come with me, son?"

The way he said it resonated through the room, making me catch my breath. The fact that Yutani was actually Coyote's *son* hit home on a level that it hadn't before. Yutani was half god—a demigod.

Yutani shook his head. "You can run faster without me. And Rafé needs to get into town as soon as possible. I'll stay here with the others."

Coyote slipped out the door, taking off without another word. Yutani watched him go.

"It's going to be like that for the rest of my life, you know?" His words were faint, almost a murmur under his breath, but in the stillness of the cabin we all caught them. He looked startled, as though he hadn't realized he had spoken aloud. After another moment, he added, "One thing I've come to realize over the past few hours is that no matter whether he's blood or not, Coyote will always come and go on his own terms. He may be my father, but he's not someone I can ever rely on."

"How do you feel about that?" Raven asked.

Yutani shrugged. "It is what it is. He is who he is. At

least he told me the truth, and he also told me why he's waited so long to tell me. I don't know how I feel about the answer—and don't even ask what it is right now. I don't feel like talking about it. But at least he did give me an answer." He turned to Rafé. "Coyote's an excellent healer. Come on, we should gather our things and be ready to go. Do you really think we can drive down the mountain tonight?" he asked Herne.

Herne shrugged. "We have to. Eventually, those guards will put out the fire I started and come looking for us. Where the hell is Kipa? Yutani is right. We need to get a move on."

"He'll be back soon." I bit my lip, torn about whether to tell them where he was. I didn't like that Herne might think Kipa had run off, when he had done so much for us.

"Spill it. I can tell you're hiding something," Herne said. He moved over to me, stroking my face as he stared into my eyes. "Where is Kipa?"

I cleared my throat. "You remember the guard we left? That you had Kipa hide?"

"He didn't go back for him, did he? The fool."

"He went because I asked him to. You and I made a promise to the man that we wouldn't kill him. Leaving him outside, tied up in the snow? That's an open invitation to hypothermia. I just can't break my word, even if it was given to someone who's on the wrong side."

Herne's gaze blazed. "That man would have been cheering for Rafé to die if we hadn't caught him and tied him up. But perhaps you're right. If Kipa can find him, we can get more information out of him. Given that Nuanda wasn't there, we need to know everything we can about him. I was hoping we would be able to shut down the compound tonight, and we may have. With all the explosions and fires, there's a good chance they'll have to move out. But my real hope—that we'd find who's behind this and that this would be the main hub of the organization—well, that's a big fat failure."

I didn't want to argue. Herne was right. If we hadn't caught him, the guard would have been cheering on Rafé's demise. I didn't understand how to reconcile my ethics when it came to lying. Oh, I was fine if the lie didn't put somebody's life in danger. But a lie like this? Where we raised someone's hopes and then dashed them? It felt akin to what I had done to Nalcops, and while I accepted the necessity for it, I still didn't feel completely settled. I needed to talk to Morgana. She would help me make sense of everything.

At that moment, someone banged on the door.

"It's me, Kipa."

Herne opened the door. Kipa was alone.

"Where's the guard? Couldn't you find him?" Herne asked.

Kipa shook his head. "He was gone. They must have found him because the slashed ropes and gag were lying on the ground. I got out of there as soon as I could, but first I scouted out the encampment again. Herne, you did one hell of a lot of damage to it. At least three of the buildings caught fire and are still burning brightly, and there's a huddle of men in the front yard. I think they're the recruits. The guards are watching them. It looks like four of the cars bit the dust. The power's out, and I'm pretty sure you took out some of the pipes to the water system because I saw frozen water coming up from a main in the center of the compound."

There was the sound of a truck outside, and I peeked out the window.

"It's Coyote. Get Rafé ready," I said.

Herne and Viktor slid Rafé onto a makeshift stretcher and as Yutani opened the door, they carried him out to the camper on Coyote's truck.

Kipa sidled over to stand beside Raven, giving her a wink. She winked back. "I think you should ride to the hospital with Rafé, to get that ankle looked at."

"I don't think I can make it into the truck," she said.

Kipa swept her up in his arms and carried her to the truck, tucking her in beside Rafé.

Herne entered the cabin again. "Pack your stuff in the car. Yutani, you ride with Coyote. Viktor, please ride in the back with Rafé and Raven and keep an eye on them. Ember and Kipa—you're with me. Let's move. We do *not* want to be on these roads when the men from the encampment start hauling ass out of here."

"They'll be leaving soon. They were rushing around, trying to salvage what they could from inside the burning buildings." Kipa slung several of the backpacks over his back and carried them out to Herne's SUV.

As we vacated the cabin, making certain that the fire was fully out and that the door was shut, it occurred to me that the case had only gotten more involved. We thought we were coming out here to find Rafé and to take down the headquarters. But it looked like we'd have to settle for saving a friend. Which, when you thought about it, wasn't really a loss at all.

IT WAS A HARROWING RIDE, BUT WE MANAGED TO REACH Port Angeles by four in the morning. Herne stopped at the hotel, dropping us off before heading for the hospital. Once there, he would pick up Viktor and Yutani and bring them back with him.

As I entered the room, it was dark. In the glow from the hall, I saw Angel spring to a sitting position with a gasp. She held her hand to her heart.

"Oh, it's you." She looked almost as though she had seen a ghost. "I was having a horrible nightmare. It was filled with fire and flame and explosions." She paused, then rubbed her eyes. She was wearing a pink nightgown, and she pulled the covers up over her shoulders as she settled back against the headboard. "Did you find him? Please tell me the truth."

I set my backpack down, wearily trundling over to her bed. But I realized that my clothes were covered with caked mud and blood, so I didn't sit down.

"Yes, we found him. He's beat up pretty bad, but he should live. He's at the hospital right now. Coyote took him there."

She stared at me, and whether it was from the surprise over hearing about Rafé, or the surprise over hearing Coyote's name, I wasn't sure. After a moment, she cleared her throat.

"When you say *should live*, do you mean he's in danger of dying?"

"He was pretty busted up. He was being beaten to a pulp by one of the members when we got there. He has a broken arm, and a broken ankle, and they think maybe some broken ribs. He looks like a mess, but he should pull through." I hated sounding so clinical, given Rafé was her boyfriend, but she wanted the truth and she deserved the truth.

She digested the information for a moment, then nodded. "If I get dressed, do you think Herne would mind if I take a cab over to the hospital and sit with them?"

"I don't think he'd mind. Herne should be there, along with Viktor and Yutani. And Raven—she hurt her ankle."

"So what happened?"

"We found the headquarters, Angel, but it wasn't what we were looking for. Herne did a pretty good job of destroying a lot of their resources, though, but this isn't their main compound, and whoever Nuanda is, he wasn't there. But I doubt they'll be able to rebuild it, so we've chased them out of there, at least."

"It's like lancing a wound. You flush it out in the air, and rinse out the infection and then look for the next place the bacteria has settled."

"I suppose every pocket that we chip away is one less place for them to hide." I shivered. "I'm cold, and tired, and I ache. I'm going to take a shower and get out of these clothes. Be glad you weren't with us," I added. "Raven and I were attacked by giant spiders when we got trapped in a pit. I'm covered with spider goo too."

"When you say 'giant,' what do you mean?"

"Think Eight Legged Freaks giant, or shelob giant. And a bunch of babies that were bigger than goliath spiders." The Amazonian bird-eating spiders were just freaks of nature as far as I was concerned, and that the babies of the etho-spiders were bigger than they are, well, that was just wrong.

"Be glad I wasn't there or I would have passed out."

I could tell she was trying to be lighthearted, trying

not to cry, but the strain was evident on her face. I stripped off my clothes and padded over to pull up a chair beside her. Spreading a towel on it, I sat down.

"Rafé will be fine. He will heal up. Please don't worry too much."

She sniffed, shaking her head as she stared at the covers. "I'm the reason he came. I'm the one who recommended that they talk to him. Yes, he made up his own mind, but in the end, he wouldn't have known about it if I hadn't said something."

"Shit happens, Angel. The people to blame are those who belong to the Tuathan Brotherhood. Without their activities, we never would have needed to infiltrate them. And here's hoping that Rafé will be able to tell us something about the organization that we didn't find out tonight." I reached out, smoothing the side of her cheek with my hand. "He'll be okay. Please, try not to worry. At least we have him back now."

She nodded, pointing toward the bathroom. "Go take your shower. Not to be rude, but you do smell like spider guts. Or something else horrible."

I headed into the bathroom to take my shower. As the hot water poured over my body, and I lathered up, all I could think about was how long the day had been, and how much we had been through. And yet, we'd only solved one of our problems. I washed my hair, squeezing the water out of it after stepping out of the tub. Wrapping a towel around my head, I slid into a clean pair of panties and slipped into my robe, tying the belt snugly at the waist. I stared in the mirror.

"It's a good thing I love my job," I told my reflection. "Because days like today make me want to quit."

My reflection, being just that, said nothing in return.

Angel was dressed by the time I returned from my shower. She glanced up at me, smiling. "Herne just texted me. The doctor says Rafé will live. He *is* pretty broken up, but nothing that won't mend. They're going to transfer him to a hospital in Seattle come tomorrow. Herne also said that the drug—the Ropynalahol—didn't catch in his system. Which means we don't have to worry about that, at least."

"I wonder if that's why they were beating him up. Maybe they realized that it wasn't effective?"

"I don't know, but Herne told me to take a cab over to the hospital if I want. He's going to stay there for a while. He said you should get to bed and get some sleep. Oh, and Raven has a sprained ankle but it should heal within a couple of days, given she's Ante-Fae."

As she left, I traded my robe for a sleep shirt and combed through my wet hair. The hotel provided blow dryers, so I pulled a chair into the bathroom and sat by the vanity as I dried my hair. The flowing air felt good against my skin, warming me up in a way that even the heater in the SUV hadn't done. I aimed the nozzle at my throat, then at my aching muscles. The warmth seeped in.

Finally, I decided I couldn't put it off any longer. I began to think about the case.

On one hand, we had mucked things up royal. We *hadn't* made any inroads on who was behind the Tuathan Brotherhood, except for Nalcops telling us it was someone named Nuanda. We had barely managed to rescue Rafé. And we weren't even sure if we had closed down the compound. On the other hand, we had practically destroyed one of their headquarters, so if they didn't close down, they'd still have a lot to explain to the park rangers who couldn't help but notice the smoke and fire. And even though he had been hurt, we had come out with Rafé still alive. We also knew—for better or worse—that there were other compounds scattered around the nation and that we weren't going to accomplish this alone.

I had been so sure the Fomorians were behind the hate group, but now I was wavering. We had only seen Fae in the compound. So were my people *truly* behind the brotherhood? Was Nuanda Fae? Nalcops had said he was connected with Lugh the Long Handed, but that didn't make sense to me, although I knew very little about the god. Were Saílle and Névé lying to us? Were they behind this? And the questions just kept coming.

Finally, my hair was dry. I turned off the blow dryer and hung it back on its hook. As I brushed my hair and braided it back for the night, it occurred to me. I hadn't wanted to even acknowledge the feeling earlier, but now I couldn't turn away from the fact that I didn't *want* the Fae to be behind this.

As much as I despised both the Light and Dark Courts, I didn't want my people to be so vile that they would create hate groups. I didn't want to be part of a race that would do that. And yet, when I really examined my feelings, I had to acknowledge that I felt that way about some of the sub-Fae. I thought nothing of getting rid of troublesome members of their species. So was I any better? Was it the nature of all sentient beings to fear and despise those unlike them?

Shaking the argument out of my head, I finally settled for accepting that every group had its bad apples, and groups holding more power usually had more bad apples than others. Not every cat hated every dog, not every bird feared every cat, but that didn't mean that danger didn't exist, that danger wasn't a reality, and it sure as hell didn't excuse mob mentality.

And none of those thoughts did anything to help me settle on who I thought was behind the Tuathan Brotherhood.

As I slid into bed, drawing the covers up, I tried to calm my thoughts. I was tired. *Beyond* tired, when I really thought about it. I needed sleep. Perhaps in the morning I would be able to make sense of things. Snuggling deep under the covers as the snow continued to come down outside, I closed my eyes and willed myself into a light trance. But actual sleep was a long time coming, and it was almost morning before I slipped into a light and restless slumber.

CHAPTER SEVENTEEN

By nine A.M., I was awake. I had managed three and a half hours of sleep and all I could think about was how much caffeine I could pour down my throat without giving myself the jitters. I pried my eyes open as the door opened and Angel entered the room. Groaning, aching in every corner of my body, I rolled to a sitting position as she sat down on her bed.

"How's Rafé doing?" My throat felt raw, as though I had been screaming too much, or been caught out in the cold for a long time. "Is he okay?"

"His arm is broken, his ankle's broken, he's got two broken ribs, and a broken nose. Both his eyes are black and blue, and he's bruised up. *But*…no internal organs were compromised. Also, the tracker that Yutani had inserted into his arm had been cut out by the brotherhood and he has an infection. So he has ten stitches and he's on massive antibiotics." She shook her head, shrugging off her coat. "He's in rough shape, and he's still sedated from surgery. He won't be able to talk for a while. Herne brought me back to the hotel, along with Raven. Her ankle's sprained, but you know that."

"Thank gods we found him before they managed to kill him." I rubbed my head. "I barely got any sleep. I'm exhausted, but I imagine Herne wants us to meet him for breakfast."

"Yeah, he asked me to tell you to get down to the restaurant. I'll change before we go."

I wrapped my hair in a chignon to keep it from getting wet and dragged myself back into the shower for another quick rinse, using the hottest water I could stand. The beads pounded on my shoulder muscles, helping release some of the tension. Then I threw on a pair of jeans and a V-neck sweater. I slid my feet into my ankle boots, because the ones I had worn the day before were still soaked through. Angel had changed into clean jeans and a peasant blouse, and she wrapped a skinny belt around her waist.

Grabbing my purse, I headed toward the door, and she followed.

Everybody was downstairs for breakfast except Raven and Herne.

"I told her to stay in bed and keep that foot elevated," Talia said. "She's watching television and I made sure that she has breakfast for her and Raj. I swear, that gargoyle is more like a dog. A happy-go-lucky dog. He was so affectionate while you guys were up on the ridge. All he wanted to do was play." She looked at me. "You look worse for wear."

"Thanks. I love you too," I said, laughing for the first time in a while. "I need more than three and a half hours of sleep to function." I waved at the waitress. "I need a quint-shot mocha and I need it stat. Extra chocolate, with a lot of whipped cream on top." As she turned, I stopped her again. "Can you shave some chocolate on top of the whipped cream, too?"

As she headed off with my order, I picked up the menu. I was starving. "Where's Herne?"

Yutani shrugged. "On a phone call. He'll be back in a moment."

Sure enough, just as we started placing our breakfast orders, Herne entered the restaurant. As he sat down at the table, looking up at the waitress.

"I'll have a stack of pancakes, eight sausage links, four rashers of bacon, and a bowl of fruit. Also, a refill on my coffee, please." He waited until she double-checked our orders and left. "That was Cernunnos on the phone. He'll be here in an hour, with Brighid's arrow. So we should be able to at least take care of the Cailleach today. I called Angus. He's still alive, so thank gods for small favors. Are you all caught up on Rafé's and Raven's conditions?"

We all nodded. Viktor looked as tired as I felt, and so did Yutani.

"Did your father take off?" Herne asked, turning to Yutani.

He nodded. "Yeah, after he dropped us off at the hospital. Coyote said he'd see me later, and I know enough to know that means when he's ready. But at least we cleared up a few things. I'll tell you about them later, when I've had a chance to process them." He paused, and then, staring at his coffee, he added, "I want to apologize if I've offended any of you lately. I know I've been kind of an asshole, and there's really no excuse. I was just so confused about what to do about my father, and so angry that I took it out on everybody else."

"How do you feel now?" Talia asked.

"I have a lot to process through, but at least I have a place to start." He shrugged, smiling sheepishly. "Forgive me?"

I stuck my tongue out at him. "I suppose. And yes, you were being an ass, but it's okay. We're all good." I glanced around the table. "Aren't we?"

Everybody nodded.

"If that's taken care of, let's move on to other subjects." Herne let out a long sigh. "We have to capture the Cailleach today. They're shutting roads down across the peninsula because of the snow. If we don't corral her soon, she'll grow too strong. My father said the arrow will work on her as long as she hasn't gained her full strength yet."

"How long does that take?" Yutani asked.

"Anywhere from several weeks to a few months after she's been released from her stone. But Cernunnos thinks we're nearing the limit."

"Why does it take one of *Brighid's* arrows to confine her to the stone?" I asked.

"Because the Cailleach and Brighid made an agreement eons ago. The Cailleach was supposed to give way to early spring, on Imbolc—Brighid's holy day. But she began pushing the limit, and finally, Brighid appealed to the Triamvinate that the Cailleach had broken their agreement. The Triamvinate gave Brighid the power to contain the Cailleach if she ever tried it again. Well, being the Force she is, the Cailleach inevitably overreached her grasp yet again, so Brighid shot her with one of her arrows, which locked the Cailleach away in the stone. She's only to be freed if the winters cease to fall as they're supposed to. I suppose, if greenhouse warming continues, the Triamvinate may decree that she be freed to work her magic. But that has not happened yet."

"Do you think you can shoot her?" Talia asked.

"If I can catch her in my sightline, I can. Brighid's also giving us a summoning stone. That will bring the Cailleach to us, but we'll have to act quickly, because it will only hold her for a moment."

"I suppose we should do this at Angus's house, correct?" I asked.

Herne nodded. "Yes. After we take care of this, we'll see if Rafé's feeling strong enough to talk. Also, Cernunnos and Morgana want to talk to us about the brotherhood."

The waitress brought our breakfasts, and we attacked the food. I was desperate for more sleep, but the moment we had the arrow, we'd have to head out. As I swallowed my mocha, the caffeine warming my blood, I decided when we got back home I would take a week off, and do nothing but sleep.

HERNE PAID FOR OUR BREAKFAST AND WE WENT OUTSIDE TO wait for Cernunnos. We huddled on the edge of the parking lot by a massive snowbank that had been plowed into a jagged embankment. I'd be happy if I never saw snow again. I knew that wasn't really true—I liked winter —but right now all I wanted was the comfort of gray skies and drizzly rain. Or clear skies and sunshine. I didn't really care which.

The snow swirled down around us. The Cailleach must have one hell of a grudge against humanity, I thought. But in my heart, I knew that wasn't true. She was the core and essence of winter, she didn't care about humans or mortals or gods—all she was focused on was bringing in the cold and the ice. It was her nature. She *was* winter incarnate.

We'd been standing there for about five minutes when a sound from the forest next to us caught my attention.

"Someone's coming," I said.

As we turned, Cernunnos emerged from the forest, followed by a woman who was almost too beautiful to look at.

She was as tall as the Forest God, with hair the color of burnished copper that fell in curls down to her butt. Her skin was pale, peaches and cream, and her eyes glistened like emeralds. She was wearing a long green velvet gown, gathered at the waist with a corset belt made of black leather. Her lips glowed with the blush of fresh peaches, and she wore a golden circlet with a triskelion over her forehead. She glided through the snow, following Cernunnos until they stood before us. Herne knelt, as did Yutani and Viktor. Talia curtsied low, and Angel and I did our best to follow suit.

"You may rise," Cernunnos said. He really didn't stand on ceremony from what I had seen of him, but it never hurt to show respect.

As we struggled upright, Herne inclined his head toward the Lady Brighid.

231

"Exalted One, welcome. We thank you for coming to our need."

When she spoke, her voice rippled through the air, sounding musical and melodic and yet infinitely powerful. "The Cailleach cannot be allowed to run rampant in the mortal world. She is too strong for both mortalkind and the animals who walk upon the face of the earth. I have warned her before. We have been down this road more than once. I will give you my arrow, dependent on a promise from all of you."

"Whatever you ask, my lady." Herne clasped his hands in front of him, waiting patiently.

"Whenever I need your help, you and your friends will attend me. There is a situation that I foresee coming, in which I will need your help." She glanced at me. "Yours especially, Ember Kearney. Give me your oath that when I call, you will come, and I will give you the arrow along with my blessing."

My stomach hit the ground. Being singled out by a goddess wasn't necessarily a bad thing, but it always led straight into the labyrinth. And the fact that she knew my name was unsettling.

I managed to find my voice. "As long as my Lady Morgana has no objections, I will be at your disposal when you need me."

Herne echoed my thoughts. "When you need us, the Wild Hunt will be there."

Brighid nodded. She held out her hand, and an arrow appeared in it. The arrow was golden, and reeked of magic. The air around it rippled, making it look like it was phasing in and out. I caught my breath. The golden shaft was beautiful, and the tip was deadly sharp.

"Herne, son of Cernunnos, may your aim be true. This arrow is for use upon the Cailleach, and the Cailleach only. It will bind her into the stone, providing you have the stone with you."

"How close does the stone have to be to the Cailleach for us to send her back into it?" Herne asked.

"Within eyesight. If you have the stone, and you can see her, then you can trap her. Now, where is the *keeper* of the Corryvreckan stone?" Brighid looked around, frowning. "I have some words for him."

I shivered. She didn't sound happy, and I felt sorry for Angus, given the scolding he obviously had coming.

Herne pulled out his phone. "I can call him out here. He's waiting in the hotel."

"Do so, now," Brighid said.

Herne put in a call to Angus, and luckily—or unluckily, as the case may be—Angus answered. "Get your ass out front to the parking lot now," Herne said. He hung up before Angus could reply.

Cernunnos motioned to me. "Walk with me for a moment while we wait," he said.

I glanced at Herne, and he gave me a nod. Nervously, I fell in stride with Cernunnos as we headed toward the street. I wondered if anybody passing by could guess that they were driving past a god. Everyone knew the gods existed, but few people ever had any interactions with them, and there were a few who clung to their outdated beliefs that the gods were demons walking freely in the world. If they ever met a real demon, though, I had the feeling they'd change their tune mighty fast. Demons existed, and far worse creatures as well.

As we wandered away from the rest of the party,

Cernunnos glanced down at me. He was massive, his muscles had muscles, and his dreads fell down to his lower back. He was wearing a windbreaker over a pair of jeans, and motorcycle boots, and though he was without his headdress, he still felt every inch the god to me.

"How are you finding life after the Cruharach? Are you at peace with your Leannan Sidhe heritage and your Autumn's Bane bloodline?"

I shrugged. "I'm getting used to both. Sometimes it's hard, because while I can tell they were always there, they weren't nearly so noticeable. They're both predatory, which is a little scary…but given I've only known the specifics a few months, I think I'm doing fairly well."

Cernunnos gave me a short nod. "Your father and mother had difficulties accepting their predator selves as well. That's partly why they're dead. I won't disparage them, they were good-hearted people, and they were loyal to Morgana and me, but they weren't survivors. And you, Ember, are a survivor."

"I suppose I am," I said.

"That's a good thing. You need to be a survivor to make it in this world, especially when you bear the lineage that you do. Don't hesitate to use your powers as you need them, but use them wisely. You don't want to end up like your grandfather, who looked to abuse his abilities."

I wasn't sure what to say.

"Cat got your tongue?" he asked with a grin.

Shrugging, I said, "It seems so. Is Brighid going to punish Angus?"

"She would be within her right to do so, given how careless he was. But I think losing his wife will be punishment enough."

"Fiona's lost, then?" I let out a soft sigh. I had been hoping we could save her.

"I'm afraid she probably is. And the sad fact is that this wouldn't have happened if he hadn't been so stubborn. I'm not entirely sure what happened—and no one will ever be—but removing the stone from Scotland was folly."

"What will Brighid do to him?"

"She'll give him a good talking-to, and he will return to Scotland. That's the thing, Ember. Destiny doesn't always take into account our wants and dislikes when doling out fate. That's true of the gods as well as mortals. Sometimes, we're called upon to do things we don't want to. Or we're called upon to carry out a duty that goes against our nature. And sometimes, we're just prevented from doing what we want. But not everyone gets to choose their lot in life."

"That seems unfair."

"Life isn't fair. Though I've seen that when this happens, the next time around on the wheel seems to offer an easier path. There are some situations where you cannot see the whole until you are off the wheel of life and looking at it from the outside. Things have a way of balancing out in The Eternal Return, even if you don't realize it at the time."

We stopped next to the road. Cernunnos watched the cars pass by as the snow swirled around them.

I turned to him. "What do you see, when you look at our world? When you visit here?"

He paused. For a moment, I thought he wasn't going to answer, but then he said, "I see forgetfulness. I see people who've lost their way, I see people who forget to look at the beauty around them. And then," he said, looking at me, "I see others who are striving to be the best they can be. Who are making the best lives they can for themselves. The world of Annwn is not so different from your world." He glanced over my shoulder and I followed his look. Angus was coming out of the hotel, walking slowly toward Brighid.

Cernunnos turned to me, giving me a slight grin. "Well, shall we go back and witness the fireworks?"

I shuddered, thinking I'd rather not, but instead I turned and followed him back to where the others were standing.

"Angus Lesley, you have abandoned your post, and as a result you have allowed the Cailleach to be freed. What have you to say for yourself?" Brighid was saying to Angus, who was kneeling in front of her.

"I am so sorry, milady. I didn't realize this was going to happen. We've been over here for over forty years, and nothing like this has happened before."

"You are one of the magic-born. Forty years is a drop in your lifetime. You should know better. Didn't your father school you on what your duties were?" Brighid's voice was harsh, though she didn't look all that angry. More, she looked disappointed.

"My father did warn me. I accept responsibility for this. It's my fault, and I'll do whatever I have to do to correct it." Angus stared at the pavement, still kneeling. His voice was contrite, and he looked shaken.

Brighid folded her arms across her chest. "These are things you cannot undo, these things that have been done. This is not my doing, but your own. The Cailleach has taken over Fiona, and the two are permanently entwined at this point. Because of your actions, you will lose your wife."

Angus let out a cry, covering his face.

"This is not my doing, Angus. It's the direct result of your carelessness. I've given Herne one of my Fiery Arrows so he'll be able to capture the Cailleach back into her stone. After he's done this, you will return to Scotland with the stone and resume your duties. Your daughter will join you there to learn the ways of the keeper of the stone of Corryvreckan. It is her duty to follow in your footsteps, so you would do well to make her aware of just how serious this position is. Your family was entrusted with it from the beginning, and so it shall remain. As your daughter will become the keeper of the stone, so will her firstborn."

Angus bent over, resting his head on the snowy pavement in front of him. "Please, Lady, isn't there any way to save my Fiona?"

"If there were, I would help you," Brighid said. "But I can see no untangling the situation. Fiona has merged with the Cailleach. They are one. So, no, there is no return for her. She is part of the storm, part of winter. Her magic has been bound up in ice and snow and mist and wind. You are not being punished, but this is simply the result of what path you have chosen."

Angus began to sob, his shoulders heaving. Herne knelt beside him, glancing up at Brighid as he placed his hand on Angus's shoulder.

"I think he understands the severity of what he did." Herne's voice was soft, and in his expression I caught a plea for leniency.

Brighid uncrossed her arms and knelt in front of

Angus. "If I could help her, I would. Truly, I would. But the gods are not omnipotent, nor are we omniscient. And we cannot undo everything that has been done. There are many ways we can help, but over some things we have no power. And the great Forces of Nature are beyond even us. So arise, Angus Lesley, and do what you must. Let your heart rest easier, for Fiona is in no pain nor discomfort, that much I will guarantee you. And neither will she be when she joins the Cailleach in the stone."

Angus looked up, his face streaked with tears. Herne stood and offered his hand to the man, helping him to his feet.

He coughed, trying to wipe his eyes. "And there's no hope that she'll ever be free of the Cailleach?"

Brighid let out a great sigh, and then shrugged. "We can *always* keep hope alive. I would tell you no, but I am no prognosticator, and who knows what the future may bring? As you keep watch over the stone, you will be watching over Fiona as well. That is the best I can tell you." She turned to Cernunnos. "It is time we left this place. I have things to do."

As she began to walk back into the forest, Cernunnos glanced back at us.

"I will speak with you in a day or two about the Tuathan Brotherhood. They're not going anywhere, so another day or so won't matter. I'm afraid that this is a far more complex issue than we first thought, and it's going to take some time to dig through the barriers they've erected between themselves and the rest of the world. Herne, call me when you get back to Seattle. And use Brighid's gift wisely." And with that, the Lord of the Forest followed Brighid back into the woods.

CHAPTER EIGHTEEN

*L*eaving Talia, Raven, and Angel at the hotel, we gathered our gear to head out to Angus's house. I was still chilled from being up on Hurricane Ridge, but at least we were within driving distance of our beds this time. I made certain that I was armed with my bow and dagger, and that everything was in good working order. I thought about asking Raven if I could borrow her blade again, but decided that poison probably wouldn't affect a Luo'henkah. As I suited up, Angel watched me. I had told her what it gone down between Angus and Brighid, and she seemed taken aback.

"What are you thinking about?" I asked.

"Fate or destiny, call it whatever you will. There's really no mercy in it, is there?"

"You're thinking about Fiona and Angus, aren't you?"

She nodded. "It just seems so harsh that he's lost her forever because of this."

"The Cailleach doesn't care. The Luo'henkah are much like elementals, only even more so. She is the core in the heart of winter, of the snow and ice and mist. There's no humanity in that, merely one of the great forces that makes up this world." I paused, glancing at her. "I feel bad for him, too. I feel incredibly sorry for him and for Fiona. But Brighid was right when she said that he caused this. Maybe he didn't know what would happen. But he was in charge of a great artifact, and he decided willy-nilly to lump it all and carry it off to a different land against instructions. Now, he has to live with the results of his decision."

"What was Brighid like?" Angel asked.

"She scared me almost more than Cernunnos. He may be Lord of the Forest but she's the Fiery Arrow. And now that I've met her, I see why she bears that title. There's something about her that goes beyond our understanding. I can't explain it, but I think I'd be more comfortable having a beer with Cernunnos than a glass of wine with Brighid."

"Do you have everything you need?" Angel asked. "You need to borrow my gloves? I see you misplaced yours."

She was right. In all the confusion and chaos at the headquarters of the Tuathan Brotherhood, I had somehow lost my gloves.

"If you don't mind, I'd appreciate it. I have no idea where mine went to." I was also wearing Raven's jacket, and I showed Angel the material. "She charmed it so that it retains heat. Pretty nifty, huh?"

"I want one!" Angel clapped her hands. "That really is amazing. I didn't know she could do things like that."

"I have a feeling there's a lot we don't know about Raven. You should've seen her take on that giant spider. She wields some pretty powerful magic. I sure wouldn't want to be on her bad side." I brushed my hair into a ponytail and shoved a hat down over my ears to keep them warm. Angel handed me her gloves, and I slid my fingers into them, making sure that I could still grab my dagger easily enough. I slung my crossbow over my shoulder and strapped a quiver of bolts on my belt. Finally, I looked around and let out a sigh.

"I guess I'm as ready as I'll ever be. I'm not looking forward to this, I'll tell you that. The Cailleach is deadly—and she's crafty. But even more than that, I just want to sit by a warm fire and pet Mr. Rumblebutt."

"We'll take some time off when we get home. Go get the Cailleach and then we can leave this place. I'm going to go visit Rafé while you're out, see if he's woken up yet." She hugged me, holding me tight. "Come back, Ember. Every time you go out there I'm afraid that—"

"I know. Every time I head out to a battle, I'm afraid it may be my last too. But I'll be back. Herne has Brighid's arrow, and he has a deadly aim. You can't beat that combination."

As I headed out, I stopped in to say good-bye to Talia and Raven, and to thank Raven for the jacket. Raj was staring out the window, looking hopeful, and I caught Talia and Raven in the middle of watching the *Fae House-wives of New York*.

As I left, I called out, "I'm not letting you live this one down."

Their laughter lifted my spirits better than any hug could.

Herne, Angus, and I rode in Herne's SUV, while Viktor and Yutani followed in Viktor's rental. As we approached Angus's house, the snow was almost too deep to drive through. The road he lived on wasn't on the snowplow route, and we were lucky to get through.

"I'm usually the one who plows the road when we get snow," Angus said. He'd managed to recover from the traumatic talk with Brighid, but he was somber in a way that spoke miles to his sorrow. He seemed resigned to his fate, but I had a suspicion that he had a whole lot of grieving to do over the next few years.

"You have the stone?" Herne asked.

"I do. Right here," Angus said, holding it up.

"Give it to Ember. I care about you, mate, and I trust that you are no coward, but I am afraid that when you see the Cailleach, you might just go a little bonkers on us, given what she's done to Fiona."

Angus let out a choked sound, but handed the stone to me. It felt heavy in my hands, chilled and polished in a way that resonated from deep within the stone.

"You mean, what *I've* done to Fiona. Brighid left no doubt in my mind that this is my fault, and what's happened to my wife lies directly on my head." He sounded like a convicted man, facing execution.

Herne turned to him, glancing over the seat. "Listen to me. I know what Brighid said, and in one respect, she's right. But ultimately, the Cailleach remains to blame. She didn't have to take possession of Fiona and she didn't have to work through her. That was a choice that the Cailleach made. Granted, it's the most natural choice for someone of her nature, but the Cailleach is the one who made the final decision."

"Thanks, but I know in my heart that if I hadn't left Corryvreckan this wouldn't have happened. I shirked my duty. I chose to blow it off like it was nothing. I just wish Fiona hadn't been the one to pay for my stupidity."

Herne stared at him for a moment, then with an almost imperceptible shift, said, "All right, let's get this show on the road. We want to be done before dark."

He hopped out of the car, shouldering his bow and quiver. As I emerged from my side of the car, Viktor crossed the driveway to help me on with my snowshoes—a new set, given both Raven and I had lost ours when we tumbled into the pit. I didn't want to use them again—they were difficult in some ways, and bulky—but the snow was too deep to wade through. Once we were all strapped into our snowshoes, Angus led the way.

"I can feel her, just like I could always tell where Fiona was." He set off into the thicket that surrounded the house, where we had encountered the padurmonstris and the schnee-hexe.

I looked around nervously, expecting the grigit to come bounding out at any minute. But it was quiet—too quiet. The trees felt watchful and wary, and the magic running through the copse had grown so thick I could barely breathe. This wasn't the magic of the padurmon-stris, though. This was the magic of the Cailleach.

"How will we know when she's near?" I asked, although in my bones I had the feeling there would be no doubt. She was everywhere around us, in the wind and the snow and ice. "Does she have to be in human form to shoot her?"

"Yes, but she already is," Herne said. "She's taken over Fiona and is using her as a vehicle."

He said it so quietly that for a moment it didn't register, and then I understood. He wouldn't be shooting the *Cailleach* with the arrow. He would be shooting *Fiona*.

I looked at Herne, and he met my gaze with a silent nod. Letting out a soft breath, I held the stone closer to me, trying to focus on anything beyond the thought that we were going to kill Fiona. Selfishly, I was grateful it was Herne who had the arrow, because I didn't know if I could do it. I didn't know if I could shoot someone who was ultimately—at heart—a good person. Fiona hadn't chosen to open herself up to the Cailleach, and even though Fiona's actual spirit—her essence--was lost inside the snowy Force, she still looked like Angus's wife.

At one point, as we pressed deeper into the thicket, I thought I saw something to the side. I paused, sweeping aside a branch of a fir tree. Behind it, I caught sight of an extremely large rabbit, almost the size of a small dog. It rose up on its haunches and met my gaze. There was intelligence behind that look, and I realized this was one of the padurmonstris. It seemed to be hiding, though, and I got the distinct impression that it was hoping I would ignore it and leave it alone. I slowly lowered the branch again, wincing as a shower of snow came tumbling off the tree, dousing me with the cold white powder.

Herne glanced at me and I shook my head.

"Padurmonstris, but I think it's hiding from the Cailleach."

"I don't blame it," Herne said.

I was beginning to wonder how large this thicket was. It seemed to be bigger once we were inside of it.

"She's near," Angus said. "I don't think you'll have to summon her, Herne." His voice echoed bleakly.

"I can feel her," I said, closing my eyes. "Why isn't she hiding?"

"Because she knows that we won't stop. She knows that this showdown will happen, regardless of her plans. If she were to just pick up and run off, Herne could summon her back thanks to Brighid. The Cailleach is afraid of no one, and she considers herself stronger than Brighid, so she's hoping that she'll beat us at our own game." Angus stopped in his tracks. "Do you know why Brighid gave you that arrow? Other than wanting to stop the Cailleach?"

I shook my head. "Why?"

"In the lore of my ancestors, it's written that when Brighid first went up against the Cailleach, the Triamvinate decreed that if the Cailleach broke free, the one onus placed upon her was that she *must* answer Brighid's challenge. If an arrow was offered in the hunt for the Cailleach, the Cailleach must face the challenge. If she wins, she goes free."

Angus looked so stricken that I wanted to give him a hug.

"That's why my family was entrusted with the stone. If she somehow avoids the arrow, if the marksman cannot shoot to a true aim, then she'll run wild. Herne must hit her in the heart."

So there was more at stake than we thought. If we missed, the Cailleach would be free to do as she would. And there would be nothing we could do about it, at least as far as Angus seemed to think.

"Why didn't Brighid give us two arrows, then? To increase our chances?"

Herne glanced at me. "These arrows cost Brighid a

great deal more than a bit of metal. Each one is infused with her blood, and when it hits its mark, she feels the pain of the victim. She feels the death caused by her own arrows. In this case, she will feel the rage and anger of the Cailleach as she is driven back into her stone, as well as any pain Fiona's body endures. All of that will reverberate through Brighid's psyche. It's not an easy thing to bear. Which is why she gave the arrow to me. I'm almost always true with my aim."

I let out a long breath. In a sense, the goddess Brighid had offered us a double-edged sword that would rebound against her. That alone sent a deep sense of reverence for her through me.

"How much farther do you think we have to go?" Yutani asked. He was looking nervously around the thicket.

"We don't," Victor said. "The mountain has come to us."

As we turned, there, facing us from beneath a tall fir tree, was Fiona. The Cailleach had come to meet the challenge.

Angus let out an anguished cry as Fiona laughed. He glanced at Herne. "Give me one last chance to get through? Please?"

Herne nodded, but his voice was brusque when he spoke. "You have one chance. And Angus, if I have to, I'll have Viktor hold you back."

Angus stepped forward, holding out his hands. My heart broke for him as I watched.

"Fiona, my wife. Please, please try to break free. This is my fault. This is all my fault. If you can hear me, Cailleach, Ice Queen of Winter, *please let her go*. If you have to take over someone, let it be me. I'm the one to blame. I faltered in my duty. Set my wife free, and I'll take her place willingly." He fell to his knees, holding out his hands, as he begged for Fiona's life.

My stomach clenched. For both Angus's and Fiona's sake, I prayed the Cailleach would have some sense of mercy, but I didn't hold out much hope. The Cailleach was a Luo'henkah, far beyond human emotions, and even her joy in being free wasn't the same as human joy. I wanted to run to Herne, to cling to him as we watched and waited, but I didn't dare interrupt him.

Herne fit Brighid's golden arrow into his bow, and now he waited.

Fiona—the Cailleach—turned to Angus, who was kneeling on the ground before her. The look in her eyes was one of swirling frost and ice, the smile on her face sly.

"You ask for mercy. And yet you have held me against my will, Keeper of the Corryvreckan stone. You have been my warden and prison keeper, like your father before you, and his father before him. And so on into the depths of history. But yet, you also gave me the chance to break free." The sly smile turned ever upward. Fiona looked over at Herne. "You are a fool, to care so much for what one man feels." With that moment, she jumped. Fiona dropped to the ground as a silver mist rose out of her body and plunged into Angus's form.

Abruptly, Angus shot to his feet and turned, his hand out. A silver beam shot forth, filled with spikes of ice aimed directly at Herne. Herne dodged, swinging his bow to bear again, but Angus was off and running. He darted behind a tree.

The wind was picking up, shrieking around us as a nearby cedar, laden with snow on its boughs, creaked and moaned as it toppled forward, falling toward us. Viktor grabbed hold of my arm and yanked me away as he stumbled back in the snow. Yutani dodged to the side, and Herne managed to jump away as the tree landed, its heavy trunk merely a couple yards from him.

I turned to Viktor. "Fiona! We have to pull her away."

Viktor nodded, leaping over the trunk and running toward Fiona's prone form. Herne was chasing Angus, bow in hand. Yutani brought out what looked like a tranquilizer gun, trying to take a bead on Angus's form. I followed Viktor as he carried Fiona over to the shelter of a nearby tree. He looked at me.

"Stay with her."

"No. There's something I can do against the Cailleach that you can't. *You* stay with her." I summoned up my Leannan Sidhe self. I gave her full rein, because I knew she could handle the snow better than I could. I had nothing on the Cailleach when it came to snow magic, but there was something I could do to disrupt her.

As I looked up, I could see the swirl of energy following Angus, and I could feel the connection between the Cailleach and the storm. If I could suck the moisture out of the air, it might have an effect on her.

I focused on the clouds, focused on the water in frozen form, and bade it to transform, because I knew I couldn't manage to make it all dissipate. I couldn't bust the clouds apart.

With a shimmer, the snow suddenly turned to heavy

rain, saturating the ground around us. It was coming down in buckets, but *rain* I could work with. I aimed it at the face of the Cailleach, to blind her with a wave of water. I wasn't sure exactly whether it was working, but Angus suddenly froze, then turned to me.

"You dare disrupt my power!" Angus's voice echoed through the copse, low and resonant.

It was then that I remembered that he had his own magic and the Cailleach could use that.

Oh crap. I started to run, heading toward the fallen cedar so that I could take shelter behind it. The Cailleach, still in Angus's body, let out a shriek, wiping the rain away from his eyes.

Herne swung around, bringing his bow up, taking a bead on Angus.

When I saw what he was doing, I froze, and began to laugh at the Cailleach, waving my hands to get her attention. As she focused on me, she held out one hand and another stream of ice spikes came sailing my way. Herne took that moment to let fly the golden arrow of Brighid, and it spun through the air, slicing a path directly into Angus's heart. I dropped to the ground, barely escaping the hail of ice. As the spikes whistled overhead, I huddled behind the tree.

A shriek echoed through the thicket, piercing the air, so loud that it made my eardrums hurt. I pressed my hands to my ears, still huddling on the ground. And then I remembered the stone. I had dropped it when I ran over to Fiona. I sat up, terrified, but saw that Yutani had managed to grab hold of it and he was holding the stone out. A silver mist was rushing toward it, escaping from Angus's body, slamming into the stone. Angus fell to the ground, the arrow piercing his heart as a pool of blood began to stain the fresh snow.

A moment later, everything fell silent around us. The Cailleach was trapped within the stone again. And Angus was dead.

Yutani stared at the stone, then silently held it out to Herne, who took it and packed it into his backpack.

"So is that it? Is she in there?" My shoulders were tense as I waited for the Cailleach to reappear. The storm had immediately begun to ease up, but I didn't trust it.

Herne nodded, his expression bleak. "Yes, we trapped her."

"And Angus?" Yutani asked.

"I don't think so, but I can't be sure. She wasn't in possession of his body long enough." He lifted his head, a bleak expression filling his eyes "I just killed one of my oldest friends."

I wanted to go to him, but he needed space. I could feel it. I ducked my head, staring down at Fiona. Viktor knelt beside her, lifting her up in his arms. He took hold of her wrist, feeling for her pulse. After a moment, he shook his head.

"She's dead."

"She was so entwined with the Cailleach that when Angus goaded her into fleeing Fiona's body, it killed her. My guess is her soul is still entwined with the Cailleach's." Herne walked over to kneel by Fiona's side. He gently brushed her eyes closed. "Rest well, in the arms of the winter crone."

There was a sound behind us and I glanced over my shoulder. Brighid was standing there, a fiery flame against the snow. Three tall elves stood behind her.

She gazed down at Angus's body, then over at Fiona, a sadness in her eyes so strong that it made me want to weep. In fact, I realized I was already crying.

Herne waded through the snow to hand her the stone.

Brighid held it up, then walked over to Angus and knelt by his body, her gown spreading across the snow like a carpet of spring moss. "Away to the Summerlands, fair Angus."

"What about Fiona?" I asked as Brighid grasped hold of the arrow and, bracing herself, pulled it out of his heart. A fresh spatter of blood spread across the snow, thin fingers of red staining the white like a blush of roses.

"She sleeps within the stone, bound to the Cailleach." Brighid looked up at me, her emerald eyes mirroring my own. "Sometimes there is no remedy, Ember Kearney. Sometimes, life is what it will be, regardless of what we hope for. Their daughter awaits my return. She will move to Corryvreckan and take over the post of her ancestors." She paused, then glanced over at the thicket. "The Cailleach left behind a part of herself."

We followed her gaze. There, dancing through the trees, was a ghostly spirit who looked like Fiona, but she was translucent, spinning through the soft snowfall, oblivious to our presence.

"Who's that?" I asked. "That can't be Fiona, not if she's tangled with the Cailleach."

"The Cailleach spun off a daughter, who will wander in Fiona's form. She's an elemental spirit, a Luo'henkah like her mother, but she's young and new." Brighid watched her for a moment. "There's nothing we can do about her. It will take centuries for her to evolve. Until then, we'll set up someone to watch over her."

"A daughter?" Herne stared at the spirit. "How is that possible?"

"Fiona was one of the magic-born, and had a great deal of power. The Cailleach must have taken hold of that force and infused a part of her own self into it. But the daughter is autonomous. I cannot control her like I can the Cailleach." Brighid stood, shaking her long red hair, her curls tossing in the wind. "But I *can* give her a name. And once a thing is named, there is a chance to gain control over it."

"What will you call her?" Yutani asked, coming to stand next to me.

"Isella, the Daughter of Ice." Brighid turned back to us. "Well done, Herne. You forfeited much with your actions, but you have saved countless lives from the Cailleach's fury. Each time she escapes, she grows stronger, and she grows more angry at her entrapment. One day I fear my arrows will no longer be able to contain her. Until that day, however, we will do what is needed to keep her under guard."

"May that day never arise," Herne said. "What about Angus's house?"

"I will arrange for the contents to be returned to Scotland, to his daughter. His other son has drifted away from the family line, in terms of duty, but his daughter holds true and she will do what her father could not."

Two of the elves respectfully picked up Angus's body, and the third scooped Fiona into his arms. They returned to Brighid's side. With that, the four of them began walking toward a particularly dense patch of undergrowth.

"I will call you when I have need of your services," Brighid said over her shoulder before vanishing in a swirl of mist and smoke.

We were alone. As we stood there, a noise behind me caught my attention. I turned to see the padurmonstris—the rabbit I had seen—peeking out. I lifted my fingers to my lips but nodded to it, and it inclined its head back toward me.

We stood there for another moment, watching as the bloodstained snow slowly vanished beneath the new snowfall. Then, as Isella spun in circles, we turned our backs on her and walked out of the thicket, leaving it to the elementals and the creatures who called it their home.

CHAPTER NINETEEN

*A*ll the way back from Angus's house, we had remained silent. There was nothing to say. We had lost both Angus and Fiona. Isella had been born, spinning off from her mother. The Cailleach was under control, but given all that had happened, it seemed a hollow victory.

Back at the hospital, we gathered around Rafé's bed. He was awake and able to talk, though he was bruised up pretty badly, and with a broken leg, broken arm, and broken ribs, he wouldn't be running around any time soon. But at least we had saved his life.

Angel sat on the bed next to him, his good hand in hers.

"Can you remember what happened? How did they find out you were a spy?" Herne asked.

Rafé tried to adjust his position. A veiled look passed through his eyes. "They knew, Herne. They knew that I was a spy. I'm not sure who told them, but somebody did. Somebody who knew what we were planning." He paused, then shook his head. "They have someone on the inside, somewhere."

The room fell silent. There were only a handful of us who had been in on the plan, and most of us were here. That meant we had an informant.

Herne paled. "Who? It can't be one of us." He gazed around the room. "Who else knew?"

"Cernunnos, Morgana…did we tell Névé and Saílle?" I asked.

"I honestly don't remember at this point." Herne's expression clouded. "We obviously have a mole, and before we do anything else, we have to figure out who it is. Yutani, could someone from the Tuathan Brotherhood have followed you back on the Dark Web?"

Yutani paused, his gaze thoughtful. After a moment, he shrugged. "I'm not sure. It would be one thing if we weren't dealing with the astral web as well, but when you factor in magic and the ability to scry, I can't guarantee that it didn't happen."

"It doesn't help that we're going to have to go further out on the Dark Web to trace them," Herne said. "It's a dangerous game, this is."

"Life is dangerous," Viktor said. "We have no choice. We can't turn away. Your father and mother made it clear this is our task to figure out."

"Before we say anything more, we should figure out if they put a trace on him," Talia said. "Yutani, can you check for that now?"

Yutani nodded. "I'll get my gear. It's in the car." He jogged out of the room.

After he left, Talia turned to Herne. "I'm going to ask you something, and I don't want you to take this the wrong way, but it's something we have to consider. Do you think that Coyote could be spinning some shade our way? Not deliberately, but Yutani *is* his son, and chaos falls in the wake of his journeys."

Herne raised his gaze to meet hers, a solemn look on his face. "That's also something we must consider. But keep the thought quiet for now. I don't want to make him feel like he has to run. He was cast out by his village when he was young. I won't have that experience repeated."

I caught my breath. The joy over saving Rafé's life was rapidly dwindling. Herne's phone rang and he glanced at it.

"My mother. I'll be right back." He moved to the other side of the room.

Yutani returned with his backpack, and he pulled out an odd-shaped device that reminded me of a Y-shaped piece of metal. He pressed a button on the handle and held it out, scanning Rafé from head to foot. A moment later, a red light flared at the end of the right fork. He turned to me, nodding and pointing to Rafé's arm, where the GPS trace we had inserted had been ripped out. I motioned for Angel to man the door, and she reluctantly moved to watch over it.

Talia joined me as Rafé held out his arm. It was the one that wasn't broken, and so Talia gently unwrapped the bandages where the doctors had stitched him up. She eyed the wound, and then turned to Rafé. He simply nodded, bracing himself.

I pulled out my dagger. I had recently sharpened the blade, so it was razor-sharp. Viktor silently handed me a bottle of disinfectant and I wiped down the blade. Herne returned and started to say something but Talia held her finger to her lips and he fell quiet.

I motioned for him to take hold of Rafé's arm and hold it steady. Viktor rolled up a towel and handed it to Rafé, helping him put it in his mouth. We couldn't wait till we were back in Seattle.

Cautiously, I slid the blade through the stitches, and the blood began to weal up through the gash as I reopened the wound. Rafé bit down on the towel, sweating as I grimaced and pulled back the flaps of skin. Yutani held a magnifying glass over the area and sure enough, there was a tiny wire inside. Given the doctors had merely thought they were sewing up a gash, I had no doubt they had missed seeing it.

Viktor motioned to Talia, who found a pair of tweezers, and she very carefully plucked out the wire as I held the flaps of skin back. Yutani nodded, holding the gadget over the wire. We had found the trace. They had removed ours and inserted their own. Talia handed it to Yutani, who took it over to the sink and washed it down the drain. He held out his detector, then let out a loud sigh.

"It's out of range. It can't hear us now. But everything we've said around Rafé since we found him is likely to be common knowledge among the Tuathan Brotherhood. They know we're searching for them on the Dark Web, and they'll be watching."

"That still doesn't tell us how they found out in the first place." I turned to Herne.

"So they had the gall to put a counter-bug in Rafé's arm." He frowned. "That was my mother on the phone, by the way. She wants to see Ember and me tomorrow, as soon as we get back to Seattle. Which means we better get on the road as soon as possible. I don't want to leave Rafé alone, so she's sending guards to watch over him till he can be transferred back to the city. They'll be here within an hour. Then, we head out and catch the ferry."

"I'd like to stay with Rafé—" Angel started to say, but Herne shook his head.

"No, sorry. I can't allow that. I don't want anything happening to you, and right now, things are just too dangerous. There are guards from the compound out there, looking for us."

Angel started to argue, but stopped as he gave her a stern look. I motioned to the others. "Let's leave them alone for a few minutes while we wait for the guards. We can sit outside in the hall."

Herne agreed to that, and so we waited for half an hour until Cernunnos's Elven guards arrived. As they took up their places in Rafé's room, we headed out to the parking lot. The snow was softly falling, but the wind had died down. I gazed across the street at a thicket of trees. For a moment, I thought I saw Fiona dancing in the stark splendor of ice and snow, but then she vanished.

As Herne opened my door for me, he whispered, "I saw her too. Isella. She's free and she's exploring her powers. Who knows what she'll become?"

I stared at the trees again, straining to catch another glimpse of her, but all I saw were snow-clad trees and a field of white. How many people could say they had been present at the birth of a goddess…or the creation of a Luo'henkah? The thought chilled me and I quickly ducked into my seat. All the way to the ferry terminal, I kept my eyes on the road, afraid that if I looked out to the side, I'd see something that reminded me of things and experiences I wanted desperately to leave behind me.

THE NEXT DAY...

HERNE AND I WERE WALKING THROUGH CERNUNNOS'S grove. A clearing surrounded by oak and ash and thorn, circled by a ring of fly agaric, the grove was near his palace in Annwn.

Here, spirits danced, and earth elementals lumbered through the land, shaking the rock and soil with their massive footsteps. Cernunnos's grove was magic incarnate, alive and ever watchful. In the center of the grove, two thrones rose, one formed from the trunk of an ancient oak and the other from the trunk of an ancient willow. Their roots were still buried deep in the ground, and the seats of power had been formed by no hand, but by the trees themselves. Pockets of emerald and peridot and smoky quartz glimmered from knotholes in the oak throne, and in the willow, sapphire and moonstone glistened, peeking out.

Cernunnos was sitting atop the oak, his chest bare. His olive skin shimmered, every muscle defined and taut, a massive map of the eons through which the Lord of the Forest had ruled. He wore a bearskin fastened at the neck by a knotwork brooch, and black jeans spanned his tree-trunk thighs. His eyes glimmered, green with gold flecks, wide-set like those of a cat's, and his hair was draped down to his thighs in coiled braids. His headdress was feathered in the shape of a hawk's head.

Beside him, on the willow throne, sat Morgana, her dark hair cascading down her back. She wore a diaphanous gown, violet with threads of dark blue running through it, so sheer I could almost see through it to her rounded breasts. Her eyes mirrored the silver of the moon. The diadem on her head shimmered with diamonds, and a faint mist rose around her, like the mists that came in off the ocean waves.

I went down on my knees before them and beside me, Herne did the same.

"Rise, children, and be seated." Morgana's voice was ethereal, reminding me of the chords of a hammered dulcimer. "You have had a weary chase. Brighid told us of your friend Angus, my son."

"I'm sorry. I wasn't able to stop the Cailleach before she spun off a child." Herne raised his head as he stood, holding out his hand to me. A bench sat behind us and we took our places, sitting hand in hand.

"So Brighid said—Isella, the child of ice and snow. She's free in the world now. We'll have to keep watch on her, but Brighid has volunteered to take care of that. Unless she causes too much havoc, we will not intervene." Cernunnos cleared his throat. "Some days, the mission schools you rather than the other way around. And the Cailleach is not an easy force to contain. Had we known about this in advance, I would have sent help with you before you even ventured over to the peninsula, but too little, too late. Angus must have known what was going on, but he didn't want to admit it."

"Who is guarding the stone now?" I asked.

"His daughter will watch over it, as she was raised to accept would happen." Morgana let out a sigh. "Now, onto other, more serious, matters. Something has happened that sheds even more urgency and worry on the issue of the Tuathan Brotherhood."

Herne let out a groan. "What more could happen?" He had told them about the trace we had found on Rafé.

Cernunnos grunted. "Corra's awake. Your mother and I are traveling to Scotland next week since she refuses to come here, but she's asked for us to attend and, given it's Corra, of course we must."

Herne paled. "Oh cripes."

I glanced at him, confused. "Who's Corra?"

Cernunnos answered me. "Corra is an ancient Scottish serpent goddess. She only wakes when there are major shifts coming to the land or the country. She's an oracle for the gods, you might say." He waited for me to say something, but I merely nodded. There wasn't much *to* say.

After a moment, he continued. "While we attend her and find out why she's waking, you are to find out everything you can about this *Nuanda*. I contacted Lugh the Long Handed, but he has no clue, or at least he's not saying. I've never fully trusted him, but there's no way to know what the truth is save for the Triamvinate forcing him to swear an answer and that's not going to happen any time soon."

The only thing I knew about Lugh the Long Handed was that he was yet another Celtic god. Herne had never really talked about him.

Herne cleared his throat. "Lovely. All right, we'll dive

into it. We're also having to delve deeper into the Dark Web—into the magical workings of it."

"Be cautious, my son," Morgana said. "There are powers there that are best left sleeping. You don't want to wake up one of the nameless ones who haunt the etheric caverns."

Herne nodded. "We'll do whatever we can to be careful. I assume after you find out what Corra wants, you'll tell me?"

"If need be, yes." Morgana paused. "Ember, I also have a task for you. I don't think you're going to like it. You must go into the cities of Navane and TirNaNog and seek out the remaining members of your family lineages. There are two items that they have kept from you—one on each side. While I can order Saílle and Névé to allow you entrance to the cities, you are the one who must retrieve your rightful heirlooms. You will need them in the coming months."

I stared at her. I had never been in the great Fae cities —I wouldn't even be allowed in if I tried, given I was a tralaeth. And now I was supposed to waltz in and demand they give me family heirlooms?

"What are they?" I asked, not even attempting to bargain my way out of her demand. Over the past months, I had learned that when the gods ordered you to do something, you did it.

Morgana stared at me for a moment. Finally, she said, "A crown and a bow. The crown is with your great-grandmother in Navane. The bow is with your great-uncle in TirNaNog."

My lips went dry. "My grandfather's brother?"

"The same, yes."

I began to shake. I didn't want to set foot in either city, let alone face the families who had contrived my parents' murders. I sought Morgana's gaze, pleading silently for a reprieve, but she slowly shook her head.

"I'm sorry, but you must do this, Ember." And so it was set.

AFTER WE LEFT THE GROVE, HERNE TOOK ME TO ANOTHER, just as lovely but smaller in size, with one throne in the center of the clearing. It was a throne of oak, similar to Cernunnos's, but smaller in stature.

"This is yours, isn't it?" I turned to him.

He nodded. "I thought you might like to see it."

"It's beautiful," I said, running my hand over the ancient oak. "I never would have imagined you sitting on a throne, and yet now that we're here, I can see it so clearly." I turned to him, suddenly hungry for his embrace. "I need you. It's been too long, and so much has happened."

He pulled me into his arms and, without a word, kissed me, his lips warm on mine, his arms encircling me, shielding me from the storms that were running rampant in our lives. As our kiss deepened, he tugged at my shirt, and I pulled away, letting him slide the sweater over my head. I shivered in the chill mists around us, but then he embraced me again and his body warmed me through. We shed our clothes, and there, under the rising moonlight of Annwn, he pulled me down to the grass and made love to me, his hands sliding over my body, his lips caressing me, his gaze focused solely on me.

"I love you," I whispered as he entered me, suddenly

aching to hear those words in return. There was a wistful feel to the grove, as if time had stopped and here we could say anything, and could hope for anything, and as long as we remained within the borders, the universe was ours.

"Ember," he whispered, slowly moving inside me, his chest pressed against my breasts. "You are my love. You are my heart."

To my core, I felt the truth of his words. And as the moon continued to rise, he kissed me and loved me until everything else faded and we were the only ones in our little world.

YULE—MIDWINTER...

THE NEXT NIGHT WE ALL GATHERED AT MY HOUSE, including Rafé, who was in a wheelchair given his broken arm and leg. Yutani had built a makeshift ramp so he could enter the house easily.

I had spent the day decorating the tree and it was shimmering under the firelight, glowing with soft hues of blue and silver and sparkling white. I glanced outside. The snow had stopped, but it was still cold, and across our side yard, the blanket of white looked comforting rather than fearsome. The lights on the trees outside the door were glowing against the night sky, and I found myself humming an old song my mother had taught me when I was little.

"Greensleeves was all my joy, and
Greensleeves was my delight..."

Yutani joined me by the window and lent his voice to mine. I glanced at him, surprised he knew the words, but he just smiled and sang a counter-balance to my melody.

"Greensleeves was my heart of gold, And
who but my lady Greensleeves."

As we finished, I turned to him and impulsively gave him a hug. He seemed surprised, but hugged me back.

"I'm glad you found your father," I said.

"I am too. Would you do me a favor? Would you tell Raven that...I won't bother her? I'd like to be friends, but I won't pressure her."

I nodded. "I'll tell her, but you might want to tell her yourself. I think that would ease some of the tension." I patted his arm and turned back to the party.

Angel had outdone herself in the kitchen. A crockpot of wassail was steaming away on the counter. A massive prime rib roast sat on a platter, surrounded by roasted carrots and brussels sprouts, while a turkey and stuffing sat on another. Dinner rolls, cranberry-raspberry sauce, and mashed potatoes and gravy completed the sides. For dessert, she'd made a chocolate-peppermint Yule log, divinity, and coconut cream pie.

Everybody was there—Herne, Talia, Yutani, Viktor and his girlfriend Sheila, Charlie, Raven—who was walking with a cane—and Kipa. Kipa and Raven were obviously getting cozier—it was easy to see, just watching them. They sat together and grinned at each other in that way that belied new relationship secrets.

"Have you decided what to do about Lazerous?" I asked Talia as we set the table for dinner. "Or is that still up in the air?" It had been awhile since she had found out that the liche who stole her powers didn't live very far from us, and we might be able to get her powers back if she wanted.

Talia shook her head. "I'm still thinking. I don't know what I want, and until I do, I'm opting to just put the matter on the shelf."

"Probably best that way." I winked at her. I headed back over to where Angel was setting out dishes of food on the long kitchen island. While the table in our large eat-in kitchen was big enough to seat all of us, the food needed to be served buffet style. "Everything ready?"

She nodded. "I think we're good. Go ahead and call everyone to dinner." She gave me a soft smile. "I'm so glad we made it back in time for Yule. And that we have a family to spend it with. I miss DJ, but he texted that he's having fun with Cooper and his foster family. They're staying up at Mission Ridge. I never thought my little brother would learn to ski."

"Did you tell him about DeWayne calling?"

She held my gaze for a moment, then shook her head. "No. There's no reason. DeWayne isn't interested in knowing his son. He just wants to get as much as he can out of him. Don't you say anything, either."

"I won't," I promised. "But I have an uneasy feeling this isn't over yet."

"So do I," Angel said. "But until we know for sure, let it be."

As we gathered around the table, with me on one end and Herne on the other, I tapped my water glass and stood. "Angel and I just want to say thank you, everyone, for joining us on this Solstice night. Life hasn't been easy lately for any of us, but you are all family. For the first time in years, we don't feel alone in the world, and we have the Wild Hunt to thank for that. So, that being said… Blessings to everyone on this, the longest night of the year. Let's drink to the return of the Oak Lord, and the death of the Holly." I held up my glass and everyone followed suit.

As he sipped his mead, Herne said, "I've actually seen them fight at both Midwinter and Midsummer. It's… impressive. I would never want to tangle with the Lords of the Seasons."

"Are they Luo'henkah?" I asked.

He shook his head. "Not exactly, but close to it. At least they're good about giving over when their half of the year is done."

We filled our plates, talking about everything except the Tuathan Brotherhood. For the evening, we wanted to forget the struggles we were facing.

After we finished dinner, with Mr. Rumblebutt getting his own special treats, we carried dessert into the living room, where we exchanged gifts in a flurry of unwrapping and laughter. Since we hadn't really had much time to shop, most of the gifts were trinkets, friend-to-friend gifts just to acknowledge the season.

But Herne held out a package to me. "Here, love."

I stared at the small box. I had given him a framed picture of us, not sure what to get someone who could have just about anything he wanted.

As I tore open the paper, I realized everyone was watching. Blushing, I lifted the velvet box out of the wrapping and opened it. Inside the jewelry box was a polished ring made out of what appeared to be bone. I glanced up at him, asking a silent question.

"I had that made from a sliver of one of my tines," he said quietly. "Let's just call it a promise ring?"

"This came from your own antler?" I slid the ring on the third finger of my right hand. It fit perfectly. "It's beautiful."

"I wanted you to have something that marks you as my own. Do you like it?" He looked so worried that I leaned over and gave him a slow kiss.

"I love it. And yes, a promise ring is perfect."

As we settled down to finish our desserts, Herne's phone beeped. He glanced at it, then slowly straightened.

"I hate to interrupt this, but Ember, turn on the TV, please."

I slowly picked up the remote and turned on the television. There was a breaking news report going on and, dreading what we were about to hear, I turned up the volume.

The reporter was in midsentence. "—This afternoon, by a split vote of three to two, the United Coalition has suspended the Fae Courts from taking part in the governance of the nation until the Tuathan Brotherhood has been disbanded and brought to justice. The Shifter Alliance, the Human League, and the Cryptozoid Association voted in favor of the suspension. The Vampire Nation and Fae Courts voted against. This comes on the heels of a manifesto published on the internet two hours ago by the Tuathan Brotherhood threatening continued violence until the Cryptozoid Alliance is removed from the United Coalition. We have reached out to Queen Saílle and Queen Névé, but neither Court has made a statement yet—"

Herne motioned for me to turn off the television. We all sat silent, waiting.

He shook his head. "I'm afraid that our vacation's just been cut short. Come Monday, we head back into the office and get to work on finding out all we can about Nuanda and who the hell he is." He held out his arm and I slid into the seat beside him. He kissed the top of my head. "I'm sorry, I know we planned to take a week or two off, but we can't."

"We also have to find out who the hell leaked the info about Rafé to the Tuathan Brotherhood," I murmured.

We went back to our desserts, but the evening wore away with a shadow hanging over it, and all I could think of was that we were facing an uphill battle. But at least we were facing it together. And on the longest night of the year, in the darkness and shadow, that felt like the strongest light we could have to hold onto.

I woke into my dreaming state, standing on an open field as I stared up into the night sky. Through the darkness, a flaming arrow soared through the air. It sailed in an arc, directly toward me, but I made no move to dodge it. The arrow came to land at my feet, and I saw that it was made of gold, and the fire clinging to it was burning pure and clear.

In the distance, the sun began to rise over the horizon, and as it crested above the mountains, the silhouette of a man rose up against the sky, spear in hand, ready for battle, and behind him stretched an army fed on anger and discontent.

I leaned down to pull the arrow out of the ground and it turned into a sword dripping with moss. The figure in the distance stiffened as the sword reverberated in my hand, and as I stood, a horn sounded. He was coming, and I turned, knowing that my sword waited to meet him in battle.

IF YOU ENJOYED THIS BOOK AND HAVEN'T READ THE FIRST five, check out THE SILVER STAG, OAK & THORNS, IRON BONES, A SHADOW OF CROWS, and THE HALLOWED HUNT. Preorder Book 7 now— WITCHING HOUR (An Ante-Fae Adventure) for a glimpse of Raven's world. There will be more to come after that.

I also invite you to visit Fury's world. In a gritty, post-apocalyptic Seattle, Fury is a minor goddess, in charge of eliminating the Abominations who come off the World Tree. Book 1-5 are available now in the Fury Unbound Series : FURY RISING, FURY'S MAGIC, FURY AWAK-ENED, FURY CALLING, and FURY'S MANTLE.

If you prefer a lighter-hearted but still steamy para-normal romance, meet the wild and magical residents of Bedlam in my Bewitching Bedlam Series. Fun-loving witch Maddy Gallowglass, her smoking-hot vampire lover Aegis, and their crazed cjinn Bubba (part djinn, all cat) rock it out in Bedlam, a magical town on a mystical island. BLOOD MUSIC, BEWITCHING BEDLAM, MAUDLIN'S MAYHEM, SIREN'S SONG, WITCHES WILD, CASTING CURSES, BLOOD VENGEANCE,

TIGER TAILS, and Bubba's origin story THE WISH FACTOR are all available.

For a dark, gritty, steamy series, try my world of The Indigo Court , where the long winter has come, and the Vampiric Fae are on the rise. The series is complete with NIGHT MYST, NIGHT VEIL, NIGHT SEEKER, NIGHT VISION, NIGHT'S END, and NIGHT SHIVERS.

If you like cozies with teeth, try my Chintz 'n China paranormal mysteries. The series is complete with: GHOST OF A CHANCE, LEGEND OF THE JADE DRAGON, MURDER UNDER A MYSTIC MOON, A HARVEST OF BONES, ONE HEX OF A WEDDING, and a wrap-up novella: HOLIDAY SPIRITS.

The last Otherworld book—BLOOD BONDS—is available now.

For all of my work, both published and upcoming releases, see the Biography at the end of this book, or check out my website at Galenorn.com and be sure and sign up for my newsletter to receive news about all my new releases.

CAST OF CHARACTERS

The Wild Hunt & Family:

- **Angel Jackson:** Ember's best friend, a human empath, Angel is the newest member of the Wild Hunt. A whiz in both the office and the kitchen, and loyal to the core, Angel is an integral part of Ember's life, and a vital member of the team.
- **Charlie Darren:** A vampire who was turned at nineteen. Math major, baker, and all-around gofer.
- **Ember Kearney:** Caught between the world of Light and Dark Fae, and pledged to Morgana, goddess of the Fae and the Sea, Ember Kearney was born with the mark of the Silver Stag. Rejected by both her bloodlines, she now works for the Wild Hunt as an investigator.
- **Herne the Hunter:** Herne is the son of the Lord of the Hunt, Cernunnos, and Morgana, goddess

of the Fae and the Sea. A demigod—given his mother's mortal beginnings—he's a lusty, protective god and one hell of a good boss. Owner of the Wild Hunt Agency, he helps keep the squabbles between the world of Light and Dark Fae from spilling over into the mortal realms.

- **Talia:** A harpy who long ago lost her powers, Talia is a top-notch researcher for the agency, and a longtime friend of Herne.
- **Viktor:** Viktor is half-ogre, half-human. Rejected by his father's people (the ogres), he came to work for Herne some decades back.
- **Yutani:** A coyote shifter who is dogged by the spirit of the Great Coyote, his father. Yutani was driven out of his village over two hundred years before. He walks in the shadow of the trickster, and is the IT specialist for the company.

The Gods, the Luo'henkah, the Elemental Spirits, & Their Courts:

- **Brighid:** Goddess of Healing, Inspiration, and Smithery. The Lady of the Fiery Arrows, "Exalted One."
- **The Cailleach:** One of the Luo'henkah, the heart and spirit of winter.
- **Cerridwen:** Goddess of the Cauldron of Rebirth. Dark harvest mother goddess.
- **Cernunnos:** Lord of the Hunt, god of the Forest and King Stag of the Woods. Together

with Morgana, Cernunnos originated the Wild Hunt and negotiated the covenant treaty with both the Light and the Dark Fae. Herne's father.

- **Coyote (also: Great Coyote):** Native American trickster spirit/god.
- **Danu:** Mother of the Pantheon. Leader of the Tuatha de Dannan.
- **Ferosyn:** Chief healer in Cernunnos's Court
- **Herne:** (see The Wild Hunt)
- **Isella:** One of the Luo'henkah. The Daughter of Ice (daughter of the Cailleach).
- **Kuippana (also: Kipa):** Lord of the Wolves. Elemental forest spirit; Herne's distant cousin. Trickster.
- **Morgana:** Goddess of the Fae and the Sea, she was originally human but Cernunnos lifted her to deityhood. She agreed to watch over the Fae who did not return across the Great Sea. Torn by her loyalty to her people and her loyalty to Cernunnos, she at times finds herself conflicted about the Wild Hunt. Herne's mother.
- **The Morrígan:** Goddess of Death and Phantoms. Goddess of the battlefield.

The Fae Courts:

- **Navane:** The court of the Light Fae, both across the Great Sea and on the eastside of Seattle, the latter ruled by **Névé**.
- **TirNaNog:** The court of the Dark Fae, both across the Great Sea and on the eastside of Seattle, the latter ruled by **Saílle**.

The Ante-Fae:

Creatures predating the Fae. The wellspring from which all Fae descended. Unique beings who rule their own realms. All Ante-Fae are dangerous, but some are more deadly than others.

- **Apollo:** The Golden Boy. Vixen's boy toy. Weaver of Wings. Dancer.
- **Blackthorn, the King of Thorns:** Ruler of the blackthorn trees and all thorn-bearing plants. Cunning and wily, he feeds on pain and desire.
- **Raven, the Daughter of Bones** (also: Raven BoneTalker)**:** A bone witch, Raven is young, as far as the Ante-Fae go, and she works with the dead. She's also a fortune teller, and a necromancer.
- **Straff:** Blackthorn's son, who suffers from a wasting disease requiring him to feed off others' life energies and blood.
- **Vixen:** The Mistress/Master of Mayhem. Gender-fluid Ante-Fae who owns the Burlesque A Go-Go nightclub.
- **The Vulture Sisters:** Triplet sisters, predatory.

The Force Majeure:

A group of legendary magicians, sorcerers, and witches. They are not human, but magic-born. There are twenty-one at any given time and the only way into the group is to be hand chosen, and the only exit from the group is death.

- **Merlin:** Morgana's father. Magician of ancient Celtic fame.
- **Taliesin:** The first Celtic bard. Son of Cerridwen, originally a servant who underwent magical transformation and finally was reborn through Cerridwen as the first bard.
- **Ranna:** Powerful sorceress. Elatha's mistress.
- **Rasputin:** The Russian sorcerer and mystic.
- **Väinämöinen:** The most famous Finnish bard.

Friends, Family, & Enemies:

- **Aoife:** A priestess of Morgana who guards the Seattle portal to the goddess's realm.
- **Celia:** Yutani's aunt.
- **Danielle:** Herne's daughter, born to an Amazon named Myrna.
- **DJ Jackson:** Angel's little half-brother, DJ is half Wulfine—wolf shifter. He now lives with a foster family for his own protection.
- **Erica:** A Dark Fae police officer, friend of Viktor's.
- **Elatha:** Fomorian King; enemy of the Fae race.
- **Ginty McClintlock:** A dwarf. Owner of Ginty's Waystation Bar & Grill.
- **Marilee:** A priestess of Morgana, Ember's mentor. Possibly Human—unknown.
- **Myrna:** An Amazon who had a fling with Herne many years back, resulting in their daughter Danielle.
- **Rafé Forrester:** Brother to Ulstair, Raven's late

fiancé; Angel's boyfriend. Actor/Fast-food worker. Dark Fae.

- **Sheila:** Viktor's girlfriend. A kitchen witch; one of the magic-born. Geology teacher who volunteers at the Chapel Hill Homeless Shelter.

PLAYLIST

I often write to music, and THE SILVER MIST was no exception. Here's the playlist I used for this book.

- **AJ Roach:** Devil May Dance
- **Air:** Napalm Love; Playground Love
- **Android Lust:** Here and Now
- **Arch Leaves:** Nowhere to Go
- **The Black Angels:** Half Believing; Comanche Moon; Always Maybe; You're Mine; Manipulation; Phosphene Dream; Death March; Young Men Dead
- **Black Mountain:** Queens Will Play
- **Bobbie Gentry:** Ode To Billie Joe
- **Bon Jovi:** Wanted Dead Or Alive
- **Brandon & Derek Fiechter:** Will-O'-Wisps; Black Wolf's Inn; Fairy Magic
- **Broken Bells:** The Ghost Inside
- **Buffalo Springfield:** For What It's Worth

- **Celtic Woman:** The Butterfly; The Voice; Scarborough Fair
- **Cher:** The Beat Goes On
- **The Chieftains:** Dunmore Lassies
- **Clannad:** Newgrange
- **Cobra Verde:** Play with Fire
- **Colin Foulke:** Emergence
- **Crazy Town:** Butterfly
- **Cream:** Sunshine of Your Love; Strange Brew; I Feel Free
- **Creedence Clearwater Revival:** Run Through the Jungle
- **Crosby, Stills & Nash:** Guinnevere
- **Damh the Bard:** Silent Moon; The Cauldron Born; Tomb of the King; Obsession; Cloak of Feathers; Lady in Black; Taliesin's Song; The Wheel; Noon of the Solstice
- **David Bowie:** Golden Years; Sister Midnight
- **Dizzi:** Dizzi Jig; Dance of the Unicorns
- **Eastern Sun:** Beautiful Being (Original Edit)
- **Eivør:** Trøllbundin
- **Faun:** Hymn to Pan; Oyneng Yar; The Market Song; Punagra; Cernunnos; Rad; Sieben
- **Flight of the Hawk:** Bones
- **Gabrielle Roth:** The Calling; Raven; Mother Night
- **Gordon Lightfoot:** The Wreck of the Edmund Fitzgerald
- **The Gospel Whiskey Runners:** Muddy Waters
- **Gotye:** Hearts A Mess; Somebody That I Used To Know
- **Gypsy:** Magick; Medicine Song; Morgaine

- **Gypsy Soul:** Who?
- **The Hang Drum Project:** Shaken Oak;
  St.Chartier
- **Hedningarna:** Ukkonen; Juopolle Joutunut
- **The Hu:** Wolf Totem; Yuve Yuve Yu
- **Huldrelokkk:** Trolldans
- **Ian Melrose & Kerstin Blodig:** Kråka
- **Jeannie C. Riley:** Harper Valley PTA
- **Jessica Bates:** The Hanging Tree
- **Jethro Tull:** Jack Frost & the Hooded Crow;
  Down at the End of Your Road; Jack-A-Lynn;
  Motoreyes; Rhythm in Gold; Overhang; Witch's
  Promise; Mountain Men; Acres Wild; Moths;
  Journeyman; Heavy Horses; Weathercock;
  North Sea Oil; Something's On the Move; Old
  Ghosts; Dun Ringill
- **Led Zeppelin:** Ramble On; The Battle of
  Evermore; Stairway to Heaven; When the Levee
  Breaks; Kashmir
- **Leonard Cohen:** The Future; You Want it
  Darker
- **Libana:** The Earth is Our Mother; Ancient
  Mother; Round and Round
- **Linda Perhacs:** Delicious
- **Lorde:** Yellow Flicker Beat; Royals
- **Loreena McKennitt:** The Mummers' Dance; All
  Souls Night
- **Low with Tom and Andy:** Half Light
- **Marconi Union:** First Light; Alone Together;
  Flying (In Crimson Skies); Time Lapse; On
  Reflection; Broken Colours; We Travel;
  Weightless; Weightless, Pt. 2; Weightless, Pt. 3;

Weightless, Pt. 4; Weightless, Pt. 5; Weightless, Pt. 6

- **Matt Corby:** Breathe
- **Motherdrum:** Big Stomp; Ceremony; Instant Success
- **Nick Cave & the Bad Seeds:** Red Right Hand
- **Nirvana:** Come As You Are; Lake of Fire; Something in the Way; Heart Shaped Box; Plateau
- **PJ Harvey:** Let England Shake; The Glorious Land; The Words That Maketh Murder; The Colour of the Earth
- **Rachel Diggs:** Hands of Time
- **Robin Schulz:** Sugar
- **Rolling Stones:** Gimme Shelter; 19th Nervous Breakdown; Lady Jane; Sympathy For the Devil; Miss You
- **Ruth Barrett:** Faeries Love Song
- **J. Tucker:** Hymn to Herne
- **Sharon Knight:** Ravaged Ruins; Bewitched; 13 Knots; Let the Waters Rise; Star of the Sea; Siren Moon; Mother of the World; Berrywood Grove
- **Shriekback:** Dust and a Shadow; Underwaterboys; This Big Hush; The King in the Tree; And The Rain
- **Snow Patrol:** The Lightning Strike: What If This Storm Ends; Life Boats; If There's a Rocket, Tie Me To It
- **Spiral Dance:** Boys of Bedlam; Tarry Trousers; Burning Times; Rise Up

- **Steeleye Span:** The Fox; Blackleg Miner; Cam Ye O'er Frae France
- **Steppenwolf:** Don't Step on the Grass, Sam; Magic Carpet Ride; Jupiter's Child
- **Strawberry Alarm Clock:** Incense and Peppermint
- **Sweet Talk Radio:** We All Fall Down
- **Tempest:** Buffalo Jump; Raggle Taggle Gypsy; Mad Tom of Bedlam; Queen of Argyll; Nottamun Town; Black Jack Davy
- **Todd Alan:** We Are the Walking Breath; Spirit of the Wind
- **Tom Petty:** Mary Jane's Last Dance
- **Traffic:** Rainmaker; The Low Spark of High Heeled Boys
- **Tuatha Dea:** Wisp of A Thing (Part 1); The Hum and the Shiver; Long Black Curl; Irish Handfasting; Tuatha De Danaan
- **Warchild:** Ash
- **Wendy Rule:** Let the Wind Blow; Elemental Chant; The Circle Song; The Wolf Sky
- **Woodland:** Blood of the Moon; The Grove; Witch's Cross; First Melt; The Dragon; Secrets Told; The Dragon; Under the Snow; Golden Raven's Eye
- **Zero 7:** In the Waiting Line
- **The Zombies:** Time of the Season

BIOGRAPHY

New York Times, Publishers Weekly, and USA Today bestselling author Yasmine Galenorn writes urban fantasy and paranormal romance, and is the author of over sixty books, including the Wild Hunt Series, the Fury Unbound Series, the Bewitching Bedlam Series, the Indigo Court Series, and the Otherworld Series, among others. She's also written nonfiction metaphysical books. She is the 2011 Career Achievement Award Winner in Urban Fantasy, given by RT Magazine.

Yasmine has been in the Craft since 1980, is a shamanic witch and High Priestess. She describes her life as a blend of teacups and tattoos. She lives in Kirkland, WA, with her husband Samwise and their cats. Yasmine can be reached via her website at Galenorn.com.

Indie Releases Currently Available:

The Wild Hunt Series:
  The Silver Stag

Oak & Thorns
Iron Bones
A Shadow of Crows
The Hallowed Hunt
The Silver Mist
Witching Hour

Bewitching Bedlam Series:
Bewitching Bedlam
Maudlin's Mayhem
Siren's Song
Witches Wild
Casting Curses
Blood Music
Blood Vengeance
Tiger Tails
The Wish Factor

Fury Unbound Series:
Fury Rising
Fury's Magic
Fury Awakened
Fury Calling
Fury's Mantle

Indigo Court Series:
Night Myst
Night Veil
Night Seeker
Night Vision
Night's End
Night Shivers

Indigo Court Books, 1-3: Night Myst, Night Veil, Night Seeker (Boxed Set)

Indigo Court Books, 4-6: Night Vision, Night's End, Night Shivers (Boxed Set)

Otherworld Series:

Moon Shimmers

Harvest Song

Blood Bonds

Earthbound

Knight Magic

Otherworld Tales: Volume One

Tales From Otherworld: Collection One

Men of Otherworld: Collection One

Men of Otherworld: Collection Two

Moon Swept: Otherworld Tales of First Love

For the rest of the Otherworld Series, see website at Galenorn.com.

Chintz 'n China Series:

Ghost of a Chance

Legend of the Jade Dragon

Murder Under a Mystic Moon

A Harvest of Bones

One Hex of a Wedding

Holiday Spirits

Chintz 'n China Books, 1 – 3: Ghost of a Chance, Legend of the Jade Dragon, Murder Under A Mystic Moon

Chintz 'n China Books, 4-6: A Harvest of Bones, One Hex of a Wedding, Holiday Spirits

Bath and Body Series (originally under the name India Ink):
Scent to Her Grave
A Blush With Death
Glossed and Found

Misc. Short Stories/Anthologies:
The Longest Night: A Starwood Novella
Mist and Shadows: Tales From Dark Haunts
Once Upon a Kiss (short story: Princess Charming)
Once Upon a Curse (short story: Bones)

Magickal Nonfiction:
Embracing the Moon
Tarot Journeys

42591252R00174

Printed in Poland
by Amazon Fulfillment
Poland Sp. z o.o., Wrocław